LION ON THE MOUNTAIN

WATCHDOG MOUNTAIN DIVISION BOOK 3

OLIVIA MICHAELS

FALCON IN HAND PUBLISHING LLC

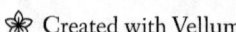 Created with Vellum

ONE

"I'm sticking every single needle I own into you," he said.

Oh, this is so not going to go well.

Wren Stapleton lay face down on a table, practically naked under a thin, white sheet, waiting to turn into a porcupine.

Why did I let Barbie talk me into coming here?

"Now it's not going to hurt, I promise. So just relax," Serge the acupuncturist said. "You're so tense! Your shoulders feel like they're cast in iron. We want soft shoulders, don't we?"

Wren wasn't sure if she was supposed to nod or answer vocally. She was afraid to move, despite Serge's promise that this wouldn't hurt. He was sticking *needles* into her—she didn't care how small they were. At least there was a hole in the table for her face, but lying face down like this was wreaking havoc with her sinuses. Or maybe it was the copious incense burning on a nearby table. The smell was supposed to make her relax but instead it made her hold back a sneeze. The last thing she wanted to do was move suddenly. What if Serge stuck a needle in the wrong place and it paralyzed her legs or something?

"Yes, we want soft shoulders," she finally said, her voice already sounding stuffy.

"Good." Serge sounded distracted. At least he was paying attention to what he was doing and not to what she was saying. "We're going to start with your ears."

"My ears? Seriously? Are my ears tense or something?"

Serge just chuckled. "Funny girl. I like 'em funny."

And then she felt the slightest pinch at the top of her ear. It actually didn't hurt.

"See? Not bad, is it?" He stuck several more needles in her ear and walked around the table to the other side of her head.

"I'm withholding judgment until this is over."

"Oh, I like 'em sassy, too. I should spank you."

Wait, what? "Um."

"Just kidding with you. Relax. I'm a professional. I thought you had a sense of humor. That's what Barbie told me."

I'm going to kill Barbie and it won't be funny at all.

"Now let's tackle those shoulders. You're going to be so relaxed when this is over you won't even recognize your own body."

"Doubtful."

"Serenity is the goal, Wren. Breathe in and embrace serenity."

"Hang on. I really need to sneeze."

"Oh, good, it's working already. Just let it out. Sneezing is a sign of relaxation."

More like a sign that this incense is going to kill me before I get the chance to kill Barbie.

The smoke had gotten stronger, and there was a foul odor underneath that didn't smell natural at all. Maybe it was burning the base it was sitting on? Her nose was too plugged to really tell.

Wren sneezed and then Serge stuck a series of needles in her back like he was making up for lost time. A couple of them made the muscle twinge underneath, but yeah, no pain. And her shoulders and back really did feel more relaxed.

This might be working.

Barbie wasn't the only one of her photography subjects who raved about Serge but she was the one who finally convinced Wren to book a morning appointment for her shoulders and back. Carting around photography equipment all day was taking its toll.

Though, Wren's shoulders were almost permanently parked up around her ears way before she ever picked up a full camera bag. She'd just ignore that little fact.

Serenity. She took another deep breath and her nose twitched at the smell.

"Just a few more to go," Serge said as he stuck another needle in.

"I need to sneeze again."

"*So* relaxed."

"No, I think it's the incense making me sneeze."

He made a disgruntled sound. "It's barely there. I don't even smell it anymore. I was thinking of lighting another cone as a matter of fact."

"Then you're totally nose-blind because it keeps getting stronger. I think it's burning the holder or something." There was definitely an acrid smell beneath the sweet sandalwood odor.

Wren sneezed, clearing her sinuses. "Wait, that's not the incense. That smells electrical."

"Huh. I think you're right." Wren heard Serge walk over to check the incense. "But it's not coming from here. Shit."

Wren listened as he walked across the room and opened the door. She assumed he was checking the hall.

A claxon sounded, and there went all her hard-won serenity. Wren *hated* sudden loud noises and a fire alarm was the granddaddy of them all.

"Serge? Is everything all right? Should I...?" Wren lifted her head and looked toward the open door.

Her acupuncturist was nowhere in sight.

"He ditched me!"

Wren sat up and looked around. Her clothes sat in a heap on the chair where she'd left them. She jumped off the table, bringing the sheet with her, and headed for the door to close it. But pounding footsteps in the hall and shouts told her she did not have time to get dressed. And was that smoke? The electrical smell was getting stronger, and now it was mixed with other chemical smells.

What about the needles in my back?

She couldn't very well slip her t-shirt on over those, could she? She reached back, trying to touch them and when her finger brushed against one, she got a horrible cringy feeling just thinking about trying to pull them out.

Just then someone stopped at the door. Thank God, Serge had not abandoned her. He could pull them out quickly.

Nope. Wasn't Serge.

"You need to get out now," some rando guy shouted into the room. "Break room's on fire."

"Shit!" After one last forlorn look at her clothes across the room, Wren grabbed her purse off the hook beside the door, slipped on her sandals, and awkwardly shuffled out of the room, trying to hold the sheet so it covered her front and her butt at least.

This is worse than a hospital gown. Thank God I didn't take off my panties. And at least she'd worn the cute ones, not her ratty old period panties. Because everyone was about to get a show.

Wren coughed as she tried not to trip down the hall toward the exit. The smell was god-awful and the smoke harsh. Her hind brain amplified her fear and she forgot she was practically naked as she started sprinting toward the open door and fresh air. Firefighters raced in past her but one stopped to escort her out. He almost put his hand on her back but stopped when he saw the needles there. She wasn't sure, but she could almost swear she heard him chuckle behind his face shield thingy.

"This way, miss." He hurried her to the exit, where the entirety of the building waited in the parking lot, facing the building. All eyes landed on her as she emerged. Looks turned from concern to humor when they got a good look at her.

Great. Wonderful. Fan-fucking-tastic.

Wren tried to wrap the sheet as best she could around her back-side without turning and giving everyone a money shot. The least the firefighter could do was give her a hand, but he was already gone, back in the building actually doing something more important than protecting her modesty, she assumed.

All she wanted to do was make a dash for her car, but the idea of driving home with *actual needles sticking out of her back* gave her the oogies. She kept her backside turned away from the crowd as she inched her way over to the waist-high brick wall enclosing the lot.

She scanned the crowd for Serge, the asshole coward who'd left her there like a helpless and pathetic baby porcupine. Maybe he could quickly de-quill her and she could disappear forever and forget this ever happened.

No Serge anywhere. The bastard had bolted.

Just my luck.

No, *this* was just her luck—the most gorgeous man she'd ever laid eyes on was heading straight for her, and not with a lustful look in his eye but supreme detachment. He was wearing scrubs or some sort of scrubs-adjacent uniform—she was no expert—and coming from the direction of an ambulance parked behind a firetruck.

And damn did he fill out those scrubs. The sleeves looked painfully tight around his upper arms. Fabric stretched across his chest and loosened as it fell toward his tapered waist. Same with the bottoms—he had thigh muscles that didn't quit.

Stop staring at his scrubs pants. I bet if you looked for it, you'd see he has a face.

Why, yes, yes he does.

Quite a face. Wow. Cool blue eyes whose gaze pierced her like the needles in her back, sending shivers down her spine. A broad, clear forehead, wide cheekbones and hollowed cheeks covered in golden whiskers that matched his tawny hair.

His name tag said *Hunt.* Because of course it did.

He's a mountain lion and I'm his prey.

Wren clutched the top of the sheet with one hand at her chest and the other at the small of her back, hoping that her panties weren't showing.

Just pretend you're at the Met Gala wearing an evening gown with a plunging back. Own it.

Uh-huh.

The Met Gala was for people like her gorgeous subjects, not for her. So were guys who looked like good old Hunt here.

He stopped in front of her, a full head taller, and studied her impassively.

"Did you inhale any smoke?" he asked. "Any trouble breathing?"

Oh yeah, breathing. Breathing is good she thought when she realized she'd been holding her breath. She inhaled sharply as she shook her head.

"Nope, breathing is not a problem. Been doing it all my life. You could say I'm an expert at it."

Right along with babbling when I'm anxious.

He reached for her hand, which was still clutching the sheet above her boobies, and she turned at the waist without thinking. The sheet started to slip on one side.

Ah, a tasteful side-boob for the nice gentleman. Good going.

"Sorry," he said quickly as he jerked his hand back. "I just want to get a pulse-ox on you." He held up a doodad with a tiny screen reading double zeroes.

"Right. Sure. Of course." Wren pointed her index finger at him, which he studied, frowning.

Is my finger that ugly? She looked at her bright red nail for chips in the polish but found none. *What's the problem?*

"Um, I'm going to have to remove your nail polish to get an accurate reading."

"Oh. That might be a problem. It's not polish, it's dip and requires grinding with a Dremel."

His lips pursed momentarily before those blue lagoons for eyes brightened. "No big, I can get a reading from your earlobe." He brushed a lock of her hair back. His thumb grazed her cheek which started an earthquake in her chest.

Then he frowned as he jerked his hand back for the second time.

Oh, God, now what? I know I don't have nail polish on my earlobes.

"Hmm. Before I can do that, let's get all those needles out of you. We'll start with the ones in your ears."

Her eyes widened. "The ones in my..." She started to raise her hand to her ear and then thought better of it. "Oh yeah, he did put some there, didn't he?"

Hunt leaned in. He had nice, fresh breath—*oh God, I'm noticing his breath, seriously?*—and studied her right ear.

"One drew some blood."

"Really? How much?" Now she was dying to touch her ear.

"Just a teeny tiny drop. It's already dried and crusted over."

Lovely. Perfect. So attractive.

Hunt took a folded blue paper towel out of his med kit and spread it open on the top of the brick wall next to them. Then he reached up to pull out a needle and she held perfectly still.

"I don't think this will hurt, but I apologize in advance if it does."

"Nothing can hurt more than my pride right now, so pluck away."

No smile from Hunt. He was laser focused on her ear as if he were doing brain surgery. She felt disappointment tug at her chest just as she felt him tug the needle from the edge of her ear.

"Got it. One down." He set the needle in the center of the paper towel. "Wait. I need to count these first so that I don't miss one or leave one behind for someone to step on." He shook his head, looking annoyed. With himself? Her? Serge? God knew; his expression was nothing but business otherwise.

Hunt studied her ears, first the right one, then he passed in front of her face—with too-brief eye contact—and looked at her left ear. He took out a Sharpie and wrote *5 per ear* on the paper towel, then wrote *R ear L ear* and *back* across the top edge and moved the needle to the spot under *R ear*.

Very logical and efficient. I like that.

Hunt touched her bare upper arm and he might as well have had a buzzer in his hand the way her skin reacted, shooting delicious sparks straight to her tummy, heart and...other places.

Please, nips, do not *poke out at him under this very thin, very white sheet.*

He gently turned her. No, actually, he very gently *tried* to turn her but she stood rooted in place.

"I, um." She giggled nervously. "Didn't exactly have time to grab my clothing."

Hunt's eyes did that widening thing again that Wren was quickly growing addicted to.

"Oh, right." He glanced over his shoulder toward the parking lot. "It's okay, I'll shield you from the crowd."

Oh, yeah. Forgot about the crowd.

Somehow, her attention had zoomed like one of her telescopic lenses into sharp focus, cropping out everything that wasn't Hunt the Lionesque Paramedic.

Including an actual burning building. That I just escaped from, mostly naked.

"Are you alright? You suddenly look pale." Hunt touched two fingers to the side of her neck. Sweet Jesus, did he have live wires running through his hands because every time he touched her he sent delicious shocks through her body.

"Pulse is racing but steady. Do you feel light-headed or faint? I should get you seated." He shook his head again, the annoyed look back in his eyes.

"No, I'm fine, just reality catching up with me, that's all."

He blew out a breath. "Let me get these needles out, get your pulse-ox, BP, hydrated, tested for shock," Hunt half-mumbled to himself. Maybe he was new on the job, reminding himself of what he needed to do? He seemed very professional otherwise. He hadn't leered at all, didn't crack a single joke when the low-hanging fruit was right there for the taking.

Darn it.

Now she felt the overwhelming urge to make him laugh. To crack that professional exterior right open and get to the warm, gooey center that must exist inside this lion.

Get a grip. Stop fantasizing.

It wasn't like she didn't spend countless hours in the presence of handsome men. Men who graced the covers of magazines, whose faces were all over the internet with headings like *Hottest Bachelors of the Year* and *Top Ten Guys We'd Like to Smother in Honey and Eat Alive.*

Problem was, they were usually boring. Or total jerks. Often both. And they'd all started looking the same to her. Haircut of the season lacquered to their heads. Faces symmetrical. Perfectly balanced. Flat-out *boring.* Total Ken dolls, really—guys who visually paired well with Barbie. Sure, the camera loved them as they pouted and sneered and only sometimes smiled, but they were always looking at the camera lens, not at Wren. She was merely the human extension of a device that took their picture and increased their fame.

So, why was she going gaga over *this* guy? Handsome men did *nothing* for her anymore. Interesting faces did.

Wren braved another good look at Hunt. Yes, he was handsome, but his face wasn't symmetrical, it wasn't perfect after all. The nose was just a tiny bit crooked, like it had been broken at one point, but whoever fixed it did a good job. Not a hint of hair gel, and the messiness wasn't contrived but looked natural, like the result of Hunt running his fingers through it. Maybe his forehead was a little too broad, his cheeks tapering too extremely? Yeah, Hunt had an imperfect but interesting face that reminded her of a lion.

But those eyes were nothing except gorgeous perfection.

Now, if she could just spark some humor in them.

Wren turned a little so that Hunt could get a look at her back and felt herself instantly flush under his intense gaze as he studied and counted the needles there. Her skin prickled as if he were touching her physically.

No, don't think about...and there goes the nips. Oh, forget it.

At least he was looking at her back.

Hunt picked up his Sharpie and added the number twelve to the paper towel beside the word *back.*

"Twelve?" Wren asked. "That's a lot. Isn't it?"

He shrugged. "I don't really know acupuncture. Is that more than what you usually get? Hold still." Hunt was back at her right ear, where he plucked out another needle and set it beside the first one.

"Dunno. This was my first time. Definitely my last with Serge."

"Serge?"

"Yeah, my acupuncturist. The jerk abandoned me when the fire alarm went off."

Hunt growled. Actually *growled* like an angry lion.

Oh. Dear. God.

Something coiled up in her stomach and she wasn't sure if it scared her or turned her on.

"I don't like that," Hunt said.

He plucked out the rest of the needles in her ear and set them aside, then attached the pulse-ox thingy.

"Ninety-eight percent, which is perfect for altitude."

Hunt unclipped the pulse-ox and wrapped a blood pressure cuff around her arm and declared her blood pressure good, too, even though her pulse was racing.

Yeah, wonder why.

"So, how'd you end up going to this Serge guy?"

She didn't want to name drop Barbie so she said, "Last time I was photographing someone, she suggested I get acupuncture and gave me Serge's name. What a mistake."

"Photographing someone?" He started on her other ear.

"Yeah, I'm a professional photographer." Wren felt herself starting to blush. "I do portraiture, photo shoots for magazines and book covers, things like that. I'm getting into real estate photography now, too." That wasn't all she photographed, but she wasn't sure if she wanted to get into her current pet project.

"And someone that you photographed suggested you need acupuncture? Last one." He removed the last needle and put it with the others.

"For my shoulders." She shrugged them, raising them toward her ears, and listened to the loud chorus of snaps and pops like firecrackers going off at midnight.

"Wow, that's bad," Hunt said.

"Thanks."

"I can see why someone would suggest acupuncture."

"Yeah, worked out really great for me, too. Totally relaxed."

The guy finally cracked a smile and snorted and it thrilled her probably way more than it should have.

"Maybe I should've left the rest of the needles in for your relaxation," he said.

She studied his face. Totally deadpan...except for a twinkle in his eye.

Like sunlight sparkling on water.

Game on. Let's see who loses it first.

"But I need a good de-quilling," she said. "It's that time of year when I shed them."

"So, now you're a porcupine? Maybe you did inhale some smoke."

"It wasn't *that* kind of smoke."

That got her the slightest grin.

Even better, Hunt started to strip for her.

He grabbed the hem of his scrubs top and pulled it up while Wren could only stare in fascination and anticipation of seeing his inevitable six-pack—oh, hell, probably an eight-pack—emerge.

But no, not today with her luck. A white tee hid paradise from her view. Wren did get a tiny glimpse of bare skin right at the top of his pants when the tee hitched up as he pulled the scrubs top over his head. Which was almost worse than nothing at all. That skin was tan and tight and she wanted more.

"Here you go," Hunt said, handing her the scrubs top. Then he turned around and blocked her from the crowd so she could slip into it unseen.

Which she did as quickly as she could. Luckily, there was a row of evergreens on the other side of the wall blocking the view on the other side. The bottom hem of the scrubs top fell mid-thigh and the V-neck showed off a little more cleavage than she was comfortable with under the circumstances, but this was way better than the drunk-at-a-toga-party look she'd been sporting before.

"Okay, I'm mostly decent now. Thank you."

Hunt turned around. Those lagoon-blue eyes did that fun and cool widening thing before he looked away at the building.

Oh yeah. Burning building. Forgot about that again.

Only, it didn't look like it was burning. While Hunt had been de-quilling her, the firefighters had done their job and put out the fire. There was still some smoke in the air and a godawful stench, but no towering inferno.

"Hey!" Hunt shouted to another paramedic standing next to a firefighter. "Anyone else?"

The guy shook his head. "All accounted for. How's your patient?"

Hunt turned back to Wren. "Hi, how are you?" Deadpan.

"I'm good, great, thanks. Very relaxed."

"She's very relaxed," Hunt shouted back. "Stunningly good vitals."

"Well, thank you," Wren said. "I take pride in my vitals."

Almost. He *almost* laughed. But then he started counting the needles on the towel as the firefighter started walking over.

"Can I go in and get my clothes?" Wren asked the firefighter. She gestured at herself in Hunt's oversized scrubs top. "I promise I did not show up here wearing this."

"I'm afraid not. There's still a lot of smoke, and just on the off chance that the structural integrity of the building is compromised, no one is allowed back in until further notice."

"Oh boy. There goes my favorite bra."

The firefighter gave Hunt a look and walked away without another word.

"You can keep it," Hunt said, looking at his scrubs top just a little too long.

"I can't keep your clothes! You need this. It's like a uniform, right?"

"It is, but I have more."

"Well, okay. But, can I at least wash it and give it back to you sometime, Hunt?" She unpinned his nametag from the scrubs top and handed it to him.

"It's Elias, actually. Elias Hunt." He stuck his hand out for Wren to shake. Then, he ran it through his hair and she was right about the naturalness of his messy hairstyle. "So... I can't really ask you out."

She blinked rapidly. *Oh. Oh wow. Ouch.*

"Okay. I wasn't asking—"

"Because it's not professional. You're kinda my patient right now."

Yeah, great, just my luck.

"But. There's this really cool place where I like to relax after work. And I know how much you're into relaxation."

Wren nodded like a bobble head. "Yeah, very much into relaxation."

"It's right in Lyons, so, if I were to see you there maybe tomorrow..." He shrugged a broad shoulder. "Or, there's this other place that's also really cool, and if you showed up there Friday *night—*"

"Wow. Two whole cool places. What are they?"

Oh God, he smiled. An actual, full-blown, gorgeous smile.

"It's up to you, depending on what you like. You know, because it's not really a date, just a couple places that you might go to, and I might be there at the same time and want to check up on you if I happen to see you."

She nodded. "Just to make sure I'm okay."

"Just to make sure you're okay, yeah, exactly."

"Because you care about my health."

"Just like any professional would care about your health after escaping a burning building, yeah."

Now *she* was trying not to smile. "So, what are these cool places where I might accidentally run into you?"

"One is a coffee shop. Low key, very public, light of day, lots of caffeine."

"Huh. Caffeine in a coffee shop. Who knew?"

He pursed his lips and nodded sagely. "They specialize in it, actually. And sometimes it gets crowded, so we might have to share a table or else I'd have to drink my coffee standing up and looking like a friendless dork."

Her chest fluttered with laughter trying desperately to escape her twitching lips. She rolled her lips in and bit down on the bottom one, not trusting herself not to burst out laughing if she tried to speak.

Finally, she gained a modicum of control. "Well, we certainly wouldn't want you looking like a friend...a friendless...dork." *Don't laugh, don't laugh, don't laugh.*

"You'd share a table with me?"

"I'd share a table with you, yes. As a sacrifice for your not-looking-dorkishness."

Now his lips twitched as he watched her. "You're a very kind person."

"I am, yes. So, what about this other really cool place? Any caffeine there?"

"Not as much. It's a bar. They have alcohol."

She lifted her eyebrows. "Alcohol in a bar? You don't say."

"It's true. *And* they have strips."

Her eyes bulged. "Excuse me, you think you're going to bump into me at a strip club?" She looked down at herself. "Sir, I think I've given you the wrong impression with my public nudity."

"*Chicken* strips." Now he was rolling his lips in and his blue lagoon eyes sparkled like the sun was shining on them again.

"So, let me get this straight. You want to meet me in a place where *live animals* strip? Isn't that illegal in this state? And to think, I let you de-quill me. Pervert."

And that did it. Elias Hunt burst out laughing.

I win, I win! Wren gave herself a mental high-five.

Elias quickly looked back at the ambulance where a couple other paramedics were watching him, arms folded. One had a definite smirk going on.

"Shit, er, shoot, I gotta go. Your vitals are fine, no signs of smoke inhalation or injuries. Do you think you need to go to the hospital for anything else?" He handed her a form on a clipboard to sign.

"Besides a chance to continue talking to you, no, I don't need a ride to the hospital this morning."

He smiled again as he put the clipboard in his kit. "The coffee shop is Riversong and the bar is Cocktails and Chicken Strips. I like to grab my coffee around noon, or I can be persuaded to eat chicken strips and drink a beer at seven on a Friday. Or both. Your choice, um..." His eyes widened. "I don't even know your name."

"It's Wren, like the bird. Wren Stapleton."

"Alright then, Wren Stapleton." Elias started walking backward, never taking his eyes off her. "Maybe I'll see you around."

"Maybe you will."

Yeah. You definitely will.

TWO

Elias blew out a relieved breath as he walked away from Wren Stapleton.

You're on the job. You're on the job. You're on the job.

Elias prided himself on his professionalism. When he'd been in the service, his teammates called him Lion for two reasons. One, the way he watched over his domain, totally in charge. He wouldn't let the tiniest thing get past him, whether it was a wisp of dust rising in the distance from an approaching enemy, or the way one of his brothers looked a little off while claiming he was fine, leading Elias to discover a health issue before it became life-threatening. He thought his attention to detail also made him a good tracker—his thoroughness and control over his impulses.

And then there was the second reason. When Lion wanted someone, he went after her without a second thought. But he saved that part of himself for when he was off the clock. He never let his impulses get in the way of the mission.

You're on the job.

Those four words were all that lay between Elias going back to work like he was supposed to, or turning back around, pulling Wren into his arms, and lifting her off her feet until those long, strong legs wrapped around his waist, then giving her a kiss so deep she'd think her soul had come loose.

Elias shook his head. He never had a problem keeping his work and playtime separated. But this woman did something to him. She blurred his edges, made him struggle against his instincts.

Elias groaned inwardly when he saw Waylon's smirk.

"'Stunningly good vitals'? Are you serious?"

"What? They were." And shouting it had made Wren Stapleton smile, which was the important thing. *No, you're on the job.*

"*Yeah* they were. So let me guess," Waylon said once Elias climbed into the rig. "You've got a date with Acupuncture Girl."

"That wouldn't be professional, would it, asking out a patient." Elias settled in beside his brother in the back of the ambo, game face back on.

Waylon pretended to look around. "I don't see her in the ambo so she's not a patient."

"She was under my care." Elias tried not to laugh as he remembered Wren calling him a pervert.

Waylon snorted. "Yeah, she was. Do you give all your patients the shirt off your back, or just the ones with stunningly good...*vitals?*"

A memory of Wren's cleavage flashed unbidden into Elias' head and he shook it away.

"She couldn't go back into a burning building for her clothes, could she? So, I loaned her my scrubs top." Elias rummaged around for another top and pulled it on, then pinned his nametag onto it.

Waylon grinned. "Yeah," he said, stretching out the word to about ten syllables. "I see that smile you're trying to hide. So when's your first date?"

"I'm not going on a date with her." Elias didn't look at Waylon as he restocked his bag. And he really tried not to imagine Wren finding one of the business cards tucked into the pocket of his scrubs top and sending him a text.

"What?"

"Nope." Elias enjoyed the skeptical look on Waylon's face.

"Then you're either blind or an idiot."

Elias shrugged a shoulder. "Like I said, I didn't ask her out because that would have been unprofessional." He paused. "But, if I happen to see her around somewhere that I might have told her about, I'll say hi."

Waylon threw his head back and laughed. "Uh-huh, now there's the Lion I know." The ambo pulled out of the parking lot. "I hope you're not taking her to Cocks and Strippers."

Shit. Elias met Waylon's eyes.

"Oh, shit, you did. Brother, why?"

"Why what?"

"Dude."

"What's wrong with the fine establishment of Cocktails and Chicken Strips?"

"Nothing at all. Never mind." Waylon took out his phone and stared at the screen.

Elias blew out a breath. "What? We pick up women there all the time."

Waylon gave Elias the side-eye. "Yeah, see, that's the thing. We pick up women there. We don't take them there on dates."

"Told you, not a date." Elias folded his arms then quickly unfolded them as Tim the driver took the ambulance around a sharp corner. Elias grabbed onto a bar. "Besides, Bear and Gabe bring Ellie and Rochelle now when we all go."

"Yeah, that's because they're *married* to them. So, you're admitting you're going on a date with her."

"No, but if she shows up there, I'll buy her a drink and dance with her if she's so inclined. Just like always. No big deal."

Waylon set his phone aside. "No big deal?" He shook his head and muttered, "Not my problem if you have a complete lack of common sense."

Elias blinked slowly. "What?"

Waylon picked his phone back up. "I'm just saying that if you want to make a good impression, you probably don't want to take her to the fishing hole."

"What makes you think I want to make a good impression?"

Waylon looked back down at his phone. "It was obvious that Stunningly Good Vitals made an impression on *you* by the way you floated back to the rig."

"I did not float back to the rig."

I totally floated back to the rig.

The corner of Waylon's mouth turned up. "Oh, my mistake."

"Yup." Elias pretended to rummage through his kit.

"In that case, if Acupuncture Girl does randomly show up at Cocks and Strips and I happen to bump into her first, I will not hesitate to ask her out. She was smokin'.'"

Elias' head jerked up. "Okay, first, she has a name and it's not Acupuncture Girl or Stunningly Good Vitals. It's Wren. Second, I... well, I didn't *float*, dammit."

Waylon laughed again. "Relax. I'm just pulling your chain. And you *floated*, dude."

Elias' phone buzzed and his heart stuttered. Was she texting him? He quickly looked at the screen. Nope, just an automated text from his internet provider saying the monthly payment went through.

Shit.

He wasn't sure which upset him more—the fact it wasn't Wren texting or that he was so bothered that it wasn't Wren texting.

Elias grinned. "Okay. Maybe I floated a little."

"I'd wonder about you if you hadn't, brother. Not kidding when I say she was hot."

And she was funny, too, Elias thought. *Clever and funny. Big, big turn-ons.*

"What are you gonna do if some woman you took home bumps into the two of you?" Waylon asked.

"Not gonna happen." *What if it happens? I didn't think this through.*

"You didn't think it through, did you?"

"Yeah, I did." *Shit.*

"Liar." Waylon laughed. "Look, if you see one, I'll run interference. I can probably handle three of your exes, but not four, so you better cross your fingers."

"I don't have one ex-girlfriend, let alone four. Jeeze, you make me sound like a man-whore."

"Brother, you danced with four different women just last Friday night."

"And I didn't take a single one home."

"That's a you problem I wasn't thinking about as I escorted a very nice lady to my truck."

Elias laughed. "So, you'll take one for the team?"

"Oh hell yeah." Waylon turned serious. "But you better not fall for her, dude. I need my wingman."

"No way. Not interested in anything serious."

"Good." Waylon scrolled on his phone.

"She probably won't even show."

"Probably not," Waylon murmured.

"But, maybe she'll come to Riversong tomorrow."

Waylon tossed his phone aside again. "Are you fucking kidding me?"

"What?"

"You're fucking kidding me. You just said you weren't looking for anything serious."

"I'm not."

"But you told her about Riversong? Where April works? Where we all hang out?"

"What's the big deal?"

"Shit. You sure *you* didn't inhale smoke? If April sees you talking to Stunning—I mean, Wren—she's going to get on the horn to Rochelle, and Ellie, and Arden, and Gina, and God help you, Stephanie." He ticked the names off on his fingers as he spoke them. "And if they aren't already at the coffee shop, it'll take like a minute for them to converge and sweep her into the posse they've got going on."

Elias reared back. "Dude. You gonna pick out the venue and the flowers and the wedding cake for us right now or when you get home tonight?"

"It's not me, it's the women. If they get one hint that Wren might mean something, they'll insta-friend her. Then, if and when you break up, you'll have a pack of furious women after you."

"Wow, okay, so after you've picked out the bridesmaids' dresses and booked the honeymoon, you'll get both our divorce lawyers lined up, right?"

Waylon put his hand over his heart and gave Elias a solemn look. "Anything for you, brother."

Elias punched him in the arm. "Fuck you."

Waylon laughed and punched him back. But he was wrong about Wren. Yeah, she was hot, but Elias wasn't interested in a relationship. He was having too much fun playing the field, just like Waylon. Seeing what his friends Bear and Gabe had gone through when they met and fell in love with Ellie and Rochelle didn't look like fun—it looked terrifying. Sure, now that they'd settled down, both couples seemed happy.

Okay, more like blissed out.

But, that life wasn't for Elias. He wasn't interested in going through the pain it took to get to a happily ever after.

As they rode, Elias tried to get his head back into the game. But images of Wren teased him—quick flashes of her creamy shoulders. Her chestnut-brown hair. The small of her back flaring out into a heart-shaped ass under the white sheet. Her long, strong legs below his scrubs top. And her eyes—sparkling and hazel and full of mischief. The way she'd joked until she finally made him break protocol and laugh. No woman—smokin' or not—ever got far enough under his skin to make him lose focus when he worked. Especially a woman he'd just met. A woman whose number he'd memorized at a glance from her paperwork.

Tempted to text her first, Elias put his phone away.

———————

IT WAS A STRUGGLE, but Elias managed to stay focused for the rest of the day, in spite of Waylon's occasional teasing.

Right up until the ambo pulled into Riversong's parking lot for their coffee break.

Elias deeply regretted telling his brother that he'd mentioned Riversong to Wren when Waylon smirked and raised his eyebrows.

"Think she'll still be wearing your scrubs top while she's ordering her coffee?"

"She won't be here." But his heart sped up foolishly when his feet hit the gravel. No way would Wren be there just a couple hours after meeting him.

But what if she is?

Jesus, play it cool.

Elias tried to remember when a woman had affected him so quickly and so hard and couldn't.

He also couldn't help looking around the shop when he walked in, but the prettiest women he saw were April standing in front of the espresso machine behind the counter, and Rochelle in her usual window seat, typing away on her computer.

No long-legged, hazel-eyed beauty holding his scrubs top in sight. Elias tried to ignore his irrational disappointment.

"Hey, guys," April said, turning around with two to-go cups in her hands. "Saw you pull in. Give me another minute to get your other drinks."

Tim practically pushed past Elias, Waylon, and their third team-mate, Andy to get to the counter first.

"I hope mine's ready already, gorgeous."

April barely shook her head at his flirting, which was unlike her. She'd always had fun bantering with the guys who flirted with her, but ever since the drive-by shooting at Riversong last winter, she acted subdued. With one exception—Shane Foti. With Shane, she'd gone from pretending to be exasperated even as she smiled and blushed, to outright avoiding talking to him. Shane still came in often, still tried to engage with April, but the wall she'd put up was higher and rockier than the red sandstone cliff overlooking the St. Vrain river outside.

Shane was another of Elias and Waylon's friends from childhood, and it was hard for Elias to watch how April's cold shoulder affected him. Despite being as close as brothers, Elias only knew a little of Shane and April's history growing up.

"Here you go," April said as she set the last two drinks on the counter. "Whose turn is it to pay?"

"Mine." Elias stepped past Tim and paid while the other guys grabbed their to-go cups. He took out some cash and stuffed it into the old-fashioned tip jar on the counter, which got him a genuine smile from April.

"Thanks, Elias."

"You're welcome. How are you?"

"Good," she chirped. "Business is picking up again, finally." April's smile remained but her eyes turned a little sadder.

Elias felt a tap on his shoulder and he jumped as his heart sped up.

She's here. She's—

He turned to see Rochelle smiling sweetly right behind him. Elias quickly hid his disappointment.

"Hey, Elias. I saw you looking around when you came in. Are you looking for Gabe? He's on his way over from the rec center for lunch." She fidgeted with her wedding ring as she spoke—a beautiful band with a mountain landscape carved on it that Gabe had their friend Ben create.

"No, I was just...looking around," he ended lamely.

Rochelle tilted her head as she studied Elias. "You sure? It looked like you were expecting to see someone."

Waylon chucked next to him. "Told you this would happen if she showed up here, didn't I?"

Rochelle's eyes went round. "She? Do you have a girlfriend, Elias?" She looked past Elias and caught April's eye. "Elias has a girlfriend."

"No, I don't," Elias said, caught off-guard. "I just loaned a patient a shirt today and she wanted to give it back, so I told her I stop by here every day."

April smirked. "*That's* a new one, Elias."

Waylon laughed while Elias tried to defend himself. "What? She didn't have any clothes on so I was being a gentleman."

That only made Waylon, Tim, and Andy laugh harder while the women exchanged incredulous looks.

"A gentleman *and* a professional," Elias added, and that made April erupt in laughter.

"Are you sure you weren't 'playing doctor'?" she asked.

"Hey, I'm a paramedic, which is way better than being a doctor." Elias pretended to be offended, but it was worth getting laughed at to see April's smile reach her eyes.

"Well, if anyone comes in here with a scrubs top, I'll be sure to get it for you."

"Oh, why do that?" Rochelle asked, eyes twinkling. "I think he'd rather retrieve it himself."

"No, I...well."

"What's her name?" April propped her elbows on the counter and rested her chin on her hands.

"And, it's starting," Waylon drawled.

"Your fault."

"What's starting?" Rochelle asked.

"The gossip grapevine. Which one of you is going to call Ellie?" Waylon looked back and forth between Rochelle and April.

Rochelle put her hands on her hips. "That's so insulting, how you just assume things." She shook her head in disgust, then smiled. "Of course *I'm* the one calling Ellie."

"And I'm calling Arden and Gina," April added. "Right after I tell Hannah."

"Then I'll call Stephanie after Ellie, and I'll text Sandra. I think that's all of us," Rochelle finished.

"Wait, no!" But their laughter drowned out Elias' words.

An alarm on Tim's phone interrupted the hilarity. "That's our next call. Time to go," he said.

"Tell Gabe we said hi," Waylon called over his shoulder as they jogged out the door.

"Be careful out there, guys," Rochelle shouted just before the door closed behind them.

WREN WASN'T at Riversong the next day either, much to Elias' disappointment. He didn't have to ask about her—April greeted him with "I haven't seen a woman with a scrubs top, sorry" before he could open his mouth.

Oh, well. It was just a shirt.

It wasn't just a shirt. He'd practiced what he wanted to say when he saw Wren, even though everything he came up with sounded corny. He'd dreamed about Wren all night and awakened sweat-drenched and aroused beyond reason.

She can't possibly be as hot as you remember. Your brain has made her into some sort of goddess and you'd just be disappointed if you saw her again. Move on.

"Hey, don't worry, brother," Waylon said as he clapped his hand on Elias' shoulder. "We'll find you someone new tonight."

Right. It was Friday, which meant Cocktails and Chicken Strips. No way she'd show up there if she wasn't taking him up on coffee first.

"Who all's gonna be there?" Elias asked. That used to mean all their brothers—Shane, Ben, Bear, Gabe, and Badger. Now it included Bear and Gabe's new wives, Ellie and Rochelle. Badger and Brianna were a maybe these days, too. Brianna had a budding music career and Badger was often on the road with her when he wasn't working as a bodyguard with Watchdog, along with Shane.

"The marrieds are staying in tonight," Waylon informed him.

"You know if Shane's going?"

April had her back turned toward them but Elias couldn't help but notice her shoulders rise halfway to her ears when he asked about Shane.

"Shane's a no."

And he watched her shoulders ease back down.

"Ben's a no, too, so it's just you and me," Waylon continued, which didn't surprise Elias. Ben wasn't much into the bar scene, preferring quieter, more nerdly pursuits. He was like their friend Bear that way—both men were big and quiet and not as likely to go out unless it was with the whole crowd.

Elias nodded. If it was just him and Waylon tonight, the objective was clear—find the hottest women and have fun. Elias smiled softly as he mentally waved goodbye to the image of Wren in his head.

"Sounds good. Hell, let's make it two women each."

Waylon punched his upper arm. "Yeah! And the Lion is back."

It would take two women at least to measure up to one Wren.

ELIAS AND WAYLON had an easy workday for a Friday, and with a whole weekend off to look forward to, Elias' mood lifted by the time he pulled into the bar's parking lot. He was ready to dance, ready to drink, and ready to feel soft hands playing with his hair and softer lips brushing his neck. Would tonight be a blonde, a brunette, or maybe a redhead? Didn't matter, so long as she could dance and was up for a good time.

He saw Waylon's truck so he headed on in to find his buddy. There he was, at a high top near the dance floor, a pitcher of beer at the ready. Walking to the table, Elias' head was on a swivel as he checked out the women clustered at tables and standing along the bar. Several checked him out in return. Their gazes swept up and down his body, lips curving up into seductive smiles. But the usual thrill of deciding which woman he wanted to pursue first just wasn't there.

None of them are as attractive as Wren.

He pushed the thought of her away as he lifted his chin at Waylon, who'd just caught sight of him. Waylon grabbed an empty mug and poured Elias a beer from the pitcher.

"Maybe this'll cheer you up." Waylon pushed the beer across the tabletop as Elias sat down with his back to the door.

"What do you mean?"

Waylon just stared. "Come on. You should have hoovered up at least three women on your way in."

"I'm waiting for someone special." Dammit, the words came out all on their own. Elias quickly took a swig of his beer. It was way too hoppy—which taught him to show up before Waylon so that he could order a normal pitcher of beer. The dude was constantly trying new things, the more extreme the better.

"You don't like it?" Waylon pointed at the mug.

"Is this actually beer or is it just straight-up pine sap? It tastes like licking a forest."

"Better than the boring shit you order." He chugged the last of his and poured another. "Don't tell me you're waiting on your patient to show."

"Told you, I don't date patients." He took another sip as if a second try would somehow magically turn this undrinkable swill into an actual beer. Surprise—it didn't. "Like I said, I'm just waiting on someone special."

Face it. She's about as likely to show up as this beer is likely to start tasting good. Time to pick up a shot of whiskey and a blonde chaser at the bar.

Elias started to stand but paused when he felt the hair on the back of his neck stand up as chills ran down his arms. But these were good chills—the kind that said something exciting was on the way. He turned around and looked toward the entrance.

His gaze immediately fell on the most beautiful woman he'd ever seen. Curling chestnut hair framed a perfect oval face. Full, luscious, red lips. Inquisitive hazel eyes that said she was up for all sorts of fun. And her body—she was model-tall but with all the curves Elias could want. He was a shameless boob-man, no denying it, and her blouse was unbuttoned far enough down to show off her ample cleavage.

"And there's someone special now. Daisy Dukes and cowboy boots." Elias pointed subtly at her but he didn't need to. Waylon was already staring as she made her way through the crowd. She outshone every woman around her.

Wren Stapleton had entered the building.

She looked around until her eyes met his and those luscious red lips parted in a dazzling smile.

And yes, Elias' memory had lied in his dreams.

She was even more gorgeous than he remembered.

"Whoa. She is way above *your* paygrade, brother," Waylon said.

"You're just jealous." Elias grinned.

"I might be. Except she only has eyes for you." Waylon grinned back. "Think I'm gonna find myself a dance partner and let you examine your patient."

"Not my patient."

But Waylon was already headed for the bar, which might as well have been on the moon as far as Elias was concerned. He stood up to face Wren and his vision tunneled. Wren took up the entire field until she was standing right in front of him.

"Well hi there," she said as she plopped her bag onto the bar stool beside Elias. "Fancy running into you here."

"Yeah. It's not like I told you where I'd be on Friday night."

"No? I distinctly remember you telling me exactly where you liked to hang out and when."

Elias tapped his chin. "Oh, that's right, I did tell you. You know, I was at Riversong this week, too."

"Were you?" Wren unzipped her bag, reached in, and pulled out his scrubs top, folded in a neat square. He hoped she hadn't washed it, that the scent of her skin clung to the fabric. She laid it on the high top and smoothed her hand over it. Elias got the sudden image of her hand stroking his chest—her long fingers gliding over his pecs and down to his abs, then lower. Hell, he could damn near feel it. He did his best to suppress an intense shiver of desire as his mouth went dry.

"Yup," he said, his voice catching lightly. "I was at Riversong yesterday and earlier today. I don't remember seeing you there."

"Well, I didn't want to give you the wrong idea about me."

"Wrong idea?"

"Mmm-hmm." Her eyes twinkled with mischief. "See, I've been to Riversong so often that I'm addicted to their cinnamon-honey lattes with a double shot of espresso. I wouldn't have been able to control myself and order just one."

Elias felt his lips twitch. "Double shot? So you're a caffeine addict."

She nodded solemnly. "Don't judge."

"Never." Elias leaned on the table. "Is that why your pulse was racing when I took your blood pressure? Too much caffeine?"

"Nope. I was relaxed from the acupuncture, remember?"

She took a step closer and Elias caught a whiff of her skin—ripe peaches in midsummer with a hint of salt. His tongue pressed against the back of his front teeth. He rolled his bottom lip in to keep from licking his lips.

"Right, you were totally relaxed. In that case, I'd hate to see your pulse when you're excited."

She focused on his mouth as she said, "Aw, what a shame."

Holy shit.

She lifted her gaze and locked onto his. "Or maybe not a shame. If you checked my pulse right now that would mean I was your patient again."

He tilted his head. "You don't want to be my patient?"

She stepped closer until he felt the warmth from her body against his chest. "Nope."

His lips twinged again. "You weren't satisfied with my care?"

"Absolutely not." She pursed her lips in an attempt to look serious but her sparkling eyes weren't fooling him.

"What was it about my care you didn't like?" Then he slapped his forehead. "Oh, right. You called me a pervert."

She pressed her lips together and looked to the side. He noticed her belly quivering with suppressed laughter. "Did I?"

Elias pressed on, just to make her laugh first. "You did. You accused me of bestiality."

She snickered.

Ha! Score one for me.

"I never said that."

"Yeah you did," he continued. "Right after you told me what a nice person you were."

Her head snapped back and her gaze laser focused on his, making his belly tighten and his cock twitch.

"Hey, you said I was nice first. And you know what? I *am* a nice person." She glanced at the two mugs on the table. "I'm so nice, that I showed up at an animal strip joint just to return your scrubs top. *And,* to prove that I'm over-the-top nice, I'm going to sit down here and share this table with you to keep you from looking like a friendless dork."

Elias snorted. Wren's eyes blazed and he realized she was keeping a laugh score, too. That did something to his chest. If he wasn't mistaken, his heart had just broken all the laws of medical science and flipped over.

"I'm not a friendless dork." He pointed to the two beer mugs on the table. "See? I have a friend."

Wren considered the mugs. "Or, it could be camouflage." She rounded the table and took Waylon's seat in front of his mug. Elias missed the heat from Wren's skin and her salty, peachy scent immediately. "This mug's empty." She reached for the beer pitcher.

Elias' hand shot out and grabbed hers before she could pick it up. Now, not only did his heart flip when he touched her, but he could have sworn he'd accidentally touched a patient receiving an electrical shock from a defibrillator. Wren looked up at him as if she'd felt the same thing.

"I can't let you drink that," he said.

"I didn't think I was your patient."

"You're not. But I wouldn't let my worst enemy drink that swill."

"Then why did you order it?"

"I didn't order it. My friend did."

Wren twisted on her seat as she looked down and around. "Your invisible friend whose lap I'm sitting on right now?"

Wren scored another point when Elias laughed.

"Why can't I drink this?" She leaned forward and sniffed the beer. "Wow. This is *not* swill. This isn't even beer. It's a pine tree disguised as beer."

"Yup, that's what I told my buddy. There's a forest in every pitcher."

She snickered again. That left them tied by Elias' count.

"So, let me buy you a real drink instead?" he asked.

Instead of answering, Wren glanced at the dance floor then turned her gaze back on him. "Do you dance?"

"I do."

She stood up. "I think I'd rather dance than drink for the moment."

"Fine by me." Elias came around the table and lightly laid his hand on the small of her back. He guided her through the bar until they stepped onto the dance floor. She rewarded him with a grin as she rose up on her tiptoes and leaned toward his ear. Her breath tickled him and this time, he couldn't suppress his shiver.

"Another reason why I wasn't happy with your care? You didn't touch me nearly enough."

Elias inhaled sharply. *Damn.* He was used to being the pursuer, leaving no doubt in a woman's mind what he wanted. Wren was outpacing him, and that was a first.

He liked it.

As she faced him, he pressed his hand against her back and drew her closer just as the first notes of Riley Green's "Worst Way" started playing. The way Wren smiled told him that she knew the lyrics too. The way her eyes locked with his told him she was feeling every word of a song about desire so strong you skip the wine and roses and go straight for the good stuff.

Elias slid his hands from her back to her swaying hips. He took his time, running his fingers along the stretch of warm, bare skin between her shirt and her shorts, luxuriating in the way her skin rippled under his fingers and her eyelids dropped to half-mast.

"How's that for touching you?" he breathed against her ear.

Wren rolled her lower lip into her mouth and let it slide back out under her teeth. "It's a good start."

She ran her fingers up his chest—lightly, teasingly, just like he'd imagined—and laced them behind his head. Her fingertips played with the nape of his neck and her thumbs caressed the sides of his throat, sending electric tingles throughout his body. Wren swayed to the music like a pendulum, her body casually brushing against his. Teasing. Infuriating. Building a fire inside him that threatened to rage out of control if he didn't maintain his composure.

He realized his body had other ideas when he found himself pulling her tightly against him, turning the teasing brushes into firm pressure. It still wasn't enough to satisfy him.

"Wren Stapleton," he murmured in her ear. "I don't want to be here with you."

She jerked in his arms and he gripped her tighter so she couldn't get away. She looked into his eyes, hers full of sudden confusion.

"That's not what your body's telling me."

"No? It's not telling you that I'd rather be with you someplace quiet and dark and as far away from other people as possible?" He grinned as warmth replaced the confusion in her eyes. "Guess I'll have to work on my communication skills."

"Oh, I see. I *feel* it, actually." She pressed against his hardness and did a little shimmy with her hips that made him groan.

"So." He swallowed hard. "What do you say you come home with me right now?" He felt slightly dizzy at the realization that his happiness depended on her answer. He never asked a woman to his home anymore, but always went to hers so that he could leave before morning.

I never get in this deep, this quickly, with anyone.

But he couldn't deny it—there was something special about Wren, from the moment she opened her mouth and made him laugh. He wanted more of her.

No. All of her. *Now.*

He waited for an answer that never came.

Wren only looked him in the eye, saying nothing. She unlaced her fingers and dropped her hands to her sides. He let go of her hips, his gut churning. *Dammit.* He'd gone too fast, made her think she was just another cheap pick-up.

What an idiot. I'm a fucking moron. Why did I tell her to meet me here?

She turned her back on him and he followed her to their table, trying to think of something to say that might salvage the evening. Wren slung her oversized purse onto her shoulder. Then she picked up his scrubs top and held it out for him. He took it.

"Wren, I—"

She smiled as she grabbed his hand.

"Drive fast, but not so fast that I lose you as I follow. I'm still new in town and the last thing I want is to get lost tonight."

THREE

Elias' hands damn near shook as he unlocked his front door. He barely registered the early summer night sounds around them—crickets chirping, the ping of moths hitting the porch light overhead, the ticking of his truck and Wren's car in the drive as they cooled down after they sped through the winding foothills to his house. No —his senses hyper-focused down to the woman standing just behind him—the heat radiating from her body, the sound of her breath coming in excited pants, the salty-sweet smell of her skin mingling with the earthy forest around them.

Elias swore he felt a spot on his back grew warmer just before she touched him there. Her hand slid up his back to his shoulder, the one he'd slung his scrubs top over. Suddenly, trying to get into his house was too much of a bother. He contemplated picking her up and carrying her around to the backyard and the hammock strung up under the trees where he sometimes slept on hot summer nights.

Wren slid her hand down from his shoulder to his hand, which was definitely shaking now. She steadied it.

Dear God in Heaven.

Elias couldn't stop himself. He turned and pulled Wren against him. Her lips parted in surprise. He tangled his fingers in her hair. *So soft and silky.* Elias tilted his head and leaned in to claim her mouth. When their lips met, he felt the same jolt of electricity he experienced the first time he touched her. And when she made a surprised little sound as he parted her lips with his tongue, his cock jumped eagerly. He turned with her in his arms and pressed her up against the door. Wren hooked one of her legs around his waist and he slid his hand down her back, over her ass, and gripped her leg. Just in time —he felt her other leg wobble as if she'd gone weak in the knees.

Oh yeah. Bringing her home had been a great idea.

Thank God he didn't have any close neighbors or they'd be watching a free show. All the same, Elias stopped kissing Wren long enough to unlock the door and get her inside.

But when the door opened finally, an unwelcome sight greeted Elias.

"Dammit. You're kidding me. What are you two doing here?"

Chuck and Penny only stared back up at him, Chuck looking guilty and Penny looking proud of herself.

Wren dropped to her knees—and not in the way Elias was imagining her a minute ago.

"Aw! Come here, you cuties."

Penny, being the shameless and assertive little Jack Russel Terrier she was, practically tripped Chuck on her way to Wren's outstretched hand. The big mutt was used to it. He wagged his entire body, not just his long tail, and looked back up at Elias to see if all was forgiven—which it most certainly was not. His floppy ears dropped as Chuck decided to press his luck again with the newcomer already enchanted by Penny. Wren let go of her tote and reached out to Chuck.

"Aren't you a pretty boy with your tiger stripes?" She ran her hand over Chuck's brindled coat. The dog's eyes nearly rolled back in his head and Elias knew the feeling.

So much for taking Wren straight to bed. Little cockblockers.

"Sorry about this. They had been stowed away in their room,"

Elias said as he draped his scrubs top over the back of the nearest chair. "But Penny is an evil genius who has yet to be stumped by a locked door when she truly wants out. Then again, sometimes the neighbor kid who watches them when I'm working forgets to lock the door."

"Oh, I don't mind," Wren said without bothering to look up. She turned her attention from Chuck back to Penny. "Did he call you an evil genius? Who's a good evil genius? That's you! *You're* the good evil genius."

Elias should have been annoyed at this turn of events. The last woman he brought home was the last woman he brought home precisely because of his dogs. Penny had pulled off a great escape that time, too, and when she and Chuck greeted Elias and his date at the door, Shayla pretended to be amused. But it was clear the date—and the budding relationship—was over. Wren was the total opposite, and God help him, Elias felt an even stronger connection to her.

However, this date might be over anyway. Wren didn't look like she was about to stop petting his dogs anytime soon.

And then, as if she'd heard his thoughts—damn, maybe he'd given it away with his body language—she stopped scratching their heads and stood up. Some of the sparkle had left her eyes and he immediately hated himself for it.

"Sorry. I love dogs, and these two are adorable." She clutched the handles of her tote bag and looked down as if he was about to scold her for insta-loving his dogs. Now that—her embarrassment—he didn't like.

"Adorable miscreants, you mean. Is it all right if I get them back into their room? Otherwise, they can get underfoot when I have company."

Her gaze snapped up to his. "Oh. Yeah, sure." He tried not to stare at the blush starting at her cleavage and climbing her throat as he wondered what caused—

Oh, yeah. Company. Shit. Now she thinks I bring women back here all the time and take them straight to bed.

Of course, that was exactly the plan with Wren. Straight to bed, and if she wanted to leave right after, no problem and probably for the best.

Except she liked his dogs. Loved dogs in general, actually. Like he did.

A little voice in his head protested at the thought of her leaving right after sex. That voice was not part of his plan. No way did Elias want to get serious with anyone. He was having way too much fun playing the field.

Frustrated with himself, he snapped his fingers and got the dogs' attention. Chuck went back to looking like he'd gotten caught murdering someone and Penny's expression was nothing but *Do you mind? I was busy soaking up my well-earned praise.*

"Come on, you two." He gave Wren an apologetic smile. "It might take a minute to get them situated. I'm going to let them out back for a minute and then try to figure out how Penny got the door open this time. Kitchen's that way." He pointed. "Make yourself at home. Grab a beer if you want."

"It's not a forest, is it?" she asked with a hopeful little smile.

"Forest?"

"Forest-flavored. The beer, I mean." She gestured toward the kitchen as she sucked in her lower lip.

"Oh, yeah, right. The pitcher of beer Waylon ordered."

"I was going for a call-back from earlier but flubbed it I guess." The confidence she'd shown at Cocks and Strippers all the way up to standing on Elias' porch faded a little more.

Shit.

Elias stopped trying to herd the dogs and looked straight up at the ceiling. He jumped like he was trying to catch a football.

"What exactly are you doing?"

"Oh, that's just me trying to catch the perfectly good call-back you lobbed at my head instead of totally missing it." He looked behind him. "Nope, there it goes. They sometimes do that, just bounce right off my thick skull and go on their way."

When he turned back around, there was that smile and sparkle in her eyes. He just stared for what felt like a full minute, feeling a little lost in her gaze.

"Gonna just get these two squared away," he finally said.

"Wait. What are their names?"

"Oh, yeah, I didn't tell you. The big guy is Chucklehead—Chuck for short—and the evil genius is Penny."

Wren grinned. "Good night, Chuck and Penny." She waved her fingers at them and they wagged their tails. Penny threw a look over her shoulder at Elias and started trotting back to Wren.

"Oops." Wren giggled and stooped as the little dog picked up speed, tail going a hundred miles an hour. "I made a tactical error."

"Naw. Penny's been looking for another loyal minion to hire. She's going to try and lowball you, but keep in mind she's worth billions in kibble stock and crypto." He kept a straight face.

"Oh really?" Wren's gaze flashed to his, and now he recognized the smile she'd given him back when she was dressed in nothing more than a sheet. *Ah, the good old days.* "How much is she paying you so I can ask for a fair wage?"

"You're better off talking to the Chucklehead about that. Don't let his name fool you. The Chuckster's a much better negotiator than me. I have to pay for Penny's food and toys as part of my deal, but he talked her into stock options, a 401K, *and* dental."

Wren's lips twitched as she quickly looked away, fighting her laughter. She gave Penny a good scratch behind the ears and stood up.

"Go on, evil genius," she told Penny. The little dog tilted her head, unable to comprehend how Wren could defy her every wish, before she turned and trotted back to Elias and Chuck.

"I'll just be a minute."

"Sure," Wren said, sounding a little distracted as she looked around his place.

"Come on, guys." At least they were smart enough to know they were done getting away with anything tonight and headed straight for their room. The dogs had the run of the house when Elias was home. When he had to leave for work or went out with Waylon, they stayed in a spare bedroom kitted out with doggie beds, toys, a water station, a TV, and a doggie door in a regular door that opened to a fenced-in kennel run.

Elias followed the dogs outside, contemplating the woman who waited in his living room. This was not how he'd expected or wanted the night to go. His dates never made him stop and think. They were all about fun—a short chase, then a quick, good time for both of them and back on their way. They didn't meet and fall in love with his dogs. They didn't make him laugh either, or think about them nonstop for days.

Once he got Penny and Chuck back inside and settled, he went back to the living room.

Wren was gone.

She faked liking my dogs, just like Shayla. A weird mixture of anger, hurt, and disappointment washed over Elias, far worse than what he'd felt when Shayla ghosted him. He shook his head. *How could I be so stupid? I thought she was different. I thought she might be someone special. I thought she—*

"Sorry, I needed the restroom," she said from somewhere behind him. He whipped around until he faced her, standing in the opposite hallway leading to his bedroom and the guest bathroom.

Wren took one look at the expression on his face and stepped backward as her smile turned to alarm. "I promise I wasn't snooping."

Elias quickly smiled, putting all the reassurance he could into it. "No, sorry, you're fine. You just startled me. My fault. I should have told you where the bathroom was." He blew out a breath. How did she manage to keep him so off-balance and flustered?

Her gaze flicked to the front door. "Maybe I should go. I have work early tomorrow."

"Please, I didn't mean to look upset. I just thought..."

"That I'd sneaked out without saying goodbye?" Wren's shoulders relaxed. A smile played at her lips again.

"Yes. Exactly."

"And it upset you that much?" She looked at him quizzically.

"Yes." He was surprised at his reaction, but it was the truth. He found he was also surprised she'd stuck around after Penny and Chuck's antics.

Wren nodded and walked toward him, her gaze fixed on his, studying him like no woman ever had. God, she was *intense*. She stopped inches from him. "Some other woman did that to you, I bet. Met the dogs, and poof! Out of your life."

Elias' head jerked back. "Did the acupuncture give you psychic powers?"

She grinned. "No. I'm just really good at reading people. I do it for a living."

"Right. Photography."

She nodded. "I have to get my subjects to open up. Show their true selves to the camera. Well, at least that's *my* goal, but it wasn't always what my subjects wanted. It was hard with actors. They put up a front like no one else. So, I had to be good at reading their moods from the second they walked into the studio."

Wren reached up and touched a spot just behind his left ear. Then slowly—achingly slowly—ran it down the side of his neck to just below his Adam's apple. He heard someone groan and was pretty sure it was himself. "I had to figure out how to get them to relax and drop the front."

"I wasn't putting up a front," Elias insisted.

"No, you weren't," Wren purred. "But, I misread you for a second. Kinda rare for me. You...throw me off my game." Her cheeks flushed pink as she looked away for a moment.

"Well, as long as we're being honest, you throw me off mine, too." Elias covered Wren's hand with his and pressed it against his chest.

"I do?"

"Absolutely."

"But, you were so professional the other day."

"I was trying my damnedest to stay professional and not sweep you off your feet and carry you to the back of the ambo for a thorough examination."

Wren snickered, then her face went completely neutral. But her eyes continued to sparkle with humor and mischief and he felt his chest tighten.

"That's not standard protocol?" she asked.

But Elias wasn't trying to make Wren crack up, not this time, and he wasn't expecting her to make him laugh either. He was being dead serious for once.

"It's not standard protocol for me." He glanced around the room. "Taking someone back to my home isn't, either."

Her eyes widened the tiniest bit with understanding. "Sorry some idiot didn't like Penny and Chuck. I think they're adorable." Wren's voice sounded throaty.

"I think *you're* adorable."

She gave him a wicked smile. "How adorable?"

"Let me show you."

FOUR

Past the point of playful teasing now, Elias gave in to the need that had been simmering between them since the moment Wren walked into Cocks and Strippers. He wasted no time as he picked Wren up and carried her down the hall. Finally he had her in his bedroom. He set her down on the floor a few feet from the bed. He hooked his thumbs into her belt loops and tugged her forward. Elias tilted his head and went in for a kiss as his fingers splayed across her heart-shaped ass. The second their lips met, he felt liquid fire coursing through his veins.

Elias' hands slipped under Wren's shirt and brushed along her ribcage, his fingers trailing a path that made her shiver. She watched him intently, dark lashes fluttering, their faces mere inches apart. Her breath hitched when his warm lips grazed her collarbone before they met hers once more. Elias followed each kiss with a gentle nip. He groaned against her lips while his hand slid down and pressed against the soft skin of her stomach, making her gasp.

Wren's hands found the hem of his shirt and pulled it up. She unbuttoned it, then ran her fingertips along the lines of his abs. Elias' tongue traced a line from Wren's collarbone down to her cleavage. Wren moaned, arching her head back, her fingers entwined in his hair as she guided his mouth where she needed him most.

They made their way towards the bed until the backs of Wren's legs touched the edge.

"Do you want this?" he asked.

She nodded as she reached for his belt buckle, all her attention focused on undoing it.

"Wren. I need you to say it."

Her fingers slowed as she looked into his eyes, puzzled.

"What is it?" he asked, afraid she'd tell him he was taking things too far, too fast.

She exhaled audibly, smiling. "It's...I'm not used to guys who ask that question."

That made him growl. "That's a damn shame. But you still haven't answered me." He dropped his hands, ready for her to tell him no, that she was ready to leave.

"Yes, Elias. I want this. Or I wouldn't be here. I walked into the bar knowing exactly what I wanted, and here we are." She tilted her head. "Do *you* want this?"

God, she was beautiful to begin with, and her open desire only made her more so.

"I've been dreaming of this moment since I first laid eyes on you. As inappropriate as that is."

Wren laughed. "I'm not your patient."

"That's what I've been saying."

"Oh really?" she teased.

Elias opened his mouth to backtrack, but she took that opportunity to kiss him.

After that, Wren took her time undressing him. He savored every moment of watching her sparkling eyes as she exposed more of his body. She pushed his unbuttoned shirt off his shoulders and stopped to take in his torso.

"You could be a model, you know."

"No thanks." He'd been told that before and always laughed it off. But the compliment coming from Wren sank deep into his heart.

With an amused expression, she shook her head and went back to undressing him. She took her time with his button fly, letting the backs of her fingers brush his boxers as she undid button after button. When she reached for the waistband of his boxer briefs, Elias could barely contain himself. He helped her slide them down with his jeans, revealing his hard, throbbing cock.

Wren took him in her hand, gently stroking him as she looked into his eyes. He could see the desire burning within her. She started to lower herself but he stopped her.

"Oh, no. That's not how this is going to go."

"No?"

"Mmm, nope."

Elias' hands delved into Wren's long hair. His fingers wove through the strands as he pulled her head back, exposing her throat to his hungry lips. God, she smelled good and tasted even better. Wren gasped as he kissed and nipped greedily at her skin. When he found a spot on her neck that seemed to set her ablaze, she dug her nails into his back.

"Oh God, Elias," she moaned as he continued to lavish attention on her sensitive skin. "I need you."

He growled low in response and savored her shivering body. His lips trailed lower, pausing only when he needed to unbutton her shirt and unhook her bra. Wren cried out as he took her nipple between his lips, suckling gently before teasing it with his tongue. Her hips bucked against him.

"That's it, baby, my hungry, hungry baby." Elias undid her shorts and watched them drop to her ankles. Her silky panties teased his cock as she rubbed against him.

"One sec," she said as she stepped to the side. She kicked off her boots with a laugh and returned to his arms.

"These need to go, too." Elias tucked his fingers under her panties and slid them down her long, shapely legs. Kneeling at her feet, he grasped her ass and pulled her forward to his mouth. She smelled so good—musky and sweet as he nuzzled her. His first taste of her hot, wet pussy made his cock twitch, but her satisfied moan made it jump. He licked and stroked her until her juices flowed free and her body tensed. Elias pulled away and she gasped.

"No, please! *Need* you."

Elias slipped a finger inside her and she immediately squeezed tightly around it. Velvet, pure velvet. He slid his finger in and out as he pressed his thumb against her clit. She gripped his shoulders and rode his finger shamelessly, head tossed back. His cock wept as he watched her take her pleasure from him. Then he went back to eating her out until her knees buckled and she pressed herself against his mouth.

"Elias, my God! So good!"

When her body went limp, he laid her down on his bed. He covered her body in kisses as he worked his way up her body. Straddling her, he opened the nightstand drawer. Elias pulled out a string of condoms, tore one off, and laid the rest of them on the nightstand. As he started to tear the foil open, Wren snatched it out of his hands.

"Not yet, bad boy," she purred. In one quick movement she sat up and grabbed his cock. "You aren't stopping me this time."

Elias groaned at her boldness. He was used to more passive women—not that he minded doing most of the work. But Wren excited him as she kept him guessing. Though there was no mistaking her intention as she leaned forward. She teased the weeping tip of his cock first with a single flick of her tongue. Then she pressed her lips against it and encircled his tip before opening her mouth for him, creating the illusion of pressing against the tightest, sweetest pussy.

"Fuck," he gasped. Then she took him all the way inside her mouth. She held him there as her tongue stroked the underside of his cock before moving back down to his sensitive tip.

As she continued to move her mouth up and down his shaft, Elias felt his body begin to tense with pleasure. He could feel the warmth of her breath against his skin, and the way her tongue teased him drove him wild. He ran his fingers through her hair, gently pulling it as she took him deeper into her mouth.

"Lord have mercy," he groaned, his voice husky with desire. "You're so good at this."

Wren looked up at him, her eyes filled with lust as she continued to pleasure him.

"Slow down, baby," he warned her. "I'm not going to last long."

But Wren didn't listen. Instead, she took him deeper into her mouth, creating incredible sensations with her tongue. Elias groaned as she licked up and down his shaft, teasing him with every stroke.

His orgasm built, the pressure growing with every passing second.

"I can't hold it, baby."

"I don't want you to. I want to taste you like you tasted me."

He groaned as he tried to hold back, but it was no use. Her mouth, her hands, and most of all, her desire, proved to be too much. With one final groan, he came undone, his body shaking with the force of his release.

Wren pulled back, licking her lips as she looked up at him. "Mmm, you taste so good," she said, a wicked smile playing on her lips.

Elias could only grin in response as he tried to catch his breath. He should have been done, ready to sleep, but his cock had other plans. He needed more of her. All of her.

He reached for the condom Wren had snatched from him but she beat him to it. She tore the package open and rolled the condom onto him slowly, taking her time as she watched him intently.

"God, you're so sexy," Elias whispered, his voice low and husky. He grasped her shoulders and pushed her down.

Wren grinned as he leaned down to kiss her deeply. Her hand snaked between them and she guided him inside her. Elias couldn't help but moan at the feeling of being connected with her. It went deeper than their physical connection as memories of watching her laugh, of seeing the sunlight play on her hair, of his excitement when she entered the bar played through his mind. He slowed his pace, not wanting their connection to end. Ever.

"Almost," Wren whispered, her eyes tightly closed.

"Look at me," he gasped. "Want to see when it happens."

Wren opened her eyes. Her gaze locked onto his.

With one final thrust, they both reached their peak together, their bodies shuddering with the force of their orgasms. Elias rolled until Wren lay on top of him. He held her tightly, not wanting to let go as they both caught their breath. Her heart beat quickly against his chest. They lay together in silence, their bodies entwined, until Wren finally spoke.

"I think I need to be your patient again."

Elias tensed. Did she regret what just happened? Was this her way of stepping back?

"Reason?"

"I think I left my body. That can't be normal."

Elias snorted. "Side effects of a spectacular orgasm include rapid heartbeat, elevated breathing rate, curling toes, tremors, and out-of-body experiences. Totally normal."

"Huh. Guess I've never had one before."

"Never?"

"Not like that." She blew out a breath which tickled his chest. "It's going to take me a while to recover."

"You know what speeds up recovery?"

"Another one?"

Damn! He loved the hopeful tone in her voice.

"Well, yes, actually, now that you mention it."

"Oh, I get it." She nodded against his chest. "I need to build up a tolerance through multiple exposures."

Elias laughed. *Dammit, Wren won again.* And to prove the point, she licked her fingertip and drew a tick mark in the air.

"Are we tied now?"

There went that adorable head tilt. "You're keeping score too?"

"Of course."

"No you're not. Because if you were, you'd know I'm ahead of you."

"I don't think so."

"You don't believe me?"

"Nope." He popped the 'P' and grinned.

"Wow, so cocky."

"We could start over and keep an official count."

"Oh, that totally means I'm ahead of you."

Elias' growl turned into an unexpected laugh as he rolled Wren over onto her back.

"Ha! Now I'm ever further ahead—" He cut her off with a kiss.

"Mmm," she said when he finally let her come up for air. "I think I'm leaving my body again."

"Yeah, you definitely need more spectacular orgasms."

"What if I have too many too soon and can't get back into my body?"

Elias' heart sped up as he made a decision. He rolled to his side and propped himself up on one elbow so he could judge Wren's reaction. "There's a cure for that too."

"Oh?"

"A big, hearty breakfast, which I should prepare for you first thing tomorrow."

Her eyes widened momentarily—her tell, he was learning—before she regained her composure.

"Let's try the multiple exposure cure in the meantime, shall we?"

ELIAS WOKE to his alarm going off at the crack of dawn. Dammit, he'd forgotten to turn it off yesterday. He hit the snooze button and the night before came back to him. Smiling as he thought about making breakfast, he started to apologize to Wren for waking her when he realized he was alone in bed.

He sat up quickly and looked toward the en suite bathroom door.

It was open, and Wren wasn't in there. His heart sped up with something akin to dread, just like it had the night before.

What the hell, man? Get a grip.

Maybe she was in search of coffee in the kitchen.

Elias got out of bed and pulled on a pair of boxer briefs before making his way down the hall. He smelled coffee brewing from his automatic coffeemaker. Maybe she was sitting at the table drinking a mug of it, not wanting to wake him up so early. He listened for any sounds, but all he could hear were the pups restless in their room. He'd find Wren first and give her a nice, long kiss before inflicting the terrible two on her.

She won't mind. She likes them.

Elias ignored the warmth in his chest at the innocuous thought.

The kitchen was empty. The coffee pot was full.

"Wren?" he called out. She wasn't in the living room or in the other bathroom—the door was open when he passed it in the hall.

Wait? Could she be...?

Elias grinned and headed for Chuck and Penny's room, certain that she was in there playing with them. He opened the door to see only his pups staring at him, tails wagging, expecting breakfast like it was any other day.

Shit. Idiot.

Elias went back to the living room to look out the front window. Just as he suspected, Wren's car was gone. He didn't see a note in the bedroom or one in the kitchen. He found his phone and checked it for texts.

Nothing.

Feeling way more upset than he cared to admit, Elias filled the dogs' food bowls in the kitchen. He couldn't remember the last time he'd had breakfast with a woman he'd just slept with. Or being as excited about the prospect of spending more time with her, getting to know her outside of the bedroom.

Last night obviously didn't mean as much to Wren as it did to him.

Of course not, dumbass. Ram was right—she's way above your paygrade.

He went back to the front window and looked out as if her car would suddenly materialize.

Just one night. That's all she wanted. But what did I expect?

His dark thoughts stopped abruptly as he looked around the living room and realized something he'd missed when he walked in the first time. It took him by surprise. His heart sped up.

"That little *thief.*"

He pressed his lips together, frustrated.

And trying hard not to laugh at her game as hope stirred back to life in his chest.

The hunt is on, Wren Stapleton.

FIVE

I've lost my mind, I've lost my mind, I've completely *lost my mind.*

The chorus sang merrily through Wren's head, over and over. It started singing as she slipped as carefully as she could out of Elias' bed while he slept. It picked up as she escaped out Elias' front door. It kept singing as she trotted to the car under the still-dark sky.

But, better the endless chorus than having to explore the dumbass thing she just did.

Or her feelings about Elias.

Nope. Back to the chorus. I've lost my mind, I've lost my mind, I've completely *lost my mind.*

As she started to open her car door, her phone rang, making her jump. She looked back at the house as if Elias could hear her phone through his walls. She quickly got into her car and glanced at the screen, saw who it was, and accepted the call.

Wren answered with, "About time you called. You're a dead woman."

"Now why?" her bestie asked.

"Serge."

"What do you mean?" Barbie sounded incredulous. "He works miracles. His hands are the hands of a healing angel. His needles are little darts of love."

"He left me to die in a fire."

"He...what?"

"The breakroom caught fire while I was naked on the table and he ran away."

"That rat bastard. I'll kill him myself. Oh, wait, I can't because you told me I'm already a dead woman."

Wren grinned. "You know what? I'll let you live long enough to kill Serge."

"You are such a kind person."

"Ha! That's what someone else told me recently." Her lady bits suddenly reminded Wren that she was the dumbest woman alive.

"That someone sounds like a guy."

"How can you tell?"

"Spill, sister," Barbie demanded.

"Where are you?"

"*Spill*, sister. Stop changing the subject. I'm in Aspen."

"I love Aspen."

"So help me God, I will charter a plane straight into Longmont if you don't. Spill. The. Tea."

Wren laughed. "If I'm not killing you outright now, I at least get to torture you a bit. Hang on." She started her car, hoping Elias wouldn't hear. Her phone connected to the speakers. Barbie's impatient huffs now filled the interior. "I'm hesitating because I also kind of owe you because of Serge."

"Oh? Ooohh. Yeah. Firemen, am I right?"

"Almost right. In this case, it was a paramedic."

Barbie paused. "Wait, did you get hurt for real? Wren, are you okay? Are you in the hospital? I can be right there." The genuine concern in her friend's voice touched Wren.

"No, I'm fine, I'm fine. I promise. I've already left the scene of the crime." Wren blushed as heat rose from her chest. The chorus kicked in twice as loudly:

I've lost my mind, I've lost my mind, I've completely lost my mind.

"Scene of the crime?" Barbie's voice went up an octave. "What is going on? Is there a policeman?"

Wren laughed. "Sorry, no. I need more coffee before I try to communicate this early. I'm leaving the paramedic's house right now."

Barbie paused. "Lyons is in the same time zone as Aspen right?"

"Last time I checked."

"Are you sure you're not an hour ahead of me? Because if you are, you're leaving really, really early in the morning. Like, it's not even morning yet, actually."

"It appears so. Hey, then why are *you* calling me this early?"

"Don't change the subject. Would you by chance be sneaking away?"

"Maybe?"

"You know, it's a real pain in the ass trying to get anything out of you," Barbie huffed. "Are you leaving this early because he's a bad lay? Or did he kick you out without breakfast? Because if he did, I'll kill him right after Serge."

That's my Barbie. Rabidly loyal.

Emphasis on rabid.

"No, he did not kick me out. And the sex was *phenomenal.*" She bit her lip, remembering the porch last night and the way her legs turned to overcooked spaghetti as he damn near kissed her very soul —a preview of all the pleasure that was to come.

"Okay." Barbie stretched out the word like taffy. "So. Why did you leave, Wrenbird?"

Good question.

Wren had been busy all week but she'd still had to force herself not to go to Riversong. She didn't want to run into Elias the Paramedic for a too-brief minute before he was back out the door and on to another emergency. She wanted Elias on his downtime when he was relaxed and they had a chance to actually talk. But as the days passed and her imagination ran away with her, Wren decided she wanted more than just talk.

She'd felt confident getting dressed for Cocks and Strippers. She practiced her walk—no, her *swagger*—in front of her full-length mirror. She was totally prepared to go home with Elias—or take him to her place. She felt great walking into the bar, her confidence only boosted when she saw the look on his face as soon as he spotted her. Then their dance, the way every touch sparked fireworks in her chest —fireworks she knew had to be going off in his chest too by the way he looked at her, lips parted, pupils dilated. His shaking hands as he tried to open his front door.

Dear Lord, that kiss on the porch. Best of her life.

Don't even get me started.

And that kiss didn't even touch everything that came after.

So why did my swagger abandon me and send me running before breakfast?

There were no red flags. His place was totally normal. *He* was totally normal. Incredibly hot, but totally just a dude. And as for Penny and Chuck, she'd never seen a more adorable pair of puppers.

I've lost my mind. Only explanation. She glanced at the passenger seat. At what she'd impulsively stolen—yes, stolen, what the heck was wrong with her?—on her way out Elias' door.

Because he was too good. Because if I didn't leave now, I'd blow off work and stay all weekend.

Instead, Wren told Barbie, "I have work today."

"At the crack of dawn? Really?"

"Really. It's good light for photography."

Barbie huffed again. "I think you're lying to me, but I don't know enough about photography to argue with you and not sound stupid."

"You never sound stupid."

"And that's why I love you. Because you are kind and say nice things to me, even when they're lies. But I still think you're lying to me right now about this situation too."

"I'm...not."

"Yeah, you are. What's wrong?"

"Nothing! Can't a girl have a little no-strings-attached fun?"

"Of course she can. But that's not *your* style."

"It's not?"

"No. Your style is to carefully observe. And then observe some more. Preferably through a telescopic lens. And then as soon as someone comes in for a closeup, you pack away your camera and go home."

"Sister, are we talking photography right now? Or did you just refer to my cootchie as a camera?"

"Told you, I don't know squat about photography." Barbie sounded smug.

"So you *are* comparing my cootchie to a camera."

"Wrenbird. I can't believe you went home with a guy and now you're leaving before breakfast when the sex was, as you said *phenomenal*." She exaggerated the word to the breaking point.

"Yeah. I kind of can't believe it, either."

But it was too late to turn around and go back. What if he was awake? How desperate would that be, walking back into his house? How needy? How much of a turn-off?

And in Wren's world, guys hated a needy woman.

"I do have work early today though," she added lamely.

"Do you at least have plans to see him again?"

Wren felt a smile steal across her lips. She glanced from the road to the passenger seat beside her.

To Elias' scrubs top folded neatly and draped over her tote.

I've lost my mind, I've lost my mind, I've completely lost my mind.

"Actually, I do, yes."

THE CHORUS DIDN'T LEAVE her alone, even when she got home.

It sang through what few dreams she had in the hour and a half of sleep she got before her alarm went off. It echoed off the shower walls. And it serenaded her as she grabbed a yogurt out of her fridge and headed for her garage. To block it out, Wren turned on the radio as loudly as she could and sang along to every song on her way to her gig.

Wren pulled up in front of a house in a secluded neighborhood in the mountains. She parked across the freshly paved street and studied the property. Just as she thought, the light would be perfect as soon as the sun rose a little higher. She went around to her trunk and unloaded her gear. She closed the trunk and set the case holding her drone on top of it—her pride and joy and current obsession, not including a certain lion-faced paramedic.

Wren was fiddling with the drone camera's aperture setting when the real estate agent who'd hired her drove up and parked behind her car.

"Good morning," Chase Brandt said as he got out of his Jeep. And wow, he'd picked up two coffees on his way. *How nice.*

"Good morning. Thanks for this." Wren lifted one of the coffees out of the carrier.

"Thank you for coming out so early." Chase pulled out the other coffee and tossed the carrier back into the Jeep.

"No problem. I think you'll be pleased when you see how the sun hits the property this time of day. That natural stone façade in the back's going to light right up."

Chase studied her. "You explored the back yard already." He kept his tone neutral but she could tell by his face she'd suddenly lost some of his trust. She tried to ignore the anxious clenching in her stomach.

"No, I wouldn't go onto the property without you here. I just looked at the photos in the previous listing, the one that didn't sell the house. And I can see why. In the wrong light, the backyard looks dark and uninviting. I'm going to change that this morning."

Chase's stern expression eased as he smiled. "Fantastic. That's what I'm looking for."

Wren's stomach unclenched. She was still new enough at real estate photography that if she wasn't careful, she'd second-guess herself out of a job. Chase was going to need handling with kid gloves —at least she was an expert at that.

Just treat him like your touchiest subjects. Don't back down, don't show fear, a little light flattery goes a long way.

"Between my photos and your charisma, this house will be sold in no time."

Placated, Chase's smile widened. "Your lips to God's ears. The remoteness doesn't always appeal to people. But the new road helps." He took a sip of his coffee while Wren set hers down and went back to her drone. She set the shutter speed to medium to minimize blurring since the wind would probably pick up as the morning got warmer. She didn't need blurry trees in the wind.

"All right. I'm ready to go. I've got half an hour of fly time before the battery dies. I brought an extra one, but I don't anticipate we'll need it. I should get all the shots we need within about fifteen, maybe twenty minutes. The weather's perfect."

Chase raised his coffee cup in a salute. "Fantastic. Just do me a favor and make sure you don't film the property off that direction." He turned and pointed into the woods opposite the house. "I went around and let all the neighbors know we'd be doing drone shots, half as a courtesy and half-hoping if anyone's thinking of selling they'd be impressed. But the guy who lives over there warned me off." He chuckled. "Then his wife asked about getting drone shots taken of their property."

Wren raised an eyebrow. "Are they thinking of selling?"

"No. They're actually building some sort of camp or B&B or something and she wants to have photos for a website once it's done."

Chase shook his head. "Just, if you go up really high, make sure you don't catch their property. The wife was sweet, but her husband was a real bear."

"No problem. Thanks for the warning." *And the possible lead* she thought. "If I do happen to catch their property, I can always crop it out later."

Satisfied with the drone, Wren set its launch pad on the ground next to the car and placed the drone on it. She'd preprogrammed a flight path that would return the drone to its launch pad as soon as the battery started getting low, a habit she'd formed even though she didn't think she'd need it today. Wren picked up her phone and inserted it into the drone controller. The drone lifted off and Chase leaned in to watch the screen on her phone as she worked.

"Right now, we've got really good ambient light. I'm going to start out low and get some shots of the front of the house first before the sun gets too much higher. Otherwise, we'll have the same problem as the previous agent did with the backyard. It'll be too backlit and appear shadowed."

Wren thumbed the gimble dial, adjusting the camera angle to forty-five degrees. She took some shots as Chase nodded.

"Looks good," he said.

Wren sent the drone higher but kept the camera angled. A high shot straight down was cool when photographing a beach, but in this case, she'd just get a flat-looking shot of the roof—not very sexy when selling a house. She took some photos then moved on. Once the drone was in place in the backyard, she turned it. Yup, the light was perfect, showing off the sandy-colored stone. The back patio begged for a happy couple enjoying coffee and croissants on a leisurely Sunday morning.

She turned her attention to the hot tub and lap pool just off the patio. The sparkling water reminded her of Elias' perfect lagoon-blue eyes. She shook off the distracting memory and tried to focus on her job. A couple of leaves floated on the pool's surface, but she could clean that up with her editing software. A few more angles, a few more shots, and she brought the drone in for a landing.

Chase had stayed quiet while she worked, but now that the drone landed, he was full of questions. He asked again about fly time, then about the cost of the drone.

If too many real estate agents decided to learn how to fly drones, she might be out of a job before she even got started. Wren tried to keep her voice light. "Are you planning on becoming a drone pilot yourself?"

"A drone pilot? I don't think I could fit into a cockpit that small." He chuckled at his own joke.

Wren smiled. "You need a remote pilot license if you want to do this professionally. Classes, tests, all that, then you need a top-notch drone. I've spent a small fortune already."

"Huh." His interest seemed to wane. *Good.* "What's the zoom like on the lens?"

"Really strong. I could have done interior photos from the back-yard through the patio door and picked up the texture of the oranges in that bowl on the counter."

"Cool. Speaking of, let's get some interior shots."

Wren carefully packed her drone up and grabbed her camera bag. She winced as she lifted it, remembering too late how much her shoulder hurt. She set the bag back down and picked it up with her other hand. She was still getting used to carrying her equipment on her other shoulder.

"Shoulder pain?" Chase asked.

"Yeah. Hazard of the occupation, lugging heavy equipment around. If I were smart, I'd get a new rolling bag. I broke a wheel on mine. But that can mess up your elbow after a while."

"Ever try acupuncture? I know a guy, works miracles."

Wren hid her smile. *Serge.* Chase ran in the same circles as Barbie, which was how she got this gig. "Thanks, but I'm looking into other options."

"You afraid of needles?"

No, but I'm terrified of fires now. Wren only shook her head.

The house was big and they spent over an hour inside, photographing every angle imaginable. The sun was well up and the day already warm by the time they finished. Back outside, Wren took a few more shots of the front of the house.

"Thanks for your help," Chase said as they walked back to their vehicles. "When can I expect the photos?"

"I'll have the best ones cleaned and uploaded to the cloud for you by Sunday night, and a video of that loop the drone made around the house." Wren had every intention of finishing in the afternoon— under promising and over delivering was the name of the game. "You're my priority today."

"Fantastic." Chase gave her a smile and shook her hand. "I'll look them over and if I like what I see, I've got a couple more properties that could use some drone photos."

Yes!

"Sounds good." She looked into the woods opposite the house. "What did you say the name of the good-cop, bad-cop couple was?"

Chase laughed. "That's a fantastic description of those two." He took out one of his business cards and wrote their names and address on the back. "If you're thinking of doing some work for them, make sure you talk to *her*. You'll get further."

"And maybe not get my head bitten off?"

Chase laughed again. "Exactamundo." He saluted her and got into his Jeep.

Wren got into her car and took a deep breath once she was behind the wheel.

That went well. She had hoped to get some more work out of Chase. He sold a lot of high-end properties all around Boulder County.

Then again, the way prices are skyrocketing, pretty much every property is high-end anymore.

Wren suppressed some old, bad memories and the shiver that always went along with them. She rubbed her aching shoulder then started her car. She had a choice—she could try and drum up more business, or she could go down into Lyons and grab another cup of coffee from a certain coffee shop first.

It might be too early still to go knocking on doors, she told herself, trying to ignore how much she wanted to see Elias again.

Now for coffee. And with any luck, a little something extra.

She sighed. *I just wish I knew what I was doing.*

SIX

She took my scrubs top.

Elias stared again at the empty chair where he'd draped the shirt the night before. His lips curled into a hungry smile. She'd escaped him sometime last night, which sharpened his desire for her. He couldn't remember the last time he'd wanted a woman so badly.

Wren knows exactly what she's doing.

Piquing his interest. Keeping him guessing. Drawing out the game when it so easily could have ended with a one-night stand like so many others.

Yeah, sure, a one-night stand, right. If I ignore the fact that I broke my pattern and brought her to my home in the first place instead of going to hers. And she's so damn funny. And she likes my dogs. He glanced down at the critters who'd just finished their breakfast and came to find him.

And most importantly, they like her.

Elias stretched like the great cat he was nicknamed after, then ran his hand through his hair until it stood up. Penny and Chuck went off to play in their dog run outside while he padded to the bathroom to take a shower. Hot water hit his pecs and he thought of the way Wren rested her hand over his heart—a light, fluttering touch that grew more confident as they danced. Water ran down his chest and over his abs in teasing rivulets as he imagined her fingers gliding over his bare skin like they did the night before. He shivered in spite of the hot water steaming up the shower's glass door. His cock hardened as his mind filled with visions of stripping Wren out of her shorts and top. Now she stood in nothing but lace in front of him, her cheeks pinking up the way they did the day he met her, only this time, the color rose from her desire, not embarrassment.

Elias stroked his cock as he turned her around in his imagination and bent her over his bed. He slid the lace panties down her long legs and undid her bra. He ran his hands over her smooth, round ass cheeks. *Smack* went his palm against her ass, 'punishing' her for stealing his scrubs top. The moan escaping her lips told him she wanted more, wanted him to toy with her before plunging his cock deep inside her wet pussy.

He stroked himself harder, picturing her soft, pink folds, her tightness once he'd buried himself balls deep into her from behind. He gripped her ass and leaned forward over her back to bite her shoulder. In the shower he pumped his cock for all he was worth, unable to contain himself while Dream Wren pressed back against him, drawing him deeper and deeper until her soft velvet walls spasmed around him. He came hot and fast and hard, her moans echoing in his ears.

"Need you," he growled as the water washed over him. "Next time, you're not getting away."

ELIAS BREATHED IN THE RICH, good, roasted coffee smell of Riversong as he walked through the front door. He'd come here on pure instinct and immediately scanned the room even though he didn't see Wren's vehicle in the parking lot. He wouldn't put it past her to park around the block, then catch him by surprise inside. But she wasn't sitting at any of the crowded tables or standing in the line snaking halfway to the front door. He tried to ignore his disappointment and the way his body felt heavier suddenly, as if he'd not quite been touching the ground before.

Low blood sugar he told himself. He'd just pour a sugar packet into his coffee.

He watched April, Hannah, and Sonny taking orders and mixing drinks until he got to the front of the line. April greeted him with a smile.

"Still no woman with a scrubs top, sorry." That had pretty much become her standard greeting for the past few days.

Elias glanced behind him to see how many people waited. "It was briefly back in my possession, but it's gone again, so thanks for keeping an eye out."

April's jaw dropped and then she gave him an even brighter smile. "We'll catch up." She winked and handed him a mug of black coffee.

"Glad to see business is back to normal."

"Thank God!" She looked past him and smiled at the next customer.

Elias paid, left a generous tip, and grabbed a couple of sugar packets. A couple was just standing up from their table to leave, so he nabbed their spot and sat down. Elias pretended to scroll through his phone while he sipped his coffee at glacial pace. He kept his attention on the front door while he tapped his foot to the jazzy music playing overhead, wishing he could pace instead.

After half an hour, he'd reached the bottom of his coffee mug along with his hope of seeing Wren. He stood to leave and found himself walking to the counter instead for a refill. The morning coffee crowd had died down, so he only had to wait behind two people. The bell rang over the front door and the familiar sensation of hair rising on the nape of his neck told Elias she was there. He turned to see Wren smiling at him as a faint blush crept into her cheeks.

"Hey," Wren said as she joined him in line.

"Hey yourself."

"So, about last night..." She trailed off. Elias couldn't help but notice her wince in pain while she shifted her tote off her shoulder and unzipped it.

"Is my property in that bag?"

She grinned and her blush turned fiery. "Not sure what came over me. Yes, it is."

He reached out and stilled her hand. "Keep it. On one condition."

She met his eyes with a worried look. "Yes?"

Elias leaned forward and whispered in her ear. "Wear it for me again. And next time, stay for breakfast."

He lingered beside her ear, breathing in her salty peach skin, feeling wisps of her hair tickling his cheek. He didn't miss the shiver that made her tremble like an aspen in the wind. When he pulled back, her eyes had gone a little unfocused. She bit her lower lip and Elias was in danger of sweeping her off her feet and carrying her out to his truck.

"A-*hem*."

Elias turned back toward the counter. April leaned on her elbows, grinning. "Next."

"A refill for me, and a cinnamon-honey double-shot latte for the lady."

Wren's eyebrow shot up. "You remembered."

April mock-frowned at Elias. "Hey, that's *my* job, to remember people's favorite drinks." She switched her attention to Wren. "And *you* must be Scrubs Top."

Elias' chest tightened as Wren's eyes went wide. She turned her head and glared at him. "Scrubs. Top?"

April growled and slapped her forehead. "Oh, God, there I go ruining lives again." She looked back and forth between Elias and Wren.

Flustered, Elias said, "I, uh... I might have mentioned meeting you at the fire. And the scrubs top. I'm sorry."

"Not at all," Wren said in a cold, crisp tone. She pursed her lips as she reached into her bag and pulled out the top. Elias prepared for The Speech. The one where Wren would tell him she never wanted to see him again, then thrust the shirt at him and march out the door.

Instead, she surprised him. Again.

Her face broke into a gorgeous smile. "Yup, I'm Scrubs Top. Guilty as charged." She unfolded the top and held it up to her body for April to see. "What do you think? Cute dress?"

April gave her a relieved laugh. "Very cute. Much cuter on you than on old Lion here."

Wren's eyes went round again. "He does look like a lion, doesn't he? It's not just my imagination." She turned back to Elias with a beaming smile that melted his heart.

"That's also his nickname," April informed her. "From when he was a kid. All his friends have them."

"Elias...sorry, *Lion*...has friends who aren't invisible?" She looked shocked but if her eyes twinkled before, they positively glittered with humor now.

April grinned. "They aren't invisible but they sometimes disappear at opportune moments."

"That checks out. The friend who apparently disappeared last night likes pine-flavored beer."

"That would be Waylon," April said without missing a beat. She looked at Elias for confirmation and he tipped an invisible hat to her. "Told you, it's my job to know everyone's favorite drinks. Waylon would like something more adventurous than Pabst."

Then April leaned across the counter and asked in a stage-whisper, "Please don't tell me Lion took you to Cocks and Strippers on your first date."

"April," Elias growled, though without any true malice.

Wren sucked in her cheeks just for a second before answering, "Nope," Wren stage-whispered back. "He didn't take me. I actually showed up there all on my own."

"Bold move." April nodded approvingly. "He a good dancer?"

"I'm right here," Elias said.

"Yes, actually, though he did almost step on my foot a couple of times." Wren went back to her stage-whisper. "He was dancing *really* close."

"Still right here." Elias had to force his laughter back down and it decided to hang around his heart as a warm ember.

"Interesting." April nodded, her lips twitching like she couldn't wait to spread the word.

"You gonna make their drinks or not, April?" Sonny shouted from where he was pouring a sack of beans into a giant grinder.

"MYOB, Dad," April shouted back with an eyeroll. Then with a smile for Wren she said, "I'll get your cinnamon-honey right away." She turned toward the espresso machine behind her.

Wren folded the scrubs top and put it back in her tote, then pulled out her wallet.

"Nope, I'm paying," Elias said.

"You are not. I owe you for flaking out."

Elias tilted his head. That was a weird thing for her to say, but more, it was the way she said it. Her humor seemed to go MIA again.

"What are you talking about? You're making this fun." He swiped his card as she pulled out her wallet. She blinked up at him as if he were the one not making any sense.

"Here you go." April turned around with two mugs in her hands.

"Is it okay if we go outside with these?" Elias lifted his ceramic mug.

"Of course. Seating's around the side. Should be a few open tables."

"No, I mean, to my truck."

Both women raised their eyebrows, then shared a look he had no hope of understanding. But one thing was clear.

Whether I like it or not, Wren just became part of the group.

"YOU ARE FULL OF SURPRISES," Elias said after he got behind the wheel.

"Me?" Wren blinked at him over her sweet-smelling coffee. "What about this amazing truck? You could have knocked me over with a feather when I saw you climb behind the wheel last night. I figured you'd drive something newer." She ran her hand over the black leather bench. "What year is she?"

Elias couldn't help the smile and warmth in his chest as she talked about his baby. "1973. She's an F100 Flairside. My dad gave her to me. His pride and joy, and now mine, too."

Wren looked around the cab. "And you take good care of her. She's perfect. I approve."

"I like taking care of beautiful things."

"I approve of that, too." She met his eyes for a tantalizingly brief moment before looking away. She was such a funny mix of bold and shy that kept Elias guessing.

"Totally unpredictable," he said.

"What?"

"You. You're totally unpredictable. You keep me guessing."

"Me? I'm incredibly predictable," she scoffed.

"Not at all."

"I'm clockwork, really."

"Absolutely nothing you've done so far is like clockwork."

"Okay, normally I'm like clockwork."

Elias turned the ignition.

"Are we going somewhere?" She smiled as she watched him.

"Just turning on the air. It's hot out here."

"Oh. Right." She sipped her coffee.

"We *could* go somewhere. If you wanted. So long as you don't sneak away again," he teased.

She looked around. "Hard to do that if I'm in your truck." Wren turned her head and locked onto his gaze. "So, did you bring me out here to scold me?" She batted her eyes.

"Scold? No."

"Spank?" And there went her lips fighting a laugh that was so contagious he almost—*almost*—joined her.

"Not enough room for that in here. And too much of an audience if I did." He tilted his head toward the outdoor seating at the side of the coffee shop. "Though, you are fond of public nudity, so maybe you like an audience?" He set his coffee cup on the dashboard. "You'd prefer putting on a public show?"

"What gave it away? Wearing nothing but a sheet? The short-shorts? The pornographic kiss on your front porch where the neighbors could see? Honestly, I thought I was being subtle."

Now he was grinning as widely as she, despite feeling the tiniest doubt that clutched at his chest.

Flaked out.

Did he have her all wrong? He thought she was playing a game, teasing him, stringing him along in the best of ways. But maybe not.

"What if I kissed you right here?" he tested. "How would that make you feel?"

Wren turned her full body in her seat until she was facing him. "Well," she drawled. "Will it be a repeat of the porch?"

"Oh no. Much more pornographic, as you put it." He stretched out his arm as an invitation. She slid across the bench, closing the gap between them. All he had to do was pull her over on top of him until she straddled his lap. He reached out and took her hands in his hand. always testing her reactions, looking for the slightest hesitation.

Wren giggled as her cheeks flamed. She dropped her chin then stared out the dashboard window. "I'd really hate to be arrested in front of my favorite coffee shop."

Does that mean back off?

But instead of scooting back, she turned and studied his face. "But, it might be worth it."

Wrong again. Damn, she knows just how to keep me on my toes.

Elias chuckled as he ran one hand up her arm and tangled his fingers in her hair. He gently guided her head forward until their lips were a breath apart. His heart decided somewhere along the way to turn into a jackhammer. He brushed his lips against hers softly, balancing his need to claim them—to claim her—and letting her control the situation.

A totally new experience for him.

Wren's fingers brushed his cheek on their way to the nape of his neck. She hesitated just long enough to make him think she'd changed her mind. Then she kissed him.

This kiss was far more controlled than the one they'd shared on the front porch but that didn't make it any less hot. Wren opened to him eagerly and he explored her sweet mouth as his fingers tangled in her hair. He was in serious danger of forgetting where he was and getting them both arrested for indecent exposure.

Elias ended the kiss to ask if she wanted to go somewhere private. All he could think about was getting Wren naked again. Instead, what came out of his mouth was, "Wren, I gotta be honest here. I'm getting mixed signals from you. Was it something I said or did?" He rubbed his chin, listening to the rasping sound it made. "Or, maybe it was the dogs?"

Wren looked surprised. "No, not at all. They're adorable."

"Then, am I pushing things too fast? We could stay here, or just go back inside and talk if that would be better."

Wren took a deep breath. "The truth is, I've been trying to figure out myself why I left without telling you." She grabbed his hand. "It's not your dogs. It's not you. I like you. A lot. Maybe I like you too much, too soon." She let go of his hand as she looked down and away. "Sorry. I sound needy and that probably scares you off."

Does it? It might have, coming from anyone but Wren. But Elias didn't feel the need to run, or to joke in order to lighten the mood, or change the topic completely. Those were all things he'd done in the past with other women. Wren made him feel completely different.

"You know, normally it might make me think twice. But not this time." He shook his head in wonder at how he felt. "I don't bring women to my house, especially not on the first date. You're the exception."

"And I don't go home with guys on the first date. Except for you." Then she shook her head. "But at the end of the day, we're just having fun here, right?" she asked lightly. "A good time?"

There she was, giving mixed signals again.

Elias should have been overjoyed that Wren wasn't taking things too seriously. He never did and that kept things light and fun. The problem was, Elias wasn't so sure if all he wanted was a good time.

Better figure that out, and soon.

Instead of answering her, he said, "I make a killer breakfast. You hungry?"

Wren laughed. "Did my stomach rumble?" She patted her belly.

"Not that I heard. But, I did promise you one. If you want."

Wren nodded slowly. "I do because I actually am starving. Breakfast would be terrific. And this time, I promise I won't disappear." She shrugged. "Well, not right away."

"Not right away?"

"I did have to work early this morning up in the hills. A real estate shoot. The agent I'm working with said there was a property nearby that might want drone footage. I was thinking I'd knock on their door later today." She chuckled. "Maybe I should take you along as a bodyguard."

Elias immediately went on alert. "What does that mean?"

She waved him off. "I'm kidding. Kinda. Chase said he'd stopped by there to let them know he'd be using a drone so please don't shoot it down, and the guy was pretty gruff with him. But his wife indicated she might want drone footage."

"Good move on the agent's part. People living in the mountains often prefer their privacy, I'll say that. Sometimes they're just weirdos. Can I ask the name? Maybe I can tell you if it's a waste of time."

"Um, sure." She pulled out her wallet, took out a business card, and handed it to him. "This couple."

Elias laughed so suddenly and so hard when he read the names that Wren jumped.

"Yeah, I'd better come with you on this one." He looked at her. "New plan. Let's grab a couple of excellent breakfast burritos here, head up to talk to them, and then I'll make you dinner instead. You'll have earned it."

SEVEN

Wren fidgeted with the crumpled up ball of foil from her breakfast burrito. Every now and then she shot a look at Elias as he drove them back into the mountains. The cocky jerk smiled back every single time.

And every single time she asked, "Still not gonna tell me what I'm in for?"

"Nope."

"Payback for stealing the scrubs?"

"Yup."

She shook her head, pretending to be more annoyed than she was. By all rights, her anxiety should have been screaming at her to jump out the truck's window at the next hairpin curve, damn the steep drop down the side of a mountain if she did. And yet, she knew Elias wouldn't put her in any danger.

Now, putting myself *into danger when it comes to my heart— that's another story.*

They'd left her car at Riversong after transferring her equipment to the truck. Elias promised he'd make her dinner and bring her back down later, but that it was, in his words 'safer and easier' to just take his truck, which they would recognize. Normally, that would send up a ton of red flags. And yet...she felt more like they were on a playful little adventure. Elias was obviously having fun with her, and when he ducked into the men's room before they left Riversong, April assured Wren she was in good hands.

So instead of being worried about where she was physically going at the moment, she worried more about where her heart was going.

Wren avoided serious relationships like the plague. She'd seen too many of her friends get close to someone only to break their hearts during cruel fights and arguments. And if there was something Wren truly hated, it was arguing. So, as soon as a relationship showed any signs of exiting the honeymoon phase and getting serious, Wren was outta there. Barbie's words came back to her.

Your style is to carefully observe. And then observe some more. Preferably through a telescopic lens. And then as soon as someone comes in for a closeup, you pack away your camera and go home.

Wren scrunched up the ball of foil even tighter. *Shit. Barbie's right about me. Well, not about my cootchie being a camera.*

Another thought bubbled up without warning.

Overexposure.

"Did you just snort?" Elias asked.

"Nope," Wren squeaked through clenched teeth.

Don't laugh. If you laugh, he'll want to know why. And if you tell him why he'll think you've lost your mind.

She squirmed in her seat like she was in church holding back a fart, while her brain kept on churning out inappropriate camera puns.

Flash.

"Okay, what's so funny?" Elias demanded.

"Nothing."

"You just snorted again."

"Did not."

Wren clamped her lips shut. Her cheeks burned from the effort not to laugh. But if her cootchie was a camera, her mind was now a drone zooming straight for Naughtyville.

Darkroom.

Private shoot.

A bubble of laughter slipped through her clenched teeth, and she quickly coughed to cover it up.

"Seriously, what's going on?" Elias pressed, his aqua-blue eyes flicking between her and the road.

"Nothing. Just...being...stupid."

Wren could feel the dam breaking. She bit down on her bottom lip hard, trying to stifle the giggles. But then her brain betrayed her with the ultimate zinger.

That did it. A laugh burst out of her, loud and uncontrolled.

"You laughed." Elias crowed, eyes twinkling with victory. "Now you've got to spill."

Wren shook her head, laughing too hard to care. "Oh, you wouldn't understand," she managed to gasp out between giggles.

"Try me." He grinned, clearly enjoying the sight of her losing her shit.

Wren's laughter slowed as she considered how to explain it without sounding completely ridiculous. She took a deep breath, wiped a tear from the corner of her eye, and gave him a wry smile.

"Okay, but if you laugh, it's two points in my favor."

Elias considered her. "So we *are* both doing this, huh?"

"Doing what?"

"Keeping a laugh score."

"You mean a laugh track?"

He grinned. "Whatever you want to call it."

"So, just to confirm—if you laugh right now, it's two points."

"Yup. Hit me."

"It's just... I have a friend. Barbie. She was making fun of me." Wren covered her face. "I can't believe I'm about to tell you this."

Elias rolled his hand in a 'come on, out with it' gesture.

"Fine." The next words rushed from her lips. "She kind of compared my cootchie to a camera."

Elias worked his jaw as his lips twitched. "A...camera? Your...cootchie?"

"Yeah. So, now my brain just keeps coming up with these really lame double-meanings."

Elias rolled his lips in as his face reddened from the effort of not laughing. "Stupid double-meanings, huh? Like what? They can't be lame if they're making you laugh."

"Flash."

Elias shrugged. "Okay." But his twitching lips continued to give him away.

Wren played along. "Damn. See? Told you they were lame."

"A little lame. Hit me with another one."

"Overexposure."

Little noises came out of his nose and he rolled his lips back in.

"Aperture."

"Aperture?"

"It means an opening." She stared right at him. "Like with the lens diameter."

Elias' chest and shoulders jumped.

"Was that a chuckle?"

"No. That was a, um, hiccup."

"Yeah, right. What happens if I say wide lens? Like, open that lens *wide* for me, baby!"

Elias' laughter filled the truck. "That's not lame, that's gold, Wren."

"Two points! I'm winning!"

He cleared his throat. "Just so you know, there's nothing wide about your *lens* or your aperture."

Wren stamped her foot, trying not to laugh. "Why, thank...thank...you." Then she lost it and cracked up. "That's the nicest thing any date's ever said about me." She grinned at him. "And, I'm still ahead."

"Negative. Ha, get it?"

"Now *that's* lame." But she still laughed, feeling a warm flutter in her chest.

"Fine, we're even."

"If you say so." Wren shook her head, grinning.

But her grin slowly dried up now that they were cruising down the road near the house she'd photographed earlier. They took the opposite fork in the road, unmarked except for a sign saying PRIVATE. She rolled the ball of foil between her hands and tried to think of how to approach her potential clients.

The trees lining the road gave way after a few minutes and opened up. Wren's eyes widened at the sight of the vast landscape stretching out before them. The mountains rose majestically in the distance, their peaks still dusted with snow even in the summer. A pristine lake shimmered in the sunlight.

"This place is gorgeous," Wren murmured, momentarily distracted from her worry.

"The people who live here sure love it," Elias said, his tone giving nothing away.

Wren shot him a suspicious glance.

Elias just smirked as he pulled the truck to a stop in front of a large, rustic cabin with a wide porch. A couple of rocking chairs sat by the door, and a pair of muddy boots were propped up against the wall, giving the place a lived-in, cozy feel. Wren could tell the cabin was old, but someone had done a lot of work to fix it up. The roof looked new and so did the addition on the back.

Before Wren could finish unbuckling her seatbelt—the process slowed down by her stiff shoulder—Elias was already out of the truck and opening her door. He held out his hand and helped her down.

As soon as they turned toward the cabin, the front door burst open and a mountain of a man stepped out, his beard thick and wild, his expression gruff and unwelcoming.

"Elias, you son of a—" the man boomed, cutting himself off as he spotted Wren. His stern eyes flicked to her, sizing her up.

Wren froze, her heart skipping a beat. Confrontation was the last thing she wanted.

But then, to her surprise, the man's face split into a wide grin. "—gun!" he finished, his deep voice rumbling with laughter. "You brought a guest. My Ellie's gonna be so happy."

So this is the grumpy Jon Behr.

Laughing, Elias hugged the big man. "Bear, meet Wren Stapleton. Wren, this is Bear. He doesn't actually bite."

Jon Behr extended a hand that engulfed Wren's. "Nice to meet you, Wren."

Still trying to process the shift from intimidating to friendly, Wren shook his hand. "Nice to meet you too, Mr. Behr."

"Just Bear like the animal," he said. "Not Jon, not Mr. Behr."

Elias chuckled at her confused expression. "It's his nickname. It suits him, don't you think?"

Wren nodded, her smile widening as she relaxed. "Definitely." Then she put two and two together. "Oh, you're part of Elias' old friend group, the one with all the animal nicknames." She grinned at Elias. "Or should I just call you Lion now?"

Bear's eyes widened and the corner of his mouth curled up. A low grumble started in his chest but by the time it got to his lips it had morphed into a deep belly laugh. He winked at Elias.

Just then, the cabin door opened again. A petite woman with sun-streaked hair and a warm smile appeared.

"Don't let him scare you, Wren. He's just a big softie," she said, coming down the steps to join them. "Elias called and told him that you all were coming and Bear was just putting on an act, like this prankster wanted." She winked at Elias. "Not that we would have turned you away or anything if we didn't know who you were," she said in a mock-stern tone directed at her husband. "We're very happy to have guests, aren't we?"

Bear snorted.

"I'm Ellie." She stuck her hand out for Wren to shake.

Wren felt the last little bit of tension drain from her shoulders as she shook Ellie's hand. "It's great to meet you. Your place is amazing."

"Thanks! We love it here." Ellie's eyes sparkled with enthusiasm. "We've been dreaming up all sorts of projects, and that's where you come in. I heard through the grapevine that you were the one flying a drone around this morning."

Wren almost staggered. "Wow, yeah. Word travels fast."

Ellie shrugged. "Small town, even though we're miles and miles away from it."

Bear wrapped his arm around Ellie. "Distance don't matter when April's got gossip."

"Bear!" Ellie frowned.

But Wren laughed. "Don't worry, I get it. I'm glad she let you know I was okay."

"I was on the phone with her right after Bear got a text from Elias. She likes you." Ellie's smile widened. "Let's get you something to drink inside, and then I've got some ideas I'd love to bounce off you."

Wren felt the familiar thrill of creative potential bubbling up. "I'd love that. And I can already picture how I'd photograph your lake."

As they headed inside, Wren glanced back at Elias, who was grinning from ear to ear. She shook her head, a smile playing on her lips. *I should have known.*

And that I can trust him.

"So... There's a house nearby for sale?" Ellie asked once they were all inside. Bear raised an eyebrow at her inquisitive tone that went beyond casual conversation. Wren wondered too.

"Yes. It's getting re-listed. It was on the market with no bites so the owners switched Realtors to Chase, the guy you met. Don't tell me you want to sell all this and buy that one instead."

"No, no. Not us."

"Put too much work into this place," Bear added.

That was obvious to Wren as she looked around the cabin. The wood trim and fireplace looked original, but the kitchen, open to the living room, was full of new appliances and definitely had a more modern layout.

"Your home is gorgeous," she told them. "I'd hang on to it, too."

Ellie was already halfway to the kitchen. Wren, Bear, and Elias followed her.

"Thanks! We have friends who've been house hunting." She pulled a couple of water bottles out of the fridge and handed them to Wren and Elias. "They're renting now down in Lyons and haven't seen anything they absolutely love yet." Ellie grabbed Bear's hand. "Wouldn't it be great to have them living nearby? Can you imagine?"

Bear's eyes twinkled, seeing his wife so excited. He nodded.

"If you don't mind, I'd love to be the one to bring them to Chase," Wren said. "I'm trying to build my real estate photo business and bringing potential buyers to an agent would help."

"Of course." Ellie nodded happily. "I'll give Gina your contact info. She and Lachlan are looking for something quiet and kind of out of the way."

"Well, that's certainly the neighborhood."

"Are you totally new to photography?" Ellie topped off Wren's water glass as she asked.

"No. I used to photograph people. For magazines and newspapers. And online."

"Oh, like for news articles?"

"More like feature stories. Human interest."

"Cool. Would I know any of your photos?"

Wren's cheeks warmed. She always felt weird talking about the details of her career with people she'd just met, hoping they didn't think she was name-dropping.

"Well, I photographed Barbie a couple months ago for Vogue."

"I don't read Vogue, but that's a big-deal magazine. Is Barbie a model or something?"

"No, not anymore. She's an actor now. Barbie Gillis? Have you heard of her?"

"Are you kidding? I love her in everything she does. What's she like in real life? Or did you only meet her the one time?"

"No, actually, she's my bestie."

Ellie's eyes rounded. "Oh, wow."

"So, she's nice?" Wren smiled and shrugged. "She's funny. Very funny person. Which, kinda goes along with someone who does comedy."

Ellie must have sensed Wren's discomfort because she didn't press. "So you wanted to do something different with your photography?"

"I did." Not that she was totally done photographing people, but she couldn't talk about her next gig, at least not yet. "It'll be fun working on your property." She took a drink of water.

"If you've got time now, I'd love to show you around."

"Absolutely." She glanced at Elias. "If you're not in a hurry?"

"Not at all. Bear and I will catch up in here," he said.

WREN AND ELIAS ended up staying for lunch at Ellie's insistence. "The least I can do is feed you after dragging you around the entire property."

They hadn't actually seen everything—Ellie owned acres of land covered in forest and craggy outcroppings—but what they did explore took Wren's breath away. So did the story of Ellie's inheritance and how she almost lost everything. Bear literally saved her life. Wren found herself wiping away a tear at the end of Ellie's story. Bear might have the size, but Wren knew Ellie was just as strong as the big man in her own way.

And the woman can cook! Wren couldn't say no to an extra biscuit with a spoonful of honey.

"Pretty soon, that'll be honey we harvest ourselves," Ellie said, glancing fondly at Bear.

"Those beehives were something else," Wren said, remembering the stacks of white boxes and the bees flying in and out of their bases. Their back legs were thick with orange, yellow, or red pollen, making them look like they were wearing bright little pairs of shorts.

"We got the bees at the end of spring, the last ones the beekeeper had, actually. Bear built the frames and boxes himself."

Elias grinned at his friend. "When does the first jar of Bear's Honey roll off the assembly line?"

"Go ask the bees," Bear said around a mouthful of fresh-caught trout from the creek cutting through their property.

"Talking to the animals is more your department." Elias pointed his fork at Bear. "This guy's other nick is St. Francis."

Bear grunted. "It's their factories, so it's up to them. One hive for sure is going gangbusters, but a couple more are gonna have to grow a lot bigger before we'll harvest any honey from them. Gotta survive the winter."

Ellie turned to Wren. "I've already promised jars to April, Rochelle, Gina, Arden, my cousin Ellen, Stephanie, Sandra... And I forget who else." She ticked the women's names off on her fingers. "I'll add you to the list."

"Oh, you don't have to do that." Wren felt her cheeks redden.

"Oh heck yes I have to. I can't leave out a friend."

Friend. Wren smiled at that. Ellie was damn near the sweetest person she'd ever met. "You should call it Ellie's Honey."

Bear pointed a thick finger at Wren. "Yeah, that's what I said, but she don't want that."

"*You're* the one doing all the work, Bear. It was your idea, too, so it's your honey. Besides, Bear's Honey sounds cute."

The big man's face turned bright red under his thick beard.

Elias pounded Bear on the back. "What's wrong, brother? Looks like you swallowed something down the wrong pipe. Maybe some of your cute honey, Honey?"

Wren stifled a giggle.

Oh, God, I'm being rude.

But then Ellie burst out laughing beside her. Bear rolled his eyes but Wren didn't miss the twinkle in them.

Elias gave him one last slap on the back. "Just be glad all the women aren't here, especially Stephanie."

"Stephanie?" Wren asked.

"Trouble," was all Bear said.

"Oh, she is not! She's lovely." Ellie stuck her tongue out at Bear. "And a good friend."

"She works with our buddy Gabe down at the rec center," Elias said as he reached for the basket of biscuits.

"Rochelle's husband," Ellie added. She passed the butter to Elias, who tipped his head in gratitude. "Rochelle and I had a double wedding earlier this year. Have her show you her wedding ring when you meet her. Ben made it himself. He's another of Bear and Lion's friends."

"What's *his* nickname?"

Ellie frowned as she tried to remember. "Oh yeah, Moose."

Elias grinned at Wren. "I'll get you a scorecard later."

"Will it have everyone's real names or their nicknames? I might need two cards," Wren teased.

Ellie patted her shoulder. "Don't worry, you'll catch right up, just like I did."

Wren felt her stomach flutter. Catching up would mean she was sticking around. Getting to know more of Elias' friends. Making them *her* friends.

'Serious girlfriend' activities.

She braved a look at Elias to gauge his reaction, not knowing what she'd see in his eyes. Acceptance or annoyance?

And which do I want to see?

Meeting his gaze was like looking into a mirror. She saw the same question for her in his lagoon-blue eyes. They both looked away at the same time.

With the same thoughtful smiles.

EIGHT

"I'm afraid I'm still full from lunch," Wren said as Elias pulled up in front of his house. The truck's tires crunched over gravel and the engine rumbled quietly before Elias turned the key. Silence settled around them.

Elias leaned back in his seat and looked at her, a mischievous glint in his eyes. "Maybe we can think of something to work up another appetite?"

Wren rolled her eyes but couldn't stop the giggle that bubbled up. "Your pickup lines are terrible, you know that?"

"Still got you to giggle. That's another point for me," he said with a triumphant grin.

Wren pretended to pout. "I forgot to keep score today."

"Oh don't worry, I still am. And I'm way ahead of you," Elias teased.

Wren cocked her head, a playful challenge in her eyes. "Somehow, I don't believe you."

Elias chuckled as he unbuckled his seatbelt.

"Ha! Point for me," Wren declared, unbuckling her seatbelt. "We're tied."

Elias narrowed his eyes "I thought you weren't keeping score?"

"So, new rule. Default tie if I forget to keep score."

"Oh, who's not playing fair now?"

Before Wren could respond, Elias lunged across the seat, catching her by surprise. He reached for her, pulled her close, and she yelped in mock protest as his lips found hers. The kiss was warm and lingering, filled with the promise of more to come. Wren's heart skipped a beat as she melted into him.

When they finally broke apart, Elias left her breathless, her pulse thrumming in her ears. The spark of mischief in Elias' eyes sent a thrill through her.

He went in for a second kiss, this time also pulling her on top of his lap.

Sharp pain ripped through her upper back. Wren yelped and broke off the kiss.

"What did I do?" Elias looked distraught as he studied her for injuries.

"Not you, promise." Wren grimaced. "It's just my shoulder. Nice time for it to act up."

"Which one?"

"Both, but the left one is barking at me right now." She waved him off. "It's okay. Sorry."

"It's not okay." He tentatively ran his hand over her shoulder to her back. "Don't ever apologize for hurting," he said. "How long has this been going on?"

"Since I broke a wheel on my rolling camera bag and had to switch to carrying my equipment. I'm dumb for not replacing it right away, I know."

"Hey." Elias frowned. "Don't ever call yourself dumb." He kissed the tip of her nose. "We should get your bags and head inside where it's more comfortable." His voice sounded huskier than before.

Wren nodded, still feeling the warmth of his kisses on her lips. "Yeah, I don't want to leave the drone in the truck."

The driver side door creaked slightly as he opened it. Wren

watched him as he walked around the truck to her side, listening to his boots crunching on the gravel. She slung her tote over her shoulder as he opened her door and helped her out. They moved to the back of the truck where her photography gear was stored. Wren started to reach for her gear but Elias stopped her.

"I can get this."

"I'm fine!" She smiled, hoping to convince him. "Besides, I don't let anybody carry my baby." She pointed at the drone case.

"Wren." His tone was full of warning.

She ignored him and reached for the drone. "See? I'm fine."

But she wasn't fine. She didn't like even this hint of an argument and it was going straight to her shoulders.

If I had my car, I'd leave the panicky little voice in her head scolded. The same one that told her she'd lost her mind. *Dumb, dumb, dummy dunce!*

"What's wrong?" Elias asked again.

Wren realized she was frowning at that little voice. She smiled. "Nothing! Told you."

Elias only shook his head. Together, Elias and Wren carefully lifted her gear out. Elias took the heavier bags, slinging them over his broad shoulders with ease, while Wren cradled the case holding her drone.

"Are you sure you want to carry that? I promise I'll be careful—"

"Nope, I've got it," Wren insisted, the familiar weight of the equipment bringing her back down to earth as they walked toward the house.

See? It's not an argument. He's looking out for you. Score a point for rationality.

Elias led the way. A sensor sent the porch light flickering on as they approached even though daylight still crept between the trees. The house was secluded, nestled among pines and aspens with only the sounds of nature surrounding them. Peace washed over Wren as she followed Elias up the steps and through the front door, the same sort of peace she felt when she first saw Ellie and Bear's property.

"Just set that on the coffee table," Elias said as he carefully set her bags down on one of the chairs.

Wren's tote started slipping off her shoulder. When she shrugged to keep it from falling, another sharp twinge shot through her shoulder and back, forcing her to stop in her tracks. She hissed and grimaced.

Elias swore and came to her side. "That's not nothing."

"Ugh. Yeah, okay," she muttered, closing her eyes to block out the pain. And the fear that Elias would start yelling at her, telling her she was an idiot and should have listened to him and let him carry everything in.

"Here, let me take those." Elias' voice came from behind her, soft and warm and steady. Soothing. She felt the weight of her tote lift from her shoulder as he took it along with the drone case. She opened her eyes and released a breath she didn't realize she'd been holding.

He set the case and tote down on the table. Wren watched as Elias clapped his hands together, rubbing them briskly until his palms must have been warm.

"Turn around," he said.

He's making such a big deal out of this.

She couldn't help but tease him, her lips curling into a grin. "Tired of my face already?"

"Mmm, never." The low rumble in his voice made her insides flutter.

The growl of a lion knowing he's got his prey at his mercy.

"Just want another look at my backside?" She couldn't resist pushing her hips back against him, and when she felt his body respond, a wicked thrill shot through her.

Elias hissed, his breath hot against her neck. "Don't distract me while I'm working."

"What are you working—oh." Wren's words dissolved into a soft murmur as Elias' strong hands gripped her shoulders, applying just the right amount of pressure. He knew exactly where the knots were, his fingers finding the tight spots like he had a map of her muscles in his head. Her body relaxed into his touch. She leaned back against him, practically purring as he worked.

Her nagging tension began to melt away under his skillful hands, but she couldn't help the small voice of doubt that crept in.

"I can't believe I'm saying this because it feels so good and I don't want you to stop, but you are never going to work that rock out from under my shoulder."

"Rock?"

"Yeah, that's what I call it. It's been there since, well, forever."

Elias' grin was almost palpable. "It hasn't met me yet. And I'm determined."

She chuckled softly. "Mmm. Yeah, I know just how determined you get."

"There you go distracting me again," he murmured, his hands never stopping their steady, soothing rhythm.

Wren's eyes fluttered closed and she let out a sigh. "Shouldn't I be lying down for a massage?" She kept her tone teasing, hoping to coax a laugh from him.

Instead, Elias paused and gripped her upper arms, his breath warm against her ear. "When I lay you down, it's going to be for more than a massage. But I want you comfortable and out of pain first so you can enjoy..."

He kissed her neck.

"Every."

Another kiss.

"Moment."

His words sent a delicious shiver down her spine as her body responded to his promise. The tender kisses he pressed just below her ear made her toes curl. But before she could sink fully into the heat building between them, he resumed his focus on the stubborn knot in her shoulder.

Wren bit her lip, torn between wanting him to keep going and knowing that this particular knot was a battle even Elias might not win.

"Just relax and let me make it all better," he whispered.

She tried to do just that, trusting his hands to work their magic, even as the familiar ache persisted.

Damn rock she thought, but with Elias' hands on her, she was content to let him keep trying. Wren closed her eyes, trying to relax and sink deeper into the moment, into his touch, but a twinge of discomfort made her wince.

Elias noticed immediately. He stopped the massage as concern crept into his voice.

"Still hurting?"

Wren sighed, opening her eyes. "It's better, but...yeah. The rock's not giving up without a fight."

Elias slid his hands from her shoulders down to her arms, his touch gentle but firm. "Then let's take this to the bedroom," he suggested.

Wren's heart skipped a beat at the suggestion and her pulse quickened with anticipation. "Are you sure that's not just a clever way to get me into bed?"

He gave her a little growl, pressing a kiss to the back of her neck that sent a shiver through her. "Told you already, I want you out of pain and relaxed first. Let's get you lying down so I can take better care of you."

His words wrapped around her like a warm embrace. She turned her head slightly, meeting his gaze over her shoulder. "You always know just what to say, don't you?"

"Well, this time, at least," he murmured, his lips brushing against hers in a soft, lingering kiss that made her knees go weak. "You know how to keep me on my toes."

And you constantly sweep me off my feet.

Wren let out a small, contented sigh. She allowed Elias to guide her down the hall toward the bedroom. He kept his arm around her, steadying her as they walked down the hallway. She leaned into him for support and comfort.

When they reached the bedroom, Elias set her gently on the edge of the bed, his hands still lingering on her arms as if he couldn't bear to break contact. "Lie down. I'll be right back. I need to check on Penny and Chuck."

"Oh!" Wren covered her mouth. "I'm a complete jerk. I'd totally forgotten about them. Are they okay?"

Elias gave her a reassuring smile. His eyes held even more warmth. "Do I need to make a list of names you can't call yourself?" He touched her lips as she started to answer. "Don't answer that. I already am, right next to the laugh tally."

"But are your doggies okay?"

Elias' eyes warmed even more. "They're fine. They have a doggie run they can get into and out of at will and they're comfortable." Elias kissed her softly. "But I love that you're worried about them." He pointed to the bed. "Now, lie down."

"Yes, sir."

She kicked off her shoes and scooted back on the navy-blue comforter, then lowered herself slowly to keep her shoulders from complaining. Wren watched the ceiling fan spin while she listened to Elias' voice grow higher in the other room as he opened the door.

"Hey, guys! You'll never believe who's back."

Wren laughed quietly, her heart thumping in her chest. He sounded so happy.

Because I'm here.

To think, I actually ran away this morning.

Watching the fan made her sleepy and she closed her eyes. It seemed like only a moment before she felt the mattress shift as Elias sat on the bed. She opened her eyes and started to sit up.

"Nope. Roll over, relax, and let me do the work."

Wren hesitated for just a moment, a small smile playing on her lips as she teased, "You're really committed to this massage idea, aren't you?"

"I'm committed to making you feel good," he replied, his tone serious now, his eyes holding hers with an intensity that made her breath catch.

I don't need any more convincing. Wren lay back on the bed, her body sinking into the soft mattress as she relaxed beneath his gaze. Elias leaned over her, his hand brushing a strand of hair away from her face as he looked down at her with a mix of tenderness and desire.

"The dogs are fine?"

Elias chuckled. "The dogs are fine. If you're good, I'll let you see them later," he teased.

"Oh, I can be good." She started reaching for his lap but he stopped her.

"Just relax," he whispered, his fingers tracing the curve of her jaw before trailing down to her neck and shoulders. "I've got you."

Wren closed her eyes and rolled onto her stomach, letting go of everything except the sensation of his hands on her skin, the warmth of his body hovering over hers, and the promise of what was to come.

Elias straddled her without letting her take any of his weight. His touch was gentle yet firm, his hands knowing exactly where to press and where to soothe, drawing out the tension. After what felt like a delicious eternity, he dipped down and whispered beside her ear.

"How are you feeling now, baby?"

Baby. Wren should have shivered at that, but she no longer had muscles, or bones, or a nervous system stuck on high. She was no longer even a human—just a puddle of warm goo under his fingers.

"Mmurff."

Elias chuckled. "Can I take that as better than you were?"

"Mmurght. Yeah."

He laughed again, his voice husky. "Ready for more?"

There was no mistaking what *more* meant.

And no mistaking, she was ready. Very ready.

She opened her eyes and propped herself up on her elbows. She looked over her shoulder and caught the look in Elias' eyes that mirrored her own desire.

"Tell me, baby. You ready? If you aren't we can just—"

"Oh, no you don't." Wren rolled over as he lifted up to give her room to move. "Can't let all your hard work go to waste."

Elias grinned as he shook his head. "Always keeping me on my toes."

He started by sinking his hands into her hair and massaging her head. As his warm hands moved lower, his touch grew more intimate, more deliberate, and Wren felt a different kind of heat spreading through her.

Without a word, Elias leaned down, capturing her lips in a deep, passionate kiss that erased any last remnants of pain or anxiety. As the kiss deepened, Elias' hands slid down her sides then back up. He lowered his body until there was no space left between them. Wren's hands found their way to his back. She clutched at the fabric of his shirt as she pulled him down even closer on top of her, wanting to feel the full weight of him, the solid warmth of his body against hers.

Elias' lips moved from her mouth to her neck, leaving a trail of heated kisses that made her breath hitch. Wren arched into him, her hands sliding under his shirt now, her fingers exploring the rise and fall of muscles along his back.

"Elias," she breathed, feeling a mix of urgency and longing.

"Shh," he murmured against her skin. His lips rediscovered the sensitive spot just below her ear that made her shiver. "I've got you, baby."

Then Elias groaned low in his throat, a growl of primal desire that sent shivers down Wren's spine.

My Lion.

Elias lifted up until he sat straddling her again. Her core clenched with need as he deftly unbuttoned her jeans. She lifted her ass and he slid them down her legs, then dropped them on the floor. He stood up and pulled off his shirt, revealing his toned chest and the abs that she'd admired last night. Her breath hitched at the sight of him.

When he undid his belt and pulled it off so quickly it made a snapping sound, she sat up and swung her legs over the side of the bed. Elias was wearing a pair of button-fly jeans and she reached for the top button. She undid it, then pulled on either side and watched each button come undone.

His erection pushed against the cotton of his boxer briefs. Wren leaned forward and nuzzled her face against it as she pushed his jeans down. Elias must have taken off his shoes and socks before coming back into the bedroom. He stepped barefoot out of his jeans and let them pool on the floor next to hers. Wren started to pull his boxer briefs down but he clasped her hands and stopped her.

"Not yet," he growled. Then he carefully lowered her back onto the bed.

Elias' fingers danced over her stomach, sending goosebumps racing across her skin. He slid one hand underneath her panties, his calloused fingertips brushing against her warmth. Helpless, she bucked against this hand.

"Oh, you *are* hungry, aren't you?" he breathed. Elias hooked his fingers into her panties, dragging them down slowly, exposing her most private parts to his ravenous gaze. He tossed them on the floor into their ever-growing pile of discarded clothing.

"So beautiful," he rasped. Storms kicked up in his lagoon-blue eyes, darkening them with hunger and desire. Wren moaned when he found her clit. He rubbed it gently until she felt herself getting closer, her body tensing under his demanding touch.

"Elias, I'm so close," she whispered, her voice barely audible. "Don't stop."

And what did the bastard do?

He stopped.

And lowered his head.

Wren felt a self-conscious blush creep up her cheeks, but it was quickly replaced by an overwhelming need when Elias gently kissed her just above her clit. She gasped, her hands fisting in the comforter as he trailed his tongue down and lathed her, lapping at her like a bowl of cream. She arched against him as he knelt between her legs and pressed her thighs down. When her climax hit, it shook her whole body. She cried out and her voice echoed off his bedroom walls. Spent, her body relaxed and the feeling of being a warm puddle returned.

But no way was she done.

Wren reached for the bedside table drawer but Elias beat her to it. With a laugh, he opened the drawer and pulled out a condom.

"Fine." Wren grinned and pulled off her shirt.

"Wren, if I let you put this on me right now, the fun would be over way too soon."

"I think you've said that before," she teased.

"Well, it's even more true now."

She looked into his eyes, and what she saw there stole her breath. His gaze was intense, filled with a mix of lust and something else— something she couldn't quite put her finger on. Vulnerability, maybe? It was there and gone so fast she might have imagined it. Then she watched as he rolled the condom onto his curving cock. He threw his leg back over her, lowered his body, and nestled his hardness between her legs.

Wren reached up, her fingers tangling in his golden hair as she pulled him back to her waiting lips.

Elias gasped between kisses, his voice hoarse with desire. "Are you sure?"

"I've never been surer," she whispered. "I need you inside me. Right now."

He squeezed his eyes shut as he growled. "Tell me how you want it, baby."

"Hard," she panted. "Fast and hard."

His eyes blazed blue when he opened them. He gave her a ferocious smile as his fingers found her clit and rubbed. The head of his cock pressed against her opening. Then he pushed inside her with one hard stroke. He continued to rub her clit as he thrust deeper inside her, faster and faster.

Wren felt his body shaking as hers trembled. Somewhere amidst her pleasure she knew he was close. Elias growled low in his throat, his lagoon-blue eyes burning with the same need that consumed her. His strong hands cupped her hips, pulling her closer, their bodies pressed together. He took her lips again, hungry and desperate. His tongue danced inside her mouth as his cock stroked her.

"Now," she cried out as her body convulsed around his hardness. Elias roared in answer, pumping into her. When he was finished, he rolled onto his side and kept her close, their bodies still connected. He laid gentle, tender kisses across her forehead until Wren sank into a deep, sweet sleep in his arms.

WREN AWOKE to the smell of breakfast cooking. She blinked and looked around the bedroom. Morning light creeped in around the blinds. Birds chirped outside the window.

Did I really sleep through the night? She had no memory of stirring after they'd made love. She tried to remember the last time she'd slept like a rock and couldn't.

She sat up carefully and stretched. Her back felt pleasantly sore, worked over from the massage. Wren reached back and ran her thumb down the side of her shoulder blade. The rock was still there, but it seemed smaller and didn't pull on her shoulder like it usually did.

Score one for the Lion.

Other parts of her felt worked over as well.

An entire weekend of great sex will do that to a girl, Wrenbird. This time the voice in her head sounded like Barbie's. Wren giggled. Lion had given it to her hot and sexy. He'd also given it to her sweet and caring. Her back was proof of that. It felt better than it had since...

Since when?

Let's just leave it at a long time.

Wren's stomach rumbled at the enticing aroma of bacon. She ran a hand through her tangled hair and wondered if there was a brush in Elias' bathroom. Then she spotted her tote bag on his dresser.

Thoughtful of him to bring it in here.

Her heart warmed. That was Elias in a word—thoughtful.

Okay, and funny. And hot. And an amazing lover. And, and, and...

She giggled again.

And calm.

She stopped giggling as her heart kicked in her chest. Anxiety threatened to close back in. But why? Calm was good. Calm was what she liked. Calm was not...

Not anything like what I grew up with.

Wren took a deep breath and threw off the comforter, determined to outrun anything negative this morning. She got out of bed and went to her tote bag. Peering in, she grinned, back in a good mood. She knew just what to do to keep that good mood going.

NINE

Elias flipped four strips of bacon over in the skillet, thinking of the woman he'd left sleeping soundly in his bed. If she hadn't left in the wee small hours of Saturday morning, this would be the second breakfast he'd made for her.

Happily.

He couldn't remember the last time he'd spent more than a few hours with a woman, let alone an entire weekend. Or how good it made him feel to know she was still in his house. Plus, they had the entire day ahead of them.

And Monday.

Elias wasn't due back at work until Tuesday.

Dude, she's not gonna want to stay. She's got her own life.

But what if?

He glanced down at the two beggars sitting patiently at his feet. Penny sat just ahead of Chuck, in charge as always.

"What do you think?" Elias asked them quietly. "Would you like having Wren stick around?"

Both dogs had perked their ears up at the first sign of attention.

Penny wiggled her entire body and Chuck's tail thumped against the tile floor.

"Yeah, I agree. Or are you just wanting bacon?"

Penny tilted her head and Chuck licked his lips.

"Uh-huh. Thought so. You guys are no help whatsoever."

Elias' phone buzzed on the countertop. He poked at the bacon before setting the fork down to pick up his phone. A group text from Gabe read:

> Need you down at the rec center at ten.

Dammit.

That could only mean one thing. Gabe wasn't texting as Gabe but as Timberwolf. And he'd included Ram, Bear, Elk, and Moose.

Someone needed their special brand of help.

It wasn't like Lyons was some lawless little town. They had a great sergeant who kept things quiet and peaceful, plus people were pretty damn good all on their own around there. But sometimes people fell through the cracks or had a problem the law couldn't handle. That's where Mountain Division came in.

It wasn't an emergency—if it had been, Gabe would have texted the number 6 and his location. This sounded like a meeting to discuss someone who could use their help and they would decide whether or not they could give it. Elias didn't hesitate to answer with a thumbs-up. The work they did often meant protecting an innocent. Sometimes it meant busting heads who wouldn't listen to reason or to a restraining order. Either way, he didn't hesitate to help. None of them did.

But dammit. Why did it have to be today?

He glanced toward the bedroom then forked the bacon out of the skillet and onto a plate lined with paper towels and turned off the burner.

"Ah-*hem*." Behind him, Wren pretended to clear her throat to get his attention.

"Hey, Sleeping Beauty," he said as he turned. The second he saw her, he stopped.

Wren cocked her hip forward, giving Elias a cheeky grin. "What do you think?"

Elias took in the sight of her wearing his scrubs top. The oversized shirt hung loosely on her, the hem brushing against her thighs, but the way she wore it made it look like it was made just to caress her curves.

He leaned back against the counter, crossing his arms as a slow smile spread across his face. "I think you wear it better than I do."

Penny let out a small, impatient whine, clearly annoyed that they were too distracted to drop fistfuls of bacon on the floor. Chuck, meanwhile, wagged his tail in a slow, steady rhythm, eyes locked on the plate of bacon.

"Sorry, guys, I'm distracting your chef," Wren said, laughing as she walked over and scratched Chuck behind the ears. Penny, not to be outdone, nudged Wren's leg with her nose, demanding equal attention. "Yes, boss," Wren said as she switched her attention to Penny who turned and sat facing away so she could get back scratches.

Elias grinned, watching the way Wren interacted with his dogs. Something deep inside him warmed and a little voice in his head whispered *this is right*.

When she stood up inches away from him, she grinned and plucked at the scrubs collar.

"You don't mind, do you? I recall you saying something earlier about wanting to see me in it again."

"Mind? Not at all." Elias uncrossed his arms and pulled her closer by the waist. "I'll be stealing it back later though."

"Oh really?" She mock-pouted. "I hope you don't mean for work today."

Damn. She did want to spend the day with him. His heart flipped over in his chest.

"I meant when I take it back off you after breakfast."

Her eyes widened and her lips curved into a smile. He kissed that smile until her lips parted and let him in.

"Deal," she breathed, her eyes still closed.

"How's your back?"

"So much better." She opened her eyes and gazed up at him through a fringe of lashes. "You did a great job. I'm hiring you as my personal masseuse. All you have to do is carry my things and rub my shoulders twenty-four seven."

Elias grinned. "Is that all?"

Wren glanced at the stove. "Breakfast is nice, too. I'll let you do that."

God, he loved her banter.

Wren dropped her act. "Seriously, thank you for making breakfast. It looks like you went to a lot of effort."

Elias shrugged. "It's just some breakfast. Eggs, bacon, toast here in a sec. I wanted to wait until you got up. Nobody likes cold toast."

"Very true."

Elias gave her a squeeze before letting her go and dropping two slices of bread into the toaster. "Figured you'd be hungry after last night."

"Starving, actually." She glanced back at the breakfast table beside the kitchen, noticing the two places he'd set up, complete with glasses of orange juice and steaming mugs of coffee. "Seriously, you really thought of everything, didn't you?"

"Just trying to take care of you," he said, giving her a soft kiss on the forehead.

Her eyes went soft and she looked away. "Thank you."

"Hey." Elias slipped his thumb under her chin and turned her face back to him. "I like this. Taking care of you."

"It's the EMT in you."

Elias shook his head. "Yeah, okay, you're right. That's why I need the scrubs top back. It's my last one since I give them out to all my naked patients on the regular."

Wren giggled.

"First point of the day goes to me." He made a tick mark in the air.

"Dang it!"

"And none of this, 'oh I didn't keep track so I win' BS."

"I didn't say I'd win. I said we'd be tied."

Elias grinned and started for the toast when it popped up but Wren beat him to it.

"Let me help at least a little bit," she said as she plated the slices and looked around for the butter.

"On the table, babe." The affectionate term rolled off his lips without thinking. He noticed her cheeks pinken along with her sweet smile and wondered if she wasn't used to being called babe.

That's gonna change.

Elias carried the rest of the food to the table and set it down. He held out her chair for her then spread a cloth napkin across her lap as soon as she sat down.

"Fancy."

"What do you mean?" He blinked at her as he sat across the table. "I spread napkins across Penny and Chuck's laps for every meal. Anything less is just savage."

Wren rolled her lips in and her shoulders shook while she sliced off a square of butter for her toast. "Right. Savage." She glanced down at Penny who'd parked herself beside the chair. "Did I steal your chair, too?"

"You did, actually, but she's playing the long game."

"Long game?" Wren took a bite of her toast as Elias plated up bacon and eggs for her. "Yeah. Letting you sit in her chair will lull you into becoming her minion."

"I see."

"Yeah. After that, we're the ones eating out of bowls on the floor."

Wren casually shrugged. "You maybe, but I've already talked her into table rights as well as stock options. Enjoy your kibble."

Thankfully, Elias had just finished sipping his coffee or he would have spewed it across the table when he laughed.

"Tied." Wren ticked off a point in the air.

God, I love you.

The thought stopped his brain. Shut it down completely.

Love? I can't love someone this quickly.

"Oh, shit, are you all right?" Wren asked, her voice full of concern.

He gave her the warmest smile he could. "Yeah, yeah, I'm just a sore loser."

"Oh. So you're already admitting defeat today? Excellent." She leaned over and mock-whispered to Penny, "You're right, that was easy."

That got her another laugh. "Apparently so."

They spent the next few minutes eating breakfast and during those minutes, Elias had never felt more comfortable with a woman. He wondered how Wren felt. Watching her, she seemed comfortable with him, too.

She picked up her glass of orange juice and looked at him over the rim as she drank. She set it down with a mischievous little smile then dabbed at her lips with her napkin.

"So. Dishes before or after you steal your scrubs top back?" She batted her lashes at him.

He looked her up and down, letting his gaze linger on the teasing bit of her cleavage showing thanks to the V-neck before meeting her eyes again. "I'll get the dishes later."

"I'll help."

"Eh, we'll see."

Wren crossed her arms. "Nope. That was the rule growing up in my house. Whoever cooks, the others clean."

"Good rule."

"It kept the peace." Her voice sounded light, but her eyes dimmed for a fraction of a second and she sucked in her cheeks. "*Do you have work today?*" she asked, abruptly changing the subject. "I can get a lift service to take me back to Lyons for my car."

Elias shook his head. "Nope. I'm off today and I'll take you to get your car, no problem." He paused. "I don't have work, but there is something I need to take care of. Kind of an errand at the rec center."

Wren raised an eyebrow, curiosity sparking in her eyes. "Oh? What kind of errand?"

He couldn't tell her outright. Elias leaned back in his chair, letting out a low sigh. "Well, I'm meeting a friend or two there, but I was also thinking. Your back seems a lot better after the massage last night, but I was wondering if maybe you'd want to try something more regular."

Wren's brow furrowed slightly as she set her fork on her empty plate. "What do you mean?"

"I was thinking that if I brought you along, we could get you signed up," he suggested, trying to sound as nonchalant as possible. "They've got weightlifting and workout classes that might help strengthen your shoulder. Plus, they've got some equipment that could work wonders for your back. Stretching, strength training, that sort of thing."

Wren looked intrigued. "You're really into this whole personal trainer gig, huh?" she teased.

Elias shrugged, grinning. "Just trying to take care of you. And hey, if you want to try yoga, they have classes."

"Yoga sounds good." She hesitated, then smiled at him. "But only if you promise not to laugh when I fall over trying to balance."

Elias touched his fingers to his chest and gave her a look of pure innocence. "Me? Never."

"That's because you'll be too busy looking at my ass in the air, right?"

"Do I *have* to answer that?"

Wren snickered. "Is this the same rec center where Stephanie works?"

"It is." He wondered what else if anything Ellie had told her about Stephanie the day before.

"Hmm," Wren mused, tapping her finger on her lips. "I *might* ask her about her yoga classes."

"Perfect," Elias said, maybe a bit too quickly, but he covered it with a grin. "Though I have to warn you about Stephanie."

"Oh?"

"She's... a little quirky."

"Quirky's good."

"I need to walk Chuck and Penny this morning, too. Do you mind?"

"Not at all, as long as I can come along." Wren stood with her plate in hand and reached for Elias' empty glass.

"Uh-uh. Dishes later." He took the plate out of Wren's hand and set it back down on the table. He looked her up and down. "First, I have a scrubs top to steal back."

"No. First, you have to catch me." Wren spun on her heel and took off running down the hall straight to his bedroom.

Elias couldn't hold back his laughter as he chased after her.

"Woo-hoo! More points for me," she shouted.

Wren was already on the bed when Elias got to the bedroom.

"Come get the top...if you dare." She made a funny-fierce face at him.

"Oh, I dare."

Eyes flashing, he stalked around the bed as she scrambled to the opposite side, laughing. Elias crouched to spring, locking his gaze with his prey—who didn't seem very prey-like as she licked her lips. He launched himself onto the bed and grabbed Wren, then pinned her under him.

"Gotcha."

"Oh dear. Whatever am I to do?"

"Hmm. You don't seem that worried."

"Hmm. I don't. Maybe because I'm not."

Elias looked deeply into Wren's playful gaze while the salty, peachy scent of her skin rose from the sheets.

How would it feel to wake up to her like this every morning?

Good. Really good.

"You caught me. Aren't you going to kiss me?" she breathed.

Elias grinned. "Nope." He swept her into his arms and got to his knees on the bed while she giggled. He backed off the bed until he stood with her cradled in his arms. "Because if I kiss you, I'm going to want to strip you. And if I strip you, I'm going to want to eat you out. And if I eat you out, I'm going to want to bury myself inside you. And if I bury myself inside you, I'm going to want to stay there a good long time. Until I've gotten you to come for me at least three times."

"Three?" She pursed her lips and covered them with her fingertips, pretending to be shocked.

"Mmm-hmm. And then it's all going to start over again. And I'll end up missing my meeting and you won't get signed up for classes."

"But I will be thoroughly and enjoyably fucked silly, so there's that."

"Ohhh...don't tempt me."

"So you're *not* stealing the scrubs top back, is that what you're saying?"

"Never said that." Elias turned and carried Wren into his bathroom. He set her down, grabbed the hem of the top, and pulled it over her head when she lifted her arms. She hadn't bothered putting on panties, so she stood stark naked and gorgeous.

"Dear God," he murmured as he looked her up and down. Waylon's words came back to him—*way above your pay grade.*

"Let's shower, then we can go from there."

"Fine by me." She rolled up onto her tiptoes and kissed him. Elias was facing the mirror and he couldn't help but peek at their reflection.

Perfection.

Not just her, but them. Together.

Elias stripped down while Wren got the water going. She stepped under the water and became his fantasy made flesh. Water coursed down her gorgeous body, which he soaped up almost reverently as his cock hardened. She stroked his length, teasing him with her soap-slicked hands until she went to her knees and took him inside her mouth. When he was close, he tried to stop her but she shook her head gently and sucked harder. His orgasm left him almost dizzy.

Elias pulled Wren to her feet and pushed her against the shower wall while he trailed kisses down her torso. She gripped his hair while he nuzzled, licked, and ate her out. He held her up when her knees threatened to give out.

They didn't—but the hot water did.

"Gahh!" Wren yelled "Cold-cold-cold-cold-cold!"

Laughing, Elias reached around her and turned off the shower. "Stay put."

She wrapped her arms around her torso and exaggerated her teeth chattering. Elias got out of the shower, grabbed a clean towel off the rack beside the shower, and wrapped Wren up.

"Oh! Nice." She snuggled into the towel. "Heated rack?"

"Yeah. The guys gave me shit for it, but it gets cold up here in the winter and I've spent enough time in the cold."

"I for one will never give you shit for a heated towel rack."

Elias wrapped a towel around his waist and opened the vanity drawer. He pulled out a pack of toothbrushes and handed it to Wren.

"I'll give you a minute. Anything else you need?"

"I'm good, thanks."

He closed the door behind him as he went into the bedroom. A glance at the bedside clock told him they'd better hustle.

Still wrapped in her towel, Wren stepped out of the bathroom as he finished getting dressed.

"Running a little behind. Not sure where you live, but I figure you want to go home for a change of clothes. I could drop you at your car and then you could meet me at the rec center."

"I don't want to make you late, so I have another idea." Wren turned to his closet and opened it. She pulled out one of his tees and a pair of jeans and held them against her front. "I'll need to roll the cuffs quite a bit, but I think these'll work."

"Do you like stealing clothes in general, or just my clothes?"

Wren stuck her tongue out at him as she draped the clothes over one arm. Then she pulled off her towel and tossed it at him. He caught it, laughing.

"Now get out. I need my privacy while I get dressed. I'm very modest that way."

Elias studied Wren when she came out of the bedroom. She was right—his clothes worked on her. She'd knotted up the bottom of his tee and it slouched just right.

And when I get it back, it'll smell like her.

Yeah, he could afford to never wash that tee again.

She was shorter than Elias, but her legs were long enough that she only had to turn the bottoms of his jeans up a couple of times, though she had to cinch her belt tightly.

Wait... Is she going commando?

Okay, never washing the jeans again, either.

TEN

The dogs ran ahead on the familiar trail snaking through the forest around Elias' house. Elias watched Penny sniff at a columbine at the side of the trail. Chuck followed close behind, his nose to the ground. The air was alive with the sound of birds—the sharp cawing of ravens, robins' morning songs, and the high-pitched whirring of hummingbirds as they darted unseen through the trees.

Wren walked at Elias' side. Their hands brushed as they walked.

"Tell me about growing up here," Wren said. "I bet you were a rule-follower."

Elias couldn't hold back his laugh. "No. Not in the slightest."

"Really?" Wren's hazel eyes sparkled as she tilted her head. She nudged a small rock off the path with her foot, her hair cascading over her shoulder in the sunlight. "But you're former military, and I've seen you in action. You're very disciplined."

"Yeah, that all came later. I was hell on my parents as a teenager."

"So what changed you?"

Elias whistled softly to get Chuck's attention, steering him away from a bush that had caught his interest. He took a deep breath, settling into his story. "It's not something I'm proud of." He shook his head as his gaze drifted to the towering pine trees surrounding them, swaying in the breeze. "I was seventeen, it was summer, and my friends and I were partying pretty hard, one last summer together before senior year. So, one night, it was my turn to bring the booze, and my fake ID got confiscated by the guy at the liquor store."

Wren giggled. "Whoops."

Penny hesitated at a fork in the trail. "To the left today, Pen. Go left. Short walk." Penny looked back over her shoulder, then started down the left hand trail.

Wren shook her head. "She's just so smart. So, what did you do then?"

"Well, to my mind, I had no choice but to raid my dad's liquor cabinet."

"Oh no."

"Yeah. And, being the dumbass that I was, not only did I raid it, but I took the most expensive bottle of bourbon in there. And, on top of that, it was a gift from his best friend."

Wren covered her mouth with both hands. "Which makes it irreplaceable," she said through her fingers.

"Yeah." He nodded. "So I took it to the bonfire party way back in the woods on Bear's parents' property. They lived on acres and acres of land, had no idea what we were up to back there. My friend Ben was the only one who paused before drinking the bourbon and looked at me. He asked how I could afford it and I just shrugged and said, 'Five-finger discount.'"

"Ooof."

"Yeah, telling you, I was bad."

"So how long did it take for your dad to find out?"

Elias sidestepped a tree root growing out of the path, guiding Wren around it as they continued around a bend and back toward his house.

"It took exactly no time. We all spent the night at Bear's since we were in no shape to drive. When I got home the next day, I had the worst hangover, so I went straight to bed right after I called in sick to my summer job. My dad knew the way dads do exactly when I'd fallen asleep, so he waited to knock on my door right then. I sat straight up in bed, hoping I wouldn't puke all over myself. And being young, dumb, and full of come, I was ready to deny everything."

"Of course."

"But my dad, he just smiled at me and sat down on the bed. 'Hey, son,' he says all friendly, 'I was going through my liquor cabinet last night.'"

"Oh no. Friendly means you're in real trouble."

Elias chuckled, watching as Penny darted after a squirrel that quickly disappeared up a tree. Chuck lumbered after her, barking in excitement.

"Ain't that the truth? So, he says, 'I'm missing a bottle of bourbon.' And that's all he says, right? Doesn't accuse me, doesn't yell, just smiles like we're talking about the weather."

"What did you do?"

"I just shrugged and I started to lie down again. And he says, 'You haven't seen it?' And I told him nope. 'I'm hoping you can help me look for it, because it's gotta be around here somewhere,' he says. Then, he gets up and opens the shade until the light's just pouring in."

"Serves you right!"

Elias laughed as they watched Penny circle back to them, her energy never seeming to wane. Chuck stared up into the tree as if the squirrel might just fall out of it.

"Yeah it does." Elias chuckled again. "So I groaned and tried to keep the contents of my stomach inside. 'You sure you haven't seen it, son?' he asks again."

Wren whistled to get Chuck's attention. He lumbered back to her side.

"And you still denied taking it?"

"Told you I was terrible."

Wren clucked her tongue. "The worst. So he made you get up and look for the bourbon during the worst hangover of your life?"

"Oh no, my dad did something way worse than that. He went back to the window and pulled the shade back down. 'I can see you're feeling poorly,' he says. 'I'll let you sleep and I'll just look for it myself. Feel better, son.' And he has the biggest look of disappointment on his face."

Wren winced as they stepped over a furrow made by a twisting stream of water, her expression mirroring the pained look Elias imagined he'd had back then. "Oh, God. So did you fess up the next day?"

"Nope."

"Oh, Elias."

"Yeah, I know. I wanted to, but I couldn't. I had it all twisted up in my head by then. You know, how dare he act like he didn't know? That shit. He never brought it up again. Never accused me, never flat-out told me he knew I'd taken it. But that disappointment in his eyes lingered." Elias shook his head, the memory heavy on his shoulders.

"But my pride wouldn't let me fix the situation. I kept on being a jackass all summer. I stayed out late, came home in the last dark before dawn or went straight to my job, just so that I wouldn't have to look my dad in the eye. Senior year started and there were no parties to go to every night. Things got real. Well, except for Waylon and me. Waylon, he was still wild, still getting in trouble. And I went right along with it." Elias chuckled ruefully, shaking his head as Penny barked at a passing chipmunk that chittered angrily back at her.

"So, what changed you guys?"

"Ben. He was the one who talked some sense into us finally. Said we needed to get serious or we'd never go anywhere, never amount to anything. It hits different when it's your friend telling you that and not your parents."

"Yeah, you're absolutely right."

"I decided I needed more discipline, so I enlisted as soon as I could, right after graduation. Me and Waylon both. And, well, all my friends eventually did, too. All that playing when we were kids, pretending we were soldiers and sailors. We made it real."

Wren slipped her hand into his. "Were your parents surprised when you enlisted?"

"Yeah, I think they were. Also, relieved that I'd decided to actually do something with my life. I became a medic with the 75th Ranger Regiment. I loved the Tactical Combat Casualty Care training and became a first responder."

"Wow. That had to be intense."

"Yeah. But I never lost anyone. I'm proud of that."

Wren glanced up at the sun filtering through the leaves. The dappled light danced on her cheeks. "I bet your dad is, too."

Elias chuckled as he shook his head. "My dad," he said fondly. "So, on my first leave, I sat down with my dad at the kitchen table on the last night. It took me that long to gather the courage to apologize to him. Before I said a word, I set a replacement bottle of bourbon on the table." Elias chuckled. His house came into view and the dogs ran ahead. "And you know what my dad did?"

Wren's eyes sparkled. "What?"

"Before I could even open my mouth to apologize, he looks me square in the eye and says with a smile, 'Hey! I see you finally found it.'"

Wren smiled so wide, the skin around her eyes crinkled. "Wow."

"Wow is right. That's my dad. All was forgiven."

Wren squeezed his hand. "I like your dad."

"I like my dad, too."

ELIAS INSISTED on carrying all her gear—even the drone—to the truck and loading it up. When he came back in to wrangle the pups into their room, he found she'd already taken care of that for him.

As if she's done it a million times. He was struck again by that feeling of *rightness.*

"They didn't give you any grief?" he asked.

"Oh, they gave me plenty. Talk about sad, mournful eyes." She imitated them—mouth turned down and big, blinking eyes. "But I told them you'd be back in time for dinner."

Just me?

His gut actually clenched.

Dude! Get a grip. Don't be so needy.

"Ready?" he asked, turning away, but not before he caught her sucking in her cheeks.

"Yeah. Sure." Her voice sounded a little flat. Then she smiled. "Penny told me she's docking your kibble though for leaving so early."

Was Wren glad to be leaving, or did she want to stay? *Mixed signals.* Or was he just reading too much into her reactions?

Get. A. Grip.

He grinned at her joke as he held the front door open. "I'm sure I deserve it."

They got to the rec center just before ten. He noticed the rest of his brothers' vehicles in the parking lot when they pulled in. He hated being the last one there, but he loved the reason for it.

Elias pushed open the door to the rec center, holding it for Wren to enter first. The sounds of the rec center hummed in the background—overhead music, a mixture of chatter, distant laughter, and the thud of basketballs hitting the floor.

His brothers stood around the reception desk. Gabe, Bear, Waylon, Ben, and Shane were all there, listening to Stephanie. The receptionist and yoga teacher was usually a force of nature with a sly smile or a quick-witted comment, but she looked uncharacteristically serious. When she glanced over at Elias and Wren, her expression changed to a welcoming smile. Gabe, Shane, and Ben looked curiously at Wren walking beside Elias. Bear nodded to her in greeting. As for Waylon, the man looked shocked.

"Looks like we're late to the party," Elias said, injecting some lightness into his voice.

"Looks like you brought a plus-one," Waylon said. Elias shot him a warning look.

But Wren looked unfazed. "Hey, Elias' bar-friend! If I'd known you'd be here, I would've brought a beer and a Pine-Sol chaser."

Elias snorted as Waylon's mouth dropped open. No one—absolutely no one—ever left that smartass speechless.

Stephanie was the first to laugh, breaking the group's shock-induced silence. "She's got your number, Waylon. When did you share a beer? Peh-tooie!"

"I couldn't get past smelling it in the pitcher," Wren said, then added, "Over at Cocktails and Chicken Strips." She gave Waylon a huge smile and stuck out her hand. "I'm kidding. It was good beer, just way too fancy for this simple PBR girl. Thanks for giving me your bar seat though, so I could talk to this guy." She bumped her shoulder against Elias. "Nice to actually meet you." Waylon shook her hand, still speechless.

"Everyone else, this is Wren Stapleton," Elias said. "Wren, you've met Bear already."

Everyone took their attention off Wren and turned it to the big man as if to say *really dude? You never said anything.* Elias pointed one by one at the rest of his brothers. "And this is Gabe, Shane, and Ben. And Waylon, officially. And this is the lovely and talented Stephanie, who is the heart and soul of this place."

She nodded at the men as they each greeted her. She extended her hand to Stephanie, her smile warm. Elias thought Wren hid her surprise well. Stephanie was in her seventies and probably not who she'd expected as a yoga teacher.

"Elias was telling me you teach yoga here and that I should sign up for one of your classes. Nice to meet you."

Stephanie took her hand, giving it a firm shake. "Nice to meet you too, dear. Gotta say, Elias has good taste."

Wren's cheeks flushed slightly, but she kept her smile. "Good taste in yoga instructors, obviously," she said, gesturing at Stephanie.

Stephanie's gaze flicked to Elias and he noted the look of approval before she looked at Wren again. "I'm not talking about myself, dear. If you could convince the big galoot to take one of my classes, I'd be shocked. What do you say we get you signed up as a member while these guys go take care of business? First week's free."

Gabe placed his hand on Stephanie's shoulder. "You sure you don't want to..." He tilted his head toward his office.

Why would Stephanie sit in on our meeting? Elias wondered. *Unless this has something to do with her?* Angered, adrenaline shot straight to his heart at the thought of anyone messing with Steph.

"I'm good, boss." Stephanie patted Gabe's hand. "I've got a new friend here to talk to."

Gabe smiled then looked at Wren. "Careful. That means you're in for an interrogation."

Stephanie rolled her eyes. "I'll behave."

Elias gave Wren a gentle nudge with his shoulder. "You good here?"

"Yeah, I'll be fine," Wren replied casually, though her eyes flicked to the group, clearly curious about them. "Go play with your friends." That got her another laugh from Stephanie.

"We'll be just be a minute." Elias grabbed her hand and squeezed it as he leaned in and kissed her.

He turned to join the other men as they headed down the hall toward Gabe's office. They joked and ribbed each other, but when the office door closed behind them with a definitive click the atmosphere in the room shifted.

Gabe didn't waste any time. "Stephanie asked me for help finding someone." He looked back and forth between Elias and Waylon standing next to each other. "Evan Roy, the guy you and Waylon saved that day at the clinic."

Elias recalled the day vividly. They'd gotten the call that a man at the rec center had suffered a possible heart attack during one of the public health clinics they held once a month. *Heart attack* was putting it lightly. Elias glanced sideways at Waylon who nodded.

"He was in rough shape," Waylon said. "Didn't think he'd make it."

"It was a miracle he survived," Elias added. They'd taken him to the hospital in Longmont while still trying to get his heart restarted. Longmont had stabilized him and the last Elias had heard, he'd been transferred to a bigger hospital specializing in cardiac care.

Gabe's tone carried a weight that made everyone listen a little closer. "Evan was a regular at the clinic. Used to bring homemade fudge in for the staff even though he couldn't eat sugar himself anymore. He came to Sue's daughter's soccer games. Sue's one of the clinic nurses," he added, looking at the rest of the men. "Always brought Stephanie flowers on her birthday. Real peach of a guy."

"Sounds like more of a friend than a patient," Shane said.

"Some get that way," Elias said.

"Especially when you loan them your scrubs top," Waylon murmured under his breath.

"Fuck off," Elias murmured back.

"Got something to share with the class?" Gabe said, looking annoyed.

"Sorry," Elias said.

Gabe continued. "They all visited him in the hospital and made sure that when he was discharged, he had help at home."

"No family?" Ben asked.

"Nope. When he came back to the clinic the first time, everyone threw a little party for him with sugar-free cupcakes."

Gabe picked up a thin stack of paper off his desk and handed it to Ben, who took a sheet and passed it on to Elias. Gabe had printed out a photo of Evan and his stats underneath—age, address, height and weight, brief background. Evan smiled out from the photo as he posed between the two nurses who helped save his life. Gabe and Stephanie flanked the three of them. Everyone held plates of cake. Evan looked like a scarecrow and Elias guesstimated that he'd lost at least thirty pounds since the heart attack.

When the sheets were all passed out, Gabe continued. "Evan came back a couple more times, but he didn't show up at the last clinic. And he's not answering his phone. Sue and Fran, she's the other nurse, stopped by his place yesterday and it looks like he's not there. They said there was a big Dumpster in the driveway full of furniture."

Bear frowned. "Hate to say it but, sounds like he died."

"Nope. When he was in the hospital, Evan gave Sue power of attorney in case that happened. She's checked all around, too. He's not dead, just missing." Gabe sighed. "Of course Stephanie's worried too. She says it's not like him to just disappear, especially after everything he's been through. If he was moving, he would've told them."

Elias crossed his arms over his chest. "He have any enemies?"

Gabe shook his head. "Not that we know of. Like I said, peach of a guy. However, he was a bit of a gambler."

"Maybe lost a bet and had to leave town quick?" Ben suggested.

Gabe shrugged. "It's a possibility. Evan liked his sports, liked going up to Central City and placing bets. So who knows? That's why Steph asked for our help. If he's in trouble like that..." Gabe trailed off.

Elias felt a chill settle in the room. *He might need muscle backing him up* went unsaid but every man in the room understood.

"That's why we're meeting. We need to figure out the best way to track him down and offer our assistance if needed. If something's wrong, he might not have much time."

Shane tapped his copy of the photo. "I can get Watchdog on it, too. See if he's hired a real estate agent for the house, what he's got in his bank account, where he's spending his money. Or if he's stopped spending money altogether, know what I mean?"

Gabe nodded, a grim expression on his face. "They'll be devastated if he's deceased." He looked down at the photo in his hands. "I'll be pretty damn upset, too."

"We've got your back on this, brother," Bear said. "Like we did with Rochelle." As he spoke, he signed the words for Gabe in ASL. They'd all been learning the language, since Gabe's injury on his final mission left him with serious hearing loss.

Gabe smiled and gave Bear a chin lift. "I appreciate it." He looked toward the closed office door. "Thanks for coming in on a

Sunday morning, guys. I know you've all got stuff to do today, so I'll let you go. Speaking of Rochelle, she should be finished with her self-defense class by now."

As everyone filed out, Waylon clapped his hand on Elias' shoulder, holding him back behind the rest. A smirk played at the corner of his mouth.

"So, Lion, you want to explain why Wren is still around? It's Sunday, brother. You're breaking protocol."

"Protocol?" Elias fought his annoyance and kept his expression neutral.

"Yeah, you know the one. Get in, get out, don't let 'em get too comfy. Instead, you spent the whole weekend with her." He gestured at the door. "And how the hell does Bear know her?"

Elias set the photo of Evan aside and crossed his arms, his gaze shifting to the door of Gabe's office, wanting this conversation to end. "Not the whole weekend. She worked yesterday."

"So you left her place late Friday night, then what? You picked her up Saturday and were like, 'Hey, let me introduce you to my friend Bear for shits and giggles'?" Waylon kept a light tone, but there was an undercurrent in his voice Elias didn't like. What the ever-loving fuck was up with him?

"That was part of her job, meeting Bear and Ellie," Elias said. "She's gonna do some photography work for them and I provided the introductions. That's all."

Waylon studied him, the lingering humor in his eyes fading into something more serious.

"Don't bullshit me, Elias. Last I saw you was Friday night, heading out the door with your hand riding just above her ass. Figured you'd take her home, show her a good time, then come in here this morning bitching that we have to work next Friday so it'll be two weeks before you can find a new honey. Instead, you two walked in through the door like you've been together forever."

Is that what we looked like? Elias shifted his weight from one foot to the other. Did it bother him, to look that way?

Or was he bothered because he *wasn't* bothered? Because it felt natural. Good.

I should just tell Waylon he's right, then get the hell out of here. Wren's probably wondering what the hell is up.

Instead, he answered, "No. I took her back to my place Friday night."

Waylon's jaw nearly hit the floor. "Wait a minute. She spent the night at *your* house?"

"Not the whole night. Like I said, she left to go to work early." He couldn't keep the grin off his face. "But she took the scrubs top with her on the way out the door."

Waylon ran his hand over the back of his head. "So you're dating a clepto."

"Dude, she's not a clepto. It's just... a thing we have going on. It's fun."

Waylon rolled his eyes. "Jesus. You are smitten, brother. What do you even know about her?"

"Plenty."

"Like what?"

"I..." Elias hesitated. "She's a photographer."

Waylon scoffed. "Shit. Even I know that about her."

"She's taken photos of famous people that end up on magazine covers."

"Already covered the photography."

Dammit. What else did he know about Wren? What did she know about him?

"Ellie likes her a lot."

Waylon pinned him with a stare. "Did I ask what *Ellie* knows about her?"

"Fine. Fuck you. I know that she's..."

Warm. Funny. Intelligent. Fucking adorable. Someone I like taking care of. Someone I could see myself with years from now.

"...Different. She fits me, you know?"

"*Fits* you? What, like the top she keeps stealing from you?"

"Again, fuck you."

"Brother. I'm just looking out for you. You sure you know what you're doing?"

"Yeah. I do." Elias held his brother's gaze. "Now, what the hell is really wrong?"

"Fuck." Waylon nodded slowly. "Yeah. Okay. If this is the real thing, I'm happy for you, brother. Don't ever think otherwise. But dammit, first it was Bear and Ellie, then T-Wolf and Rochelle. And Shane's all hung up over April and won't even come out to Cocks and Strippers without the whole group. And Ben's just a big nerd. The meat market's never been his scene so he's no good to me."

"No good to you?"

"Yeah! He doesn't know how to reel them in." Waylon gave Elias' shoulder a good-natured shove. "But you, you're my wingman, brother. You're not supposed to get all domesticated, too. Besides, I don't want to lose my wingman to a life of Sunday brunches and Netflix binges while I'm still out there having fun."

Oh. I get it now.

Elias shoved him back. "You won't lose me."

Waylon grinned, a glimmer of his usual good humor returning. "Yeah, you say that now. But if you coulda seen yourself walking in. Giving her that kiss before we all went back here." He shook his head. "Like I said, happy for you. Truly. But if it doesn't work out, you know where to find me Friday and Saturday nights. That's never gonna change."

He's gonna hate me saying this.

"Never? Brother, it's been how many years since—"

Waylon crossed his arms, all humor gone from his eyes. "Breaking the other protocol now. We don't talk about that. About *her*."

Elias lifted his hands, palms out. "I know. But I'm just saying—"

"You aren't saying a damn thing I need to hear, okay? My life is great, just the way I want it. Love my job, love my house, love my nights out." He smirked. "Love my freedom."

Elias picked the sheet of paper back up. "Roger that. I hear you loud and clear."

I'm hearing that after all this time, you're still hurting, brother.

"So." Waylon gestured to the door. "After you. She's waiting. Better hurry before she changes her mind. Way above your paygrade, I'm telling you."

Elias couldn't hold back his smile. "Yeah, she is."

"Take her someplace nice, huh? Maybe get to know her?" Waylon smirked. "What flowers she wants for the wedding, what colors, shit like that. She'll appreciate it."

"Shut up, man." Elias shoved Waylon ahead of him into the hallway.

"What? You said I get to pick out the flowers and honeymoon and shit. And I look great in a tux. Just mad I didn't go ahead and buy that one I rented for the last wedding. Now I gotta turn around and rent it again."

Buy it, brother Elias wanted to say. *So that you can wear it the day you get married.*

"Or." Waylon stuck his pointer finger in the air. "I can have your woman steal one for me. Is she wearing your jeans right now? *Dude.*"

Elias was still chuckling when they got to the end of the hall and he saw her again. Wren stood at the receptionist desk, but now Gabe, Rochelle, and Sandra had joined her. They were all laughing at Stephanie, who appeared to be fanning Rochelle with a thick paperback.

Wren looked like she belonged there. Hell, like she'd been there forever.

In my life.

In my heart.

ELEVEN

Wren watched the guys disappear down the hall, wondering what their meeting was all about. She also wondered at the shocked look on Waylon's face.

Did I read Elias all wrong?

Waylon was far from hostile, but Wren had learned to smell a confrontation brewing from a mile away and was quick to defuse the situation. She thought she'd been successful, considering they were all joking with each other, including Waylon.

"Don't worry about them," Stephanie said, breaking into her thoughts. "Let's get you signed up." She grabbed her keyboard off to the side and slid it across her desk until it was in front of her. "Gimme your deets, girl. Full name, address, phone, email."

"Wren Stapleton." She gave Stephanie the rest of her info.

"Any health concerns that might interfere with doing a physical activity?"

"Just my shoulder." Her hand automatically went to her shoulder and rubbed it. "But that's why I'm taking your class, to see if I can strengthen my shoulder and work out this knot."

Stephanie looked up. "Noted. We'll start you out slow in the beginners class. I can suggest a personal trainer as well."

"Sounds good."

Stephanie looked back down at her keyboard and typed away. "Allergies?"

"Just an allergy to fancy pants beer."

Stephanie snorted. "Girl, I like you." Her fingers kept flying as she asked more questions.

"There. All signed up," Stephanie announced as she opened a file drawer and pulled out an info packet. She handed it to Wren with a smile. "Class schedules start on page five and go alphabetically, so you'll just want to jump straight to page thirty-eight for yoga." She tilted her head toward Gabe's office. "I'm teaching a class later today but I imagine you've got other plans already."

Do I?

When she'd joked earlier about Penny and Chuck being upset that Elias was leaving them, she'd casually suggested he'd be coming back to his house alone for dinner, giving him an out but hoping he'd correct her.

He didn't. Instead he'd looked away and asked if she was ready to go.

Of course he's tired of you.

It was plain as day on every man's face when they walked in. Shock that Elias was still with the woman he'd gone home with on Friday night. Even more shock that he'd introduced her to Bear.

Waylon did everyone a favor and said the quiet part out loud.

The Lion bagged his prey and now I'm just going to bore him.

I should do Elias a favor and grab a lift to my car at Riversong so he can enjoy the rest of his weekend without me being all clingy.

Wren looked toward the front door, almost envisioning a car coming to pick her up before Elias came back out and things got awkward.

"Something wrong?" Stephanie asked. Her smile looked fixed in place while her eyes gleamed with concern.

"Sorry." Wren gave her a quick smile, a well-worn reflex. She was ready with another joke to relieve the tension but instead she found herself saying, "I'm not sure what the plan is."

Stephanie's smile relaxed into something more genuine. "I can tell you the plan doesn't involve taking your first yoga class today."

It was Wren's turn to smile for real. "You don't think so?"

"No, sweetie. I don't think Elias is going to let you out of his sight after they're done."

That reassured her a little. But there was still that nagging little voice in her head.

Nothing good ever lasts in your life.

And Elias was the best thing that happened to Wren in a long time.

"You guys are old friends, huh?" she teased Stephanie, changing the subject.

"Actually, no, not old friends. Really only got to know all the little critters this year."

Wren grinned. "The nicknames."

"Cute, aren't they?" Then Stephanie's face lit up like she'd just thought of something. "Hey, you fit right in with your name."

"Oh, right. Wren like the bird. I hadn't even thought of that."

"Lucky you. I keep angling to join the club but for some reason they're resistant to calling me Cougar."

Wren's eyes went wide before she almost bent in half, laughing. She set the info packet on the desk because she was likely to spill the folder's contents all over the floor if Stephanie kept making her laugh like that.

"Hey!" Gabe shouted from down the hall. Wren looked up and watched him coming out of his office followed by the other men. "Knew you couldn't stay out of trouble, Steph. What are you laughing at?"

"Nothing, boss!" Stephanie shouted back. She winked at Wren, who gave her another reflexive smile. All her attention was on the fact that Elias and Waylon weren't among the other men.

Are they just talking? Or is there a problem? The anxiety she'd managed to get under control flared inside. She felt flushed, and hoped it didn't show.

Shane, Ben, and Bear only stopped long enough to tell her and Stephanie goodbye before they were back out the door. Gabe lingered by the desk.

"All is well?" Stephane asked Gabe.

"All is well," he assured her.

Wren was about to ask Gabe about Elias and Waylon when two women in workout clothes came running up to the desk. They had similar features and Wren figured them for sisters or maybe cousins. The younger woman looked like she was in her very early twenties while the other woman looked somewhere around ten years older.

Gabe held out his arm to pull one of the women into a hug and Wren realized who they were—Gabe's wife Rochelle and her little sister, Sandra. Ellie had told Wren about them the day before. Sandra especially, since she was an amateur photographer.

Rochelle laughed at Gabe. "You don't want to hug me right now, I'm covered in sweat." As she spoke, she signed the words.

Gabe grabbed the woman anyway and pulled her close. "I don't care, babe." He planted a kiss on the top of her head.

"Stephanie," Sandra exclaimed, a joyful smile on her face. "I just finished the book you recommended. I could *not* put it down." She looked at Wren. "Are you a reader? Steph's got the best recommendations."

"Absolutely," Wren said.

"Oh, here we go." Gabe laughed. "Hope you like 'em spicy."

"Sure do. Lay one on me, Stephanie."

"By the way, this is my wife Rochelle and her sister, Sandra," Gabe said, making introductions. "Wren is...she came in with Elias."

Great. He's not sure what to call me. Which made her feel ridiculously awkward.

"Nice to meet you." Wren nodded at Rochelle and Sandra. "So, where's *my* book recommendation?" Wren said quickly, turning the attention back on Stephanie, who was pulling a thick paperback out of her desk drawer.

"Well, I don't usually read historical romance, but this one," Stephanie clutched the book to her chest, "is amazing."

"Really? What's it called?"

Stephanie turned the book to show Wren the cover. "It's called *The Fate of a Pineapple.*" She closed her eyes and pretended to swoon.

Gabe started laughing. "The what of the what?"

"*The Fate of a Pineapple,*" Stephanie repeated. "Oh, you're a man. You have no idea." She turned to Wren. "Not only is it a historical romance, but it's," she lowered her voice, "reverse harem."

Gabe cupped his ear and leaned in. "I didn't catch that, Steph," he said, obviously teasing her.

"You weren't supposed to."

"Anything that makes my wife blush and raises her temperature like whatever you said just did, I gotta know what it is."

Rochelle's eyes widened and she pretended to slap Gabe's arm. "I did not!" Then she stage-whispered, "But gosh, it's *so* hot in here all of a sudden," as she fanned herself with her hand.

"Wait, here you go." Stephanie started fanning her with the book, the three hot, brooding guys in frock coats and bare chests on the cover doing absolutely nothing to cool her down. Wren found herself relaxing as she laughed with the rest of them.

It's a shame. I could get used to this.

Just then she looked toward the hall and caught Elias walking with Waylon, watching her. The look on Elias' face said everything. His relaxed smile, his shining, lagoon-blue eyes focused solely on her.

Maybe I have it all wrong. He looks like he could get used to this, too.

She waited for her instinct to run to rear its head. For the tiny voice to remind her she was out of her mind for staying. That Elias actually wanted to keep her. For thinking this could work.

Instead, she watched him coming closer with a look in his eyes that said *don't you* dare *run. You're mine.*

As he walked, Elias folded up a sheet of paper and put it in his pocket. He never once broke his gaze with Wren. He and Waylon got to them just in time to hear Gabe ask, "Three guys at once?"

Both men stopped in their tracks, eyes wide, and looked at their friend.

"Come again?" Waylon asked.

"*And* again. And one more time," Stephanie said, not a trace of embarrassment on her face.

Which sent Wren, Sandra, and Rochelle back into hysterics.

Elias grabbed Wren around the waist, ostensibly to keep her from falling over from laughter. Keeping his arms around her, he maneuvered behind her and pulled her tightly against his chest, as if he held her like this in front of his friends all the time. He rubbed his rough, stubbly cheek against her temple, raising goose bumps. Wren leaned back into him and felt his heartbeat against her back, strong and steady.

See? she told the mean little voice in her head. *This is okay. This is better than okay. This is good. Now, I'm going to play with him.*

"So, how does reverse harem even happen in historical romance?" Wren asked, both curious and just to yank Elias' chain. "They weren't exactly into polyamory back then."

It worked, judging by the way he jumped.

"Oh, believe me, it happens," Stephanie answered. "People can be ingenious when they want something."

"So what's the story about?"

"Or does it even have one?" Gabe teased.

Stephanie fixed him with a frown. "Of course it does! It starts out with this family that is trying desperately to get into the inner circle of the *ton*."

"What's the *ton*?" Elias asked.

"British high society in the Georgian era. Like that *Bridgerton* show on Netflix."

"Right, the *ton*." Elias let go of Wren to slap his forehead, but Wren was almost positive he still had no idea. He confirmed it with a goofy look as he wrapped her back up again.

"Exactly," Stephanie said, ignoring his antics. "*Anyway*, this family is stretched to the absolute max of their budget, and they want to impress the *ton*, so they decide to throw a big party with a pineapple theme. Back then, pineapples were a mark of wealth and aristocracy because they were so hard to get. People actually rented pineapples for centerpieces."

"No way!" Wren asked, incredulous.

Stephanie nodded. "Mmm-hmm, they did. So, in this story, the heroine, who is the oldest daughter in the family, can't afford to outright buy an actual pineapple, so she decides to secretly rent one for this party as sort of a gamble to win over everyone. She's hoping, of course, to find her match and to make matches for her younger sisters."

"Isn't that the mother's job?" Rochelle asked.

"Her mother is a complete idiot. She lets her oldest daughter run things, and for the most part, she's done really well. So the heroine disguises herself and goes to rent a pineapple."

"Wait a minute, so there was a store where you can rent pineapples?" Elias asked, looking confused.

"Dozens. You have no clue," Stephanie said with mock exasperation. "So, she goes and rents a pineapple. She's promised it will be delivered on the night of her party. But the villain in the story, a woman from one of the snootier families she's trying to impress, has followed her. Then, when they're at the party, our heroine is carrying around this pineapple, showing it off, and everyone is very impressed."

Elias snorted.

"It would be like, I don't know, showing off your new Lotus or your Ferrari," Stephanie said.

"I don't want a Lotus or Ferrari. I don't need one. I have my trucks," Elias said, sounding proud.

"You have a second truck?" Wren asked.

"Yeah. I had it before my dad gave me his."

"It's a wonderful truck," Wren said, and earned a squeeze. "Sorry, please continue."

"So the party is going incredibly well. The sisters are all talking to eligible bachelors. There's dancing. The food is great. Everything's wonderful. Right up until the end. And that's when the villain goes up to the heroine, looks at the pineapple, and says, 'Now is the perfect time to carve that open, so we can eat it.'"

"Oh no!" Wren exclaimed.

"Oh yes," Stephanie continued. "So the heroine is standing there, dumbstruck. She has no idea what to do. This thing is rented. If she carves it up, she's out the money. But if she doesn't carve it up, she has to admit that she rented it, and she will be made a fool. She's looking at her sisters who are doing so well, talking to these bachelors. It's all gonna be ruined. So the choice is clear."

"She cuts up the pineapple, doesn't she?" Wren asked, feeling sick to her stomach.

"She sure does. She walks over to the table, plops down the pineapple. She has no idea what she's doing, right? And of course, the villain is goading her on. 'You know how to carve a pineapple? Surely your staff does it for you.' Then she looks around and says, 'but I don't see any staff here at the moment.' That's because they can't afford full-time staff and the villain has paid them off to leave early."

"Oh, she's a real bitch," Sandra muttered.

"A complete and utter bitch." Stephanie nodded in agreement. "So the heroine is standing there with a knife, looking at this pineapple, having no idea what to do with it. She's sick to her stomach, trying not to throw up because everything's gone so wrong. Everybody is staring at her. Some people are snickering, other people are looking on, horrified. She realizes... they *know*. They know she rented this thing. But in for a penny, in for a pound. She lays the pineapple on its side on a platter, takes the knife in both hands, imagines the pineapple is the villain's head, and she *thoomp!* chops off the top. It's like she's foreseen the French Revolution and the guillotine right there, and the villain is Marie Antoinette."

Everyone laughed.

"She's never had a pineapple, of course. So she's not peeling it first. She's just sort of chopping it up, making a complete hash of it. And the villain is watching her and making comments like, 'That's certainly an interesting way to dress a pineapple. I've never seen it done that way before. You must have been to parties that I've never attended.' On and on. Finally, she's got this butchered pineapple lying there. She's putting the pieces onto another platter that someone has mercifully brought to her. Everyone gathers around for a piece."

Wren was really getting into the story. "Please tell me with her head held high, she offers the first piece to the villain, right?"

"Right," Stephanie said.

"Classy move. Power move."

"And the villain turns up her nose and says, 'Honestly, pineapple does not agree with my constitution. Judging by the look on your face, I don't think it agrees with yours either.'"

The women groaned. They booed. They hissed.

"Oh, she is the *worst!*" Rochelle exclaimed.

Stephanie nodded slowly. "The story only gets better from there. This is all basically the first couple chapters. From here on, the heroine declares revenge on the villain. But at this point, she's also destitute."

"Don't tell me," Sandra said. "A man steps in to help her. He offers her money in return for her love. Or maybe just her body?" she asked, amused.

"Oh, very good, very good. Yeah, not just any man, but the villain's brother."

"Ohhh," they all said.

"This sounds like so much fun," Rochelle added.

"It is. I'm just getting to the part where she's meeting the second man who's going to be in her harem." Stephanie grinned evilly. "But...no more spoilers."

"All right, I'm running out right now and buying a copy," Sandra said.

"Me too," Wren added, just to tease Elias. But she had to admit—she was hooked.

"We could all get a copy and do a book club," Sandra said excitedly as she looked from one woman to the next. Then she looked back and forth between Gabe and Elias. "You guys want in, too?"

"No way," they both protested.

Stephanie put her hands on her hips. "I'll have you know, Dr. Boyfriend reads romances with me. He thinks of them as instruction manuals."

"Oooh..." the women chorused.

"Hey, I'll join," Waylon said, his voice only laced with a little sarcasm. "Looks like I'll have plenty of free time coming up."

Stephanie gave him a funny look but didn't say anything as she studied him. Then she glanced at Elias.

Rochelle tapped her sister on the shoulder. "Are *you* going to have time for a book club? Don't your classes start soon?"

"Wow, it's like I have a Regency big sister breathing down my neck," Sandra joked. "I'll tear through that book in a weekend. I've got plenty of time."

"Oh, that's right," Wren said. "I was talking to Ellie yesterday and she says you're going to school for photography."

"Yup! I've got an art history class that I'm looking forward to, and a few general classes that I'm not. Then I have to apply for a spot to get a BFA with a focus on photography. The program's limited to only a few students at a time."

"Would an internship with a photographer increase your chances?"

"Absolutely, but like I'm gonna find one before I start my classes. Maybe I can apply for a spot sometime late next year."

"Or, you could intern with me right now and get a head start on the competition," Wren said.

Sandra's eyebrows rose. "You're a photographer?"

"She is," Elias said before Wren could reply. "Real estate now, but she did professional portraiture before that. Celebrities, actually." He spoke in a confident, almost pompous tone, all the while looking at Waylon, who smirked back, shaking his head slightly.

What's that about?

"Yeah, I did," Wren said, taking on her own professional tone as she stepped out of Elias' arms. "I still do, but I wanted to back away for a while, do something different. Real estate's paying the bills right now, but I have another project going." *Something that has more meaning than photographing celebrities* she wanted to add. "I'd love to schlep you along this week, if you're free."

Sandra looked excited. "Oh, I will *make* the time. Wow, thank you."

"Here's my card." Wren dug into her tote, found her wallet, and took out a business card. "Kind of old-fashioned, I know. Text me at that number so I have you in my contacts and I'll let you know when it's happening."

Sandra took the card and pulled her phone out of the gym bag slung over her shoulder. "*When* it's happening?"

"It's..." She didn't want to give too much away, not with whatever weirdness was going on between Elias and Waylon right now. Plus, she didn't want to put Sandra on the spot. She'd talk to her later in private, gauge if this project was going to be a good fit. Wren had offered the internship without giving it a single thought, caught up in the moment.

"The timing might change, depending. It's all up to the subjects' availability."

Waylon nudged Sandra. "That means flighty celebrities, I'm guessing."

"Actually, no." Wren gave him a tight smile. "At least, not this time." She turned her attention to Sandra. "Hope that's okay."

"Yeah, anything and everything's great. I've done a lot of travel photography, but real estate, portraits, doesn't matter. I can learn something from all of it."

"Awesome. I'll text you."

Anxiety spun up in her head. Wren glanced at Elias, hoping he'd get the clue she wanted to leave. Right now, before there was any more weirdness between him and Waylon. What if they started arguing right here in front of everyone?

"Ready to go, babe?" Elias mercifully asked. He had a wide smile, but there was plenty of uncertainty in his eyes. Her stomach knotted and her shoulders tightened until she felt the rock pulling.

Why the uncertainty? Is he trying to think of ways to ditch me today?

He and Waylon *must* have been talking about her. That's why they'd hung back when the other guys walked out.

Waylon doesn't like me and talked him out of... whatever this is we're doing here. And now Elias is going to ditch me. I've read everything wrong.

Again.

"Yeah, I'm ready." She gave everyone a goodbye smile and nod. "Nice to meet you all."

"Hey, don't forget your info packet." Stephanie nudged it toward her. "I'll be expecting you in my beginner's class, young lady."

Even if the look Stephanie was giving her was supposed to be joking—and judging by everyone's laughter, it was—Wren could still see a spark of seriousness in her eyes. The woman really wanted her there.

"Of course." Wren took the brochure and put it in her tote.

When they got to Elias' truck, he opened her door for her and then jogged around to the driver's side and got in. He started to open his mouth to say something, but Wren cut him off.

"I've got work to do today on the drone footage for Chase and I'm already behind, so do you mind taking me to my car?"

For once, she couldn't think of anything funny to say, so she smiled and braced for a fight.

Instead, Elias turned the key in the ignition. "Yeah, sure, if that's what you want."

It's not what I want. Not at all.

But judging by Elias suddenly going cold now that they were away from his friends, saying those words would undoubtedly start a discussion she didn't want to have.

And that discussion will lead to a disagreement, and down the road we'll go, straight into an ugly fight. And that's not how I want to remember this weekend.

She'd learned long ago that nice things could disappear at a moment's notice, usually surrounded by fighting. Nice things didn't last. Not for her.

So instead, Wren rode the mercifully short distance to Riversong with her heart behaving like her name—a bird trapped and fluttering against the bars of its cage.

Elias stayed quiet through the drive. He parked next to her car and still didn't say a word as he moved her equipment from his truck to the trunk of her car. Not until he opened her car door for her and she started to get in.

"Wait. Can we talk?"

The bird in her chest that had replaced her heart went into full panic mode. *Can we talk* never led to good things, ever. Even if those lagoon-blue eyes looked hurt instead of angry. Because that's where hurt always went—straight to anger. Then to lashing out at whatever caused the hurt. Or whoever.

"It was a great weekend, Elias." She stroked his cheek. "Thank you. For everything."

She got into her car without looking back.

Classes with Stephanie would have been a riot but she'd no doubt run into Elias at the rec center—probably because of Stephanie, judging by that look she gave Wren. So, that was out. Now all she had to do was figure out how she could avoid him while still working with Sandra. Oh, and that drone and photography job for Ellie and Bear.

Well, at least he has his scrubs top back. I won't have to return...

That's when she realized she was still wearing his shirt and jeans. She actually laughed.

Well, shit.

I guess that's just me. A bird in lion's clothing.

Sure, *now* she thought of something clever to say.

TWELVE

Elias tossed the empty stretcher into the ambulance with a force that made it rattle against the metal floor, his frustration boiling over. He yanked off his gloves, tossing them into the biohazard bin with a snap, the motion more aggressive than necessary. He could feel Waylon's eyes on him, assessing, waiting. The man knew him well enough to keep his mouth shut at least.

Tim came around the side of the ambo. "What the hell? Everything okay back here?"

Waylon stretched his arms and spoke before Elias could. "Yeah, the Lion's just cranky."

Cranky doesn't touch it.

Tim knocked twice on the side of the ambo. "Well, next stop's Riversong. My turn to pay. That should cheer you up." Tim smiled. "Always cheers me up." He turned and jogged back around the driver's side.

Waylon climbed into the back of the rig ahead of Elias. "Someone really needs to tell Tim he has a less than zero chance with April."

Elias just growled. "Love makes you stupid."

They rode in silence to Riversong, which was the last place Elias wanted to be right now. Bad enough he'd spent the rest of Sunday and all of Monday mentally watching Wren drive away, her last words ringing in his ears with such finality in her voice.

It was a great weekend, Elias. Thanks. For everything.

Was.

Which meant done.

Not even a last kiss.

Now, they were returning to the scene of the crime, the place where he stupidly let her go without an explanation.

The ambulance parked at the back of the lot. Waylon opened the door. Elias grabbed a tablet before he climbed out. Tim was already halfway across the parking lot, followed by Andy. As Waylon started to follow the other two men, Elias stayed put and scanned the parking lot instead, looking for Wren's car, hating the way his heart sped up, hoping he'd see her leaning against the driver's side, his jeans and shirt folded in her hands.

Nothing.

"You coming, Hunt?" Andy called when he looked back and noticed Elias still standing at the ambo.

Elias held up the tablet. "Gonna finish this. Just grab my usual, thanks."

"Same," Waylon said. He stopped walking, turned, and headed back toward Elias.

"Don't need a babysitter," Elias bit out, avoiding eye contact as he stared at the tablet, attempting to complete the last run report.

Waylon leaned against the side of the ambo and casually crossed his arms. "Okay, that's enough, brother," he finally said. His voice was low, calm, the same tone he used to talk down anxious patients on their way to the ER.

"I'm fine." The words on the screen swam in front of him, refusing to settle into any coherent order. He ran his hand through his hair.

"You aren't acting fine, and you sure as hell don't look fine."

Elias clenched his jaw, his finger hovering over the tablet. The concern he heard in Waylon's voice—a far cry from the teasing banter they usually exchanged, especially on the job—grated on him.

"Just drop it, man," Elias muttered. He forced himself to focus on the tablet. He was being unprofessional, and that was unacceptable. He'd been thinking non-stop about Wren from the moment he watched her pull out of Riversong's parking lot without so much as a glance backward. He'd asked himself a thousand times what he'd done wrong. She'd seemed so happy joking with everyone inside, and then it was like someone in her head had turned on the air conditioner and she froze up. But he couldn't afford to think about Wren now. Not at work.

Maybe not ever.

"This wouldn't have anything to do with Wren, would it?"

"I said drop it, Ram."

"It has everything to do with Wren. You're not going inside because you don't want to face April," Waylon pressed, straightening from his lean and stepping closer. "Brother, what happened? You don't want to take one look at April and see...what? That Wren told her you guys had a fight or something?"

Elias froze, his hand squeezing the tablet until his knuckles turned white. He didn't answer right away, not trusting himself to speak. The silence stretched between them, thick with tension.

"No fight. Haven't even talked to her since Sunday."

Waylon's brows furrowed. "Dude, it's Tuesday. The way you were wrapped around her at the rec center, I figured you'd be calling in today with a—" he made a fist and pretended to cough, "—horrible cold, hack-hack, wheeze-wheeze."

Elias shook his head and let out a bitter laugh.

"So let me ask you again—what happened?"

There was no deterring Ram. He'd keep pushing until Elias gave in.

Best to shut it down now.

"I don't know. One minute, everything was fine, like you said. We were all laughing and joking with Stephanie. The next, I'm getting a weird vibe like she wants to leave immediately and not because she wants me to jump her bones. So, we're in the truck and before I can ask what's going on, she's telling me to take her straight to her car. When we got here where she left it, I told her we needed to talk and that's when she said goodbye like it was no big deal. Like this weekend meant nothing."

He set the tablet aside before he crushed it, then pinched the bridge of his nose.

"Maybe it did mean nothing," Elias continued, the words spilling out in a rush. "Maybe you were right, Ram. Maybe I'm just a good time for a weekend and nothing more. A professional wingman."

"Hold up," Waylon interrupted, his tone firm. "That's not what I said, and you know it."

Elias stared at him, his frustration giving way to confusion. "Then what the hell did you mean?"

Waylon sighed. "Look, Elias, I was giving you shit before because that's what we do. But I never meant to make you doubt what you've obviously got with Wren. From what I've seen, she's not just some weekend fling. You know that, too, or else you would have shrugged her off and wouldn't be acting all bitchy today."

Elias opened his mouth to argue, but Waylon cut him off.

"Listen to me, Lion. You're a damn good man. A far cry from when we were teenagers."

Elias almost winced.

"And you've found something special with Wren," Waylon continued. "I know she feels the same way. I could see it, the way she looked at you when we came out of Gabe's office. I might have had my doubts before, but that cinched it."

"Yeah? What did you see? How did she look at me?"

"Dude, like you hang the fucking moon in the sky. So I don't get why you just let her drive away like that. And now you're telling me you haven't called her? I told you—take her out, get to know her, didn't I?"

"But she left. She didn't even want to talk."

"If you didn't stop her right then and there, sounds to me like you're the one who didn't want to talk. Why?"

Elias felt the words hit him, sinking in deep. *Good question.* He wanted Wren, and for more than just fun. But Waylon was right—he let her go without a fight.

"I guess she figured out she's above my paygrade."

Waylon punched the side of the ambulance. "Are you fucking kidding me right now? This is not you." He studied Elias. "So which is it?"

"Which is what?"

"Which is it that's keeping you from chasing her? Is it your pride that won't let you call and find out what's wrong?" Waylon narrowed his eyes. "Or are you scared?"

Elias reared back. "Scared? Why the hell would I be scared?"

"You've never been in love. And the thought of even coming close to it scares you."

Fuck. "It was only a weekend."

"A weekend unlike any you've ever had with a woman before, am I right?"

"Damn straight."

Waylon's jaw visibly tightened. "I've been there. When it hits," he grinned ruefully and shook his head slowly, "nothing else like it. You *know* it's right, even if it's irrational. Even if it's..." He looked away, but not before Elias caught the bitter look in his eyes. Waylon didn't have to finish his sentence for his brother to know.

Even if it's doomed to end.

Waylon shook it off and snapped right back to his carefree self. "I don't think it's your pride for once, is it?"

Elias shook his head. But he still had too much pride to admit out loud Waylon was right—he was scared. Scared of fucking up. Scared of not being enough and hurting Wren, who in his eyes, was the perfect woman.

"Maybe she's scared, too," Waylon suggested, his voice softening. "Hell, maybe she's got her own shit to work through. But that doesn't mean she doesn't care about you. Man, I could see it. We all could."

Fuck, fuck, fuck.

Waylon was right. He'd let his fears color his perceptions, filter them through a lens of self-doubt. What if Wren was feeling the same way? What if she was just as scared as he was? Maybe when she left early the first night, it was out of her own insecurity, not to tease him. But what would someone as perfect as her have to be insecure about?

Waylon clapped a hand on his shoulder, breaking Elias out of his thoughts. "So stop acting like the damned Cowardly Lion, brother. You've never backed down from a challenge before, so don't start now. Go after her. Hang onto her with both hands, and don't let go until you've got the answers you need."

A surge of determination flooded through Elias, washing away the uncertainty and doubt. Waylon was right. He needed to see Wren again, to talk to her, to figure out what the hell had gone wrong.

"As much as it pains me to ever admit this, you're right. Abso-fucking-lutely right. Thanks, Ram," Elias said, his voice steadier now, conviction replacing the earlier doubts.

"Anytime, brother." Waylon gave him a knowing grin. "Besides, those *were* your jeans she had on, weren't they?"

Elias chuckled. "Yeah, they were."

"So you gotta get 'em back, right? Though, gotta say, her ass was way better-looking in them than yours."

"Stop looking at my woman's ass."

"*There* he is." Waylon punched Elias' arm.

Elias laughed and shoved Ram like they were kids again. Brothers who always had each other's backs, and always would.

"So call her, man. Right now before April shuts Tim down for the billionth time and sends him out the door with our coffees."

Elias took out his phone, called her, and put the phone to his ear, while plugging the opposite one. He turned away from Waylon for privacy, but his brother was already getting into the back of the ambo.

The phone rang. And rang. And rang. Then of course it went to voicemail.

"Hello! Thanks for calling Wren Stapleton Photography. I'm busy on a shoot right now but if you'll leave your name and number I'll get right back to you. Have a picture-perfect day!"

Elias grinned at her corny pun.

"Hey, it's Elias." He turned and glanced up at the entrance to Riversong. "I just want to say, I really love..."

Our weekend together. The way your eyes light up when I make you come. How you put up with my dogs. Your goofy sense of humor. How you look at me like I mean something. You.

"...that pair of jeans you swiped from me."

The part of him that knew he was no better than a wingman prompted him: *But what I love more is the way your ass looked in them. See you at Cocks and Strippers sometime maybe.*

"But what I love more is..."

Tim and Andy stepped outside, coffees and a bag of breakfast burritos in hand.

"...the way your..."

Elias had about fifteen seconds before they rolled out.

"...the way your smile lit up the entire rec center. And how good it felt to hold you while you laughed. Pure joy, baby. Not sure what happened after that, if it was something I said or did wrong, but I want to fix it, Wren. I want to see you again. I want to talk. Like, really talk. Get to know you." He chuckled. "Beyond your fondness for stealing my clothes. Call me."

He disconnected and took his coffee from the cardboard holder Tim held out. "Thanks, man. Any luck with April?"

"Naw, didn't even try." But to Elias' surprise, Tim actually looked cheerful. "I'm letting it go. I met someone else last weekend. Might be some potential there."

"Dude, that's great news."

Tim looked fondly at the coffee shop. "Yeah. I hope someone brings April some joy someday. She's a sweet gal under the snark."

As they climbed into the ambulance, Elias felt a sense of calm settle over him. His heart told him he'd see Wren again, no matter what. He'd talk to her, find out what was going on in that beautiful mind of hers.

And this time, he wouldn't let her go without a fight.

THIRTEEN

The rest of Wren's weekend didn't go so great, either. She cleaned up the property photos and drone footage for Chase and uploaded it without a problem, and he replied with a glowing email, telling her to clear her calendar because he was definitely going to have more work for her. That should have been cause for celebration, and to be sure, she was proud of her work. But her victory rang a little hollow without sharing it with Elias, or even Ellie, April, and especially with Stephanie. She liked all the women she'd met over the weekend. She thought she'd started something special with Elias, but her life's refrain went through her head—*nothing good ever lasts*.

Speaking of the women I met over the weekend. Wren finished composing an email to Sandra, detailing Tuesday's photo shoot—one close to Wren's heart. After talking to Sandra on the phone for an hour, Wren came away confident that she would take the shoot seriously and treat it with the respect that it deserved. Sandra had pointed Wren to some of her travel photos on her social media account. She'd snapped some gorgeous landscapes, but the photos that convinced Wren that Sandra was the woman for the job were much more intimate portraits of the people she'd met on her travels.

She'd also told Sandra that the shoot might happen later in the week instead, or might not happen at all, but Sandra assured her she'd show up anytime, anyplace.

Wren hit 'send' and closed her laptop. She stood and stretched, then rubbed her gimpy shoulder. *It'll be nice having an assistant again, and this time, I can call the shots.* When she'd worked for a fashion magazine, she'd had an assistant whose job it was to fetch and carry during shoots. She wanted to be a photographer and Wren was more than happy to give her pointers, but management was not so happy, and told Wren to stop wasting the company's time and money because it wasn't her job to train someone they'd never promote. Now, Wren was free to teach Sandra anything she wanted to know, in return for carrying her equipment.

The only drawback to using Sandra was of course, Elias. Wren fell asleep that night thinking of ways to dodge the topic. And pretending it didn't hurt.

TUESDAY MORNING, Wren checked her messages and saw the shoot was still on.

"Good," she said to herself. She called Sandra to let her know.

"I was just about to call you," Sandra said by way of hello. She sounded distraught, her voice a little muffled. "I know I said I'd be available no matter what, and I still am today, just not all day."

"What's wrong? Is everything okay?"

"Yeah, yeah, I'm just an idiot. I was eating popcorn late last night and chewing on a kernel that didn't quite pop, and managed to crack one of my fillings. Maybe the whole tooth."

Wren flinched and covered her heart. "Oh, that sounds painful."

"A couple of ibuprofens are keeping the pain at bay. But if I don't do something about it right away I'm afraid it's going to get infected. The earliest appointment I could get is this afternoon, and the next available one is three days from now."

"I totally understand. The shoot's still on today, and I'm planning on setting up at eleven. If you're still up for it, you could come for the morning and then go to your appointment, but if you can't make it at all, I'll grab you for the next one."

"The appointment's at one, so I'll be there at eleven, help you set up, and just duck out early. Thank you *so* much for understanding."

"Of course! I'll show you everything I can before you go."

"Thanks again." Sandra's relief was palpable.

"Sure. I'll meet you in the parking lot. Call me if anything changes."

"Will do."

Wren disconnected, still feeling residual anxiety over Sandra's situation as if it were happening to her. Again, she was glad she'd made the decision to step away from the magazine and strike out on her own, where she could have more control over her life. Even if it wasn't as glamorous as shooting supermodels and superstars, it felt both calmer and richer.

She met Sandra promptly at eleven. Sandra was already waiting in her car in the parking lot of the YMCA in Denver. As soon as Wren parked beside her, she jumped out of her car and made a beeline for Wren's trunk.

"I'm so sorry," Sandra apologized again.

"It's all right," Wren reassured her. "But are you sure you're okay?"

"Yup!" Sandra opened the trunk, and before Wren could say anything else, Sandra was already pulling out her camera bags.

"Hang on, I just bought a collapsible dolly," Wren said.

"I see it." Sandra grabbed the folded-up dolly and soon she had a stack of cases and bags ready to go.

"Kit Larson is the reporter we're working with today," Wren told Sandra as they crossed the parking lot to the building. "She used to cover the fashion and celebrity beat for *Mile High Marker*."

"Oh, yeah, the weekly out of Denver."

They got to the front door and Wren held it open while Sandra pushed the dolly through. "She does more longform features now and asked if I'd do the photography for this one. I met her when she interviewed Barbie Gillis last year."

Sandra paused to look at Wren. "Barbie Gillis. How cool was that, photographing her? I bet she made you laugh."

Wren blushed, feeling the usual awkwardness whenever Barbie came up. "She's a friend of mine, ever since our first shoot together. She insists on me being the photog for any of her appearances. Or at least I get first shot at it."

They stopped at the front desk and checked in. The receptionist pointed them toward a meeting room. Kit had texted earlier, saying she decided it was better to do the first interview away from the camera, but to go ahead and start setting up as soon as they got there. Wren wasn't surprised. She just hoped everything would still go as planned.

The quiet room at the Y felt like a world away from the chic studios or multi-million-dollar celebrity houses Wren was used to using. The walls were a muted beige, adorned with motivational posters that had seen better days, their corners curling slightly. A row of fluorescent lights flickered overhead, casting a harsh glow on a ring of folding chairs.

"Let's get all but two of these chairs put away off to the side by that desk, and then we'll set up the lighting." She grabbed the back of a chair. "Sorry this isn't very glamorous."

Sandra waved her off then folded a chair. "It's all part of it, right?"

They got the chairs moved—Sandra insisting on doing most of the work, then Wren decided how to set up the room.

"We'll want to start with the lighting. The key light needs to be set up at a forty-five degree angle to the subjects' faces and at eye level, which we can adjust later once they get here. Then let's get the umbrella and strobe set up over here, and the fill light will go on the opposite side." Wren explained the hows and whys as Sandra unpacked and set up lighting equipment, then the camera's tripod.

Wren tethered her camera to her laptop so she could check the shots right after she took them and adjust lighting or poses as needed. Sandra listened attentively and asked great questions.

Wren adjusted her camera lens, synching the shutter speed to the strobe lights. The familiar and precise motions usually energized her, but today her hands felt heavy, as if the weight of her thoughts had transferred to them. In her head, she couldn't stop replaying Sunday with Elias. How she'd said goodbye before he'd had a chance to tell her it was fun, but over.

Her hands stilled as she reflected on her pattern. All her life, she'd been afraid to stay somewhere or with someone too long. She left before there was a chance for everything to go bad, or to be taken from her. The combination of pushing Elias away before he could hurt her first, and now the purpose of this photo shoot, brought everything into sharp focus.

"Wren, you okay?" Sandra's voice cut through her thoughts, bringing her back to the present.

"Hmm?"

"You have a serious look on your face. Did I set everything up correctly?"

"Yeah, you did a great job. I just got a little lost in my thoughts for a moment." Wren forced a smile, pushing her sadness down where it couldn't reach her voice. She couldn't afford to let her personal life interfere with her work today. She was here to help Kit tell an important story, one that would help people, even save lives, and that required her full attention.

Sandra tilted her head, studying Wren with concern. "You sure you're okay? Anything you want to talk about?"

Wren let out a soft laugh, the sound almost foreign to her ears. "I'm good. Just the subject matter today. It's...a little personal to me."

Sandra nodded, a touch of surprise in her gaze. Before her assistant could dig any deeper, Wren plunged into a lecture on shutter speed as she returned her focus to her camera, adjusting the settings, making sure everything was perfect. It was easier to concentrate on the technical details than to let her mind wander back to Elias. Or to her childhood.

The door to the room opened, and Kit Larson entered, followed by a man holding the hand of a little boy who looked like his Mini-Me. Kit smiled warmly at Wren and Sandra.

"Are you ready for us?" she asked softly, as if she were afraid to startle anyone. She turned her smile to the little boy who looked pensively around the room at the lights and the camera. Wren didn't think he could be more than four years old. His father looked pensive too. He hunched his shoulders, head ducked, as if he were about to receive a blow between his shoulder blades.

The karate chop of life sucking Wren thought. She didn't need to hear the details of Kit's interview to know what the man and his son had just been through. *Are still going through, or else they wouldn't be here.* They'd lost their home through sudden, unmanageable debt.

"We sure are ready," Wren said, instinctively crouching down until she was at eye level with the little boy. In his other hand he clutched a tan-and-brown stuffed animal of some sort. "My name is Wren. What's yours?"

The boy looked up at his father for reassurance as he brought the stuffed animal to his face and pressed it against his mouth. It looked like a hedgehog.

"This is Arthur," the man said, mustering a smile for his son. "I'm Matthew." He squeezed his son's hand. "Wren is going to take our picture today, Art."

"Do you want to help me take a picture of your daddy first?"

Arthur nodded, the hedgehog never leaving the vicinity of his mouth.

"Okay. I'm going to teach you and Miss Sandra here," she nodded at Sandra who smiled and waved at Arthur, "how to take a good picture. Matthew, can I get you to sit in the folding chair right over there?"

Matthew nodded and leaned down. "Okay, buddy, this'll be fun. Go ahead." He let go of his son's hand and crossed the room. Sandra meanwhile grabbed an extra chair for Arthur to stand on behind the camera. Wren stood and helped the little boy up onto the chair.

"Now, look at your daddy on this screen." Wren tapped on the camera. Arthur hesitated. Then Matthew crossed his eyes and stuck out his tongue. His face went from sad to goofy, then straight to genuine joy as his son's giggle bubbled into laughter.

Arthur dropped the hand holding the stuffed hedgehog. "Do it again, Daddy!"

Matthew obliged and Wren showed Arthur where to press the button to take the photo.

"Got it!" She smiled at Arthur and pointed to the laptop on the little table beside her. "Here comes the photo you took on the big screen. Can you see it?"

Matthew's face popped up on the screen, eliciting another round of laughter from Arthur.

"Let's take a couple more, and then will you let me take your picture too?"

Arthur nodded enthusiastically. They took a few more silly pictures of Matthew, then Wren told him to go sit with his dad. Arthur hopped down from the chair and darted across the room to his dad's big smile and open arms. In the first couple of photos, both of them smiled for the camera. But as the camera kept snapping, Matthew's self-consciousness faded and his expression settled into the same, somber look he had on his face when he walked in. The very one Wren wanted to capture. Sandra was off to the side, holding a reflector to soften the shadows, one eye on Wren, waiting for cues. Wren nodded for her to put the reflector down.

There. That's the one. Same expressions, but with sharp shadows behind them now, menacing.

"And, I think we're done." Wren straightened up and smiled at Matthew and Arthur. "Thanks so much for being so patient."

Matthew nodded as he stood, gently slipping his son off his lap. "Just so long as people know what's happening. Maybe we can spare someone else." He turned to his son, who had run over to Kit for a candy bar reward. "Ready to go, bud? Daddy's got to get to work."

Arthur scampered to his dad's side.

"What do we say?"

"Thank you," Arthur shouted as they left the room.

"Thank you," Kit said. "Both of you."

Arthur smiled and waved goodbye. All three women waved and smiled back. The moment he was out of view, their smiles faded.

"Can I ask what their story is?" Sandra said as she walked to the laptop where Kit had already joined Wren. "I mean, I know they lost their home, but what happened?"

Kit nodded. "It's a sad one. They're living in a room upstairs right now, and lucky to get it. Matt and Arthur used to live in a lovely home in Centennial with Matt's wife, Lena. Right up until she got sick."

"Oh no." Wren's stomach clenched.

"Congenital heart disease. She had a defect that went undetected until she was twenty-seven. By then, her heart valves were shot. She had great insurance through her job, went to the hospital, had surgery, and it looked like everything would be all right." Kit dropped her gaze to the images on the laptop. "Unfortunately, after she went home, she had a stroke. She ended up back in the hospital, but she was in a vegetative state. Too much damage from a brain bleed. She lasted just over a month before she passed."

Sandra covered her mouth. "That poor little boy. And Matthew, too."

"Medical bills?" Wren asked.

Kit's gaze snapped to hers, knowing what she was really asking. "Exactly. Matt thought he was keeping up with them, but somehow missed a payment, lost the low interest rate, and it snowballed from there. The hospital refused to work with him."

"They lost their home," Wren whispered, fighting back hot tears.

"They did."

Wren felt nauseous and dizzy as old memories surfaced. She was about to excuse herself and find a bathroom when Sandra's phone chimed.

"Shoot, sorry." Sandra pulled it out of her pocket and silenced it. "That's my alarm telling me I need to get going." She smiled apologetically at Wren and Kit.

"No worries," Wren said. "I hope your tooth isn't cracked."

"Me too." Sandra rubbed her cheek. "If you're still here when I get done, I can help you pack up." She looked around the room. "It's a lot of stuff."

"Don't worry, it'll be okay. I'll walk you out." She hoped the fresh air would clear her head and settle her stomach.

Sandra picked up her purse. "It was nice meeting you, Kit."

"You too."

When they got to the hall, Sandra laid her hand on Wren's upper arm. "You looked really upset in there and now you're white as a ghost. You sure you're okay? I could cancel—"

"Don't you dare." Wren gave her the brightest smile she could muster. "The room was stuffy and I should have had a little more to eat for breakfast. I'll be fine with some fresh air and a snack."

Sandra held the front door open for Wren. "Promise?" The caring tone in her voice went straight to Wren's heart, calming her.

"I feel better already." She stepped outside and took a deep breath. The air was sweet thanks to a large planter full of red and pink petunias beside the door. "Now, go get your tooth taken care of. And thank you."

"Thank *you*, Wren. I'll text."

"Sounds good."

Wren watched her until she got into her car. Then she closed her eyes as she leaned against the rough wall of the building. The cool concrete felt good against the back of her sweaty neck.

I can handle this. I need to handle this. On the count of three, we're going back in. One, two, three.

Wren opened her eyes, turned, and grabbed the door handle

before her thoughts could stop her. She smiled and nodded at the receptionist as she marched back to the room.

Move, don't think. Just keep moving forward.

WHEN WREN WALKED BACK into the meeting room, Kit was still standing next to the laptop but she was frowning down at her phone.

"Everything all right?" Wren asked.

Kit looked up from her phone. "Yes. Our second guy is running a little behind. He lives here too, and slept through his alarm. He says he'll be down in a few minutes. I was afraid he was getting cold feet. He's very shy, very self-effacing. That's why I told you today might not happen, but we're two for two." She looked at the door. "If he shows up."

"Let's take a look at the photos in the meantime." Wren woke her laptop back up and started scrolling through photos of Matthew and Arthur.

"This one," Wren said, tapping the screen. "This one tells the story." She studied the way Matthew's world-weary smile contrasted to his laughing son on his lap. *Such sweet, guileless innocence.* "A little boy who lost his world when he lost his mother, then lost everything else to medical bills afterward, but his father shields him as best he can. And sometimes, he succeeds."

Kit nodded beside her. "It makes you want to protect them both."

"Exactly."

A slow grin spread across Kit's lips. "You have a gift."

Wren tsked. "I get lucky sometimes, that's all."

"No, you really do. That's why I tagged you for this assignment. I always thought your celebrity photos really brought out the parts of their personalities we never see. Their vulnerabilities." She ran her hand through her short, spiky black hair. "Watching you with Arthur,

I can see how you make people feel at ease. I couldn't get him to smile upstairs, but getting him to take a photo of his dad first was inspired."

Wren shook her head. "It was all Matthew making faces. That's usually *my* fallback—make 'em laugh."

Two voices outside the door caught their attention—one sounded like the receptionist and the other a man's voice.

"That must be him," Kit said.

A moment later, the receptionist appeared in the doorway, guiding an older man in with her. Evan moved with a slow, deliberate pace, his shoulders hunched slightly, as if the weight of the world rested on them. His clothes, though clean, were worn, and his sunken eyes carried a weary expression that Wren immediately recognized— the look of sleepless nights spent worrying.

"Wren, this is Evan Roy." Kit kept her tone gentle but professional. "Evan, this is Wren. She's the photographer I was telling you about."

Evan nodded, offering Wren a small, polite smile along with his hand. "Lovely to meet you." His soft voice was laced with a beautiful Scottish accent.

"Likewise," Wren replied, her photographer's eye already noticing the deep crow's feet etched into his face on either side of his pale blue eyes, and the way his hand trembled slightly as he extended it to shake hers. She could see the story he carried in his face and in every gesture. Kit could capture it with her words, and Wren would do her best to capture it in his face while he spoke.

"Here now, I've brought you a little something." In his other hand, Evan carried a resealable plastic bag. "They let me use the kitchen, so I made you fudge. Can't eat it myself. I'm a diabetic, but I love it so."

Kit's face broke into a smile as she took the bag. "Yes, you were telling me on the phone how much you love candy and making sweets. Thank you so much."

"It looks delicious," Wren added.

"I used to make it for my nurses." Evan smiled fondly. "They work public clinics and I used to go every month."

"But not now?" Kit asked as she led him to one of the folding chairs while Wren got behind her camera.

"Oh, no. No. I don't want them burdened with my troubles." Evan patted down his sparse grey hair.

Kit sat down in the chair next to his. She took out both a small recorder and a notepad with a pen. "We'll get to your troubles in a minute, but I'd like to ask you how they would be burdened."

Evan looked down at his hands. "That's where it all started, at that public clinic. And I'm afraid they'll blame themselves. I'm..." He raised a trembling hand and brushed at his eyes. "I'm not as grateful as I should be now. And no fault of theirs."

"Tell me about it then," Kit said softly. "Whose fault is it?"

Wren tried to be as unobtrusive as she could while still capturing the emotions flickering across Evan's face as he spoke. She zoomed in on his hands as they clenched and unclenched while he told his story in a measured tone, every word carefully chosen.

"I was feeling poorly that morning, but I didn't want to miss the clinic." He smiled sweetly. "The batch of fudge I'd made the night before was especially good."

Wren captured his smile, along with the pain in his eyes.

"When I got there and sat down for my exam, the nurses knew something was amiss. I told them I thought it might be a spot of indigestion. Sue, she was the nurse taking care of me, took my blood pressure, and the last thing I remember was her saying, 'This isn't right.' Then a terrible pain tore through me, like someone had wrenched my left arm out of its socket. I don't remember, but they say I clenched my fists, like this."

Fists clenched, Evan bent his elbows and brought his hands to his chest while he threw his head back. Wren captured the fearful grimace on his face and his rigid body. Evan relaxed and brushed away another tear. Kit reached into her purse by her feet, then handed Evan a travel packet of tissues. He smiled self-consciously and thanked her.

"They thought I was having a seizure, but it was a massive heart attack. They got me down onto the floor and did CPR until the medics showed up. They saved my life. But Sue told me later they thought that was the last they'd see of me alive. They took me to the nearest hospital first, then I was flown to Milestone Hospital, closer in to Denver. They specialize in hearts."

Evan's mild expression changed, filling with anger. "But they have no heart themselves, I can tell you that." His voice dropped an octave, and became shaky with emotion.

"Tell me what happened once you got to Milestone."

"They put me on ice, dropped my temperature down to stop any further damage, put me in a coma. Then came the surgeries and the long hospital stay as I recovered. It all added up, as I discovered. Much more than I can ever pay."

Kit nodded in sympathy. "What about Medicare? Aren't they supposed to cover you?"

"You might hear it in my accent, but I'm from Scotland. I'm a U.S. citizen now, but I haven't been in the country long enough to have paid into the system for ten years, so I don't get full benefits. I was not married to an American so I don't have spousal pay-in, and I have no children. Medicare pays up to ninety days in the hospital, but I went past my ninety-day mark, and was charged over eight-hundred dollars per day after that."

Wren suppressed a shudder. She couldn't imagine how much debt Evan was in.

"That does add up," Kit said.

"It does."

Kit crossed her leg and shifted in her seat. "What about a payment plan? Hospitals offer those all the time."

"If you ladies and God above will pardon my language, that is where Milestone Hospital is screwing me. They call it Milestone Hospital, but for me, it has been a millstone tied to my neck instead."

Kit glanced at Wren. She didn't have to say a word for Wren to understand.

I'd bet every last dollar Lena was a patient at Milestone, too.

"What happened?" Kit asked as her pen flew across the page of her notebook.

"I was pointed to their website by their billing department. I followed a link and signed up for an interest-free loan offered through the hospital. I kept up with my payments just fine, thankful to be alive. And then came a letter saying I was behind on payments and my zero-percent interest rate was gone. I went to see them, statements in hand, to show them there'd been a mistake."

Evan squeezed his eyes shut and cleared his throat. Wren captured every ounce of pain rolling off him.

"They wouldn't talk to me beyond saying I owed them tens of thousands of dollars. They said my loan had nothing to do with them anymore. That's when I discovered the truth. My loan went to a lender that might as well be a shark. While I thought all my medical bills had been consolidated, they'd not paid for my hospital stay. When I tried to explain what had happened, *Millstone* threatened to destroy my credit score."

"Which is a lie, and illegal in the state of Colorado," Kit said.

Evan nodded. "Didn't know that then. The interest on the loan skyrocketed to thirty-two percent."

Wren gasped, then covered her mouth. "I'm sorry."

Kit checked her notes. "The maximum allowable interest rate in Colorado is forty-five percent."

"That's criminal," Wren practically growled.

"They said if they could put a lien against my house, the interest would be forgiven, so I consented. I still couldn't keep up, so I lost my house to them. And almost everything I own is gone now too."

A wave of nausea rolled over Wren. She swallowed down bile as her forehead broke out in tiny beads of sweat.

Evan covered his face with both hands as his shoulders shook. Kit immediately leaned over and patted his shoulder. "Take as much time as you need."

He uncovered his face and pulled another tissue. "It's not just my house and my things I've lost, mind you. I haven't been back to the clinic since. I can't face those nurses who saved my life and tell them I wish they'd let me die."

The rest of the interview became unintelligible for Wren as she blocked out their voices. She hyper-focused on photographing Evan instead, determined that anyone who saw the anguish on this sweet man's face would be devastated by it, that her photos would move people to take action against this injustice.

"I think that about covers it," Kit said as she put her notebook and recorder in her purse. She looked up at Wren. "Do you need any more shots?"

Wren looked at Evan. "I got some good candids but are you up for me taking a few more that are a little more posed?"

"Anything you need." Evan looked around. "I'd meant to bring my stack of statements down thinking I could hold them up in a picture, but I must have left them in my room upstairs. My memory's not what it was before the heart attack." He looked suddenly drained.

"I can run up and get them for you," Kit offered. "If you trust me."

"Lass, there isn't anything in my room worth stealing. Here." He pulled out his key. "Number twelve, left side of the hall toward the end. They'll be on my bed most likely."

Kit wrapped her hands around his hand and held it before she took the key. "Thank you. I'll be right back." She stood up and left the room.

Wren did something she almost never did. She came out from behind the camera and sat in Kit's empty chair beside Evan.

"I just want to say that I... I really feel what you're going through. And it's okay to ask friends for help. I bet those nurses would be thrilled to hear from you."

Evan shook his head. "I don't want them to see me like this."

Wren sighed. "What if they read the article and see you in it?"

"It's a risk I'm willing to take if it'll help out anyone else. Maybe I'll have moved on from here before it's published."

Wren reached out and took Evan's hand. "Is there anything *I* can do to help you?"

Evan gave her another of his sweet smiles. "Try the fudge and tell me if I've still got the knack."

Wren smiled and looked away quickly in case a tear decided to leak from the corner of her eye. She stood up and walked back to the table holding the laptop where the bag of fudge lay next to it. She took out a piece and popped it into her mouth. Rich, chocolate sweetness spread over her tongue.

"It's delicious, Evan. Absolutely perfect."

"Thanks, lass."

"Here they are," Kit said as she walked in. She handed the bills to Evan, and Wren took the last pictures of him holding them up, his face somber.

Kit had escorted Evan upstairs and Wren was disassembling her gear when her phone alerted her to a message in voicemail. She'd silenced any incoming calls during her shoot. It was probably Barbie calling to check on her, or maybe Chase. She was so preoccupied with Evan's and Matthew and Arthur's stories that by the time she had everything on the dolly, she'd forgotten about the message.

Later that night, just before bed as she was putting her phone on the charger, she noticed the missed call.

Elias.

Her heart sped up and her mouth went dry as she connected to her voicemail. She listened to the message. Then she listened to it again, feeling her smile grow and her insides warm. She laughed on the third and fourth listens.

Wren changed out of her sheep shirt and into Elias' borrowed t-shirt. And then she texted one word back:

Yes.

FOURTEEN

She said yes.

The first thing Elias had done when he woke the next morning was check his phone, hoping for a message from Wren. He'd tossed and turned all night second-guessing himself, thinking that he'd been a fool to reach out.

He opened his texts, heart pounding, half-expecting to see nothing. But there it was—a sweet and short message from Wren: *Yes.*

Relief washed over him as he stared at the screen, reading the single word over and over. A simple *Yes.* Just three letters, yet it felt like she'd thrown him a lifeline. He wasn't entirely sure what it meant —whether she wanted to talk things out, to give him one last chance, or just hand over his jeans and t-shirt then walk away for good. He wanted to believe it was more than just a polite response, but doubt crept in. Maybe she just didn't want to hurt his feelings.

But she said yes.

Before he let his doubts take over, he texted back.

I'll call you tonight after my shift.

He watched three dots bounce while she answered.

> Sounds good. Be safe!

Elias smiled at that. Safe or not, it would be one long shift.

AS THEY RODE out on their first call, Elias pushed all thoughts of Wren to the back of his mind, focusing instead on prepping for a car accident. Elias secured a trauma bag on the bench next to him. His hands moved almost on their own from muscle memory.

Waylon glanced over at Elias, his brow furrowed in concern as he checked the equipment one last time. "Everything okay?"

"Yeah, actually," Elias answered, grabbing a C-collar from the compartment above.

"You look like you didn't sleep, and I can tell you're keyed up."

"No, I'm good, brother." The familiar scent of antiseptic and the slight hum of the road beneath them filled the space as he adjusted the collar, readying it for use.

"Wren again?"

Elias couldn't help but grin. "I'm talking to her tonight."

Waylon smiled back, giving him a quick nod. "Good luck."

The rest of the shift kept them busy. They dealt with the usual chaos—two more car accidents, a couple of heart attacks, and a call about a kid undergoing possible anaphylactic shock that turned out to be a false alarm but had everyone's adrenaline spiking. No paramedic ever wanted to fail a kid. All the while, Elias' mind kept wandering back to Wren despite his best efforts. To what he would say when he spoke to her.

Elias didn't even wait to get home to call her. As soon as they got back to the station and he'd changed into his civvies, he took out his phone and hit the call button.

The phone rang once. Twice. Then—

"Elias?"

Her voice caught him off guard. He'd been half-expecting her voicemail again because she'd changed her mind.

"Hey, Wren." He ran his hand through his hair. *Keep it light.* "I was just calling to check up on my jeans. You know, making sure they're adjusting well to their new living situation."

Wren's laugh made his heart skip. She didn't even try to hide it. "Your jeans are doing just fine and so is your t-shirt. I'm feeding them three times a day and taking them for walks. They've even made friends with my slippers, which usually growl at strange clothing."

"Sounds like they're settling in," he teased, leaning back against the locker room wall as his shoulders relaxed. "But I gotta say, my scrubs top misses them. It keeps scratching at the door and looking at me with big, sad eyes."

"Oh dear. I hadn't meant for that to happen. Poor thing."

"Actually, there's a good chance that it misses *you* more than my jeans and t-shirt." Elias swallowed. "I sure do." He took a breath, trying to ease into asking her what went wrong without losing the light mood. "Wren... About that message I left you. I meant it. I really do want to see you again. To talk. Get to know each other better."

"I want that too," she replied, her tone softer and more serious.

"But first." He paused, hoping he wasn't pushing too hard and scaring her off. "I think we need to clear the air about Sunday. I was ready to spend the rest of the day with you, but you said goodbye like you didn't want to see me again."

"What exactly was going on between you and Waylon?" Her question came out of the blue and threw him off completely.

"Waylon? What do you mean?"

"I was getting a weird vibe when you told everyone what I do for a living. The tone of your voice—it was like you were trying to impress Waylon with the whole photographing celebrities thing. And before that, you guys hung back in Gabe's office. Were you talking about me? Does," she hesitated. "Does he maybe not approve of me?"

Now Elias understood. He chuckled with relief. "No, baby, that's not what was going on. Okay, yeah, Waylon and I were talking about you in Gabe's office. He was curious about what was going on with us. Normally, I would have just taken you straight to your house from Cocks and Strippers. Left without spending the night. Don't get me wrong, I would have left you happy, but I still would have left." He grinned. "Kind of the way you sneaked out Saturday morning."

"Is that it? Me leaving—is that the problem you were talking about with him? Or about my habit of stealing your clothes?" She said it lightly, but Elias was tuned in, and he could hear the slight undercurrent of worry.

Now is not the right time to tease. "No, baby, no, I'm messing all of this up."

Elias dragged his hand through his hair until it stood up on end. "What I'm trying to say is, I told Waylon that you were different. That I'd taken you back to my place instead of going to yours. He was skeptical because he didn't think I knew you well enough for that. I think what you were picking up on was that I was trying to convince him that I do know you well enough. And that was the moment I realized I didn't. I don't know where you grew up, or your favorite color, or any of that."

"So, he wasn't trying to talk you out of seeing me?"

"God, no. He actually told me I needed to get to know you. But I wouldn't give a damn if Waylon approved of you or not. All I know is that I think you're amazing. You're funny, and sweet, and smart. When I'm with you, the rest of the world just sort of falls away. And from the second I saw you...I felt like I already knew you." He swallowed past a lump in his throat. "Does that sound crazy?"

She paused long enough that Elias was afraid she'd disconnected.

"It's not like me to get so caught up in someone, either," she finally said. "So, it doesn't sound, or feel, crazy to me at all. Which is why I think it freaked me out a little," she admitted with a nervous laugh. "Made me feel like something this good couldn't possibly last. So, I walked away first to keep from getting hurt."

Elias nodded, even though she couldn't see him. "I get it. Trust me, I've been thinking the same thing. That I wasn't good enough for you. That I was the one who didn't measure up."

"Wow. We're two of a kind, aren't we?" She laughed again.

Elias closed his eyes and pressed his head against the wall as he listened to the sweet sound of her laughter. It was a little louder this time, and without any nervousness.

"Yeah, we are." He opened his eyes and took a deep breath as the tension in his chest eased. "This is a good thing, and I want it to last, too."

"You're not just saying that?"

"Wren, I don't say things I don't mean. Especially not to someone who has a hostage situation with my clothes."

She laughed again, and the tension in his chest eased a little more.

"Hostage situation, huh? I told you, I'm taking very good care of your clothes."

"Right, three meals a day and walks."

"Exactly." He listened to her sigh. "Okay, so what do we do next?"

"I'm working the rest of the week. How about you bring my jeans and t-shirt back to their rightful owner on Saturday?" he suggested, his tone light but his heart hammering. "Come over to my place, spend the day hanging out with Penny and Chuck. We can take them for a longer walk. I think they miss you, too. We could have dinner too, if you'd like that. No pressure, just... Us getting to know each other."

Another pause, but this time it was shorter, and when Wren answered, he heard the smile in her voice, loud and clear. "I'd like that. Saturday sounds perfect."

Elias let out a breath he hadn't realized he was holding. "Great. It's a date then. And Wren?"

"Yeah?"

"I can't wait to see you."

"I can't wait to see you either, Elias."

––––––––––––––

TWENTY-FOUR HOURS LATER, Elias stood on his front porch, laughing. In one hand he held a large manila envelope he'd found taped to his door, along with a note:

Dear Elias,

I realized that I'm not a very good kidnapper (clothesnapper?) and that I'm falling down on the job. Enclosed, please find proof of life along with an article of MY clothing so that we can do a proper hostage swap on Saturday. Though I have to say, your jeans tend to hug me every time I put them on, and so does your t-shirt when I wear it to bed. What I'm saying is, they might not want to come home. Sorry not sorry.

Yours in Stockholm Syndrome,
Wren

In his other hand, he held three 8x10 glossy photographs pulled from the envelope which made him laugh even harder. There they were in the photos—proof that his jeans and t-shirt were alive and well. In the first photo, they were outside and posed so that it looked like an invisible man was wearing them and leaning against a tree. In the second photo, they were laid out on Wren's bed, kicking back and watching TV with a bowl of popcorn, her pair of slippers posed so that they looked like dogs begging for a stray piece of popcorn.

But he liked the third photo the best. Wren, her hazel eyes sparkling with their usual mischief, wearing his jeans and tee and holding a handwritten sign that said:

Miss you.

The envelope felt too light to be holding much in the way of clothing, but something lay at the bottom, wrapped carefully in tissue paper. He tucked the note and photos under his arm, pulled out the bundle, and tore the tissue paper open.

Five minutes later, with Chuck and Penny at his feet, Elias sat in front of his computer, composing an email:

Dear Clothesnapper,

Thanks for the proof of life, especially the third photo. While I appreciate the hostage-swap gesture, you still have me at a huge disadvantage. You've only presented me with one hostage while you have two. I demand a second hostage of the same caliber from you before Saturday, or else you will never see this one again.

Yours in Stockholm Syndrome,

Elias

P.S. You are NOT getting a photo of me wearing this hostage. Ever. Sorry not sorry.

"Take that," he said as he hit 'send' then picked up the silky, lacy, sexy-as-hell panties that weighed less than the tissue paper she'd wrapped them in.

"Nope, not wearing these." His lips curved into a sexy smile. "But you definitely will before I rip them off you again."

Friday night, exhausted, coming home hours late from his shift—a full moon on a Friday night always brought extra trauma and drama —Elias' mood lifted immediately when he saw another envelope and note tacked to his door. He heard Penny and Chuck pacing and scratching at the other side of the door. Of course they'd gotten out again. *The kid must have forgotten to lock the door again.* He unstuck the envelope and note, then went inside to see what trouble they'd gotten into.

Coffee grounds, eggshells, and a torn-up coffee filter all over the kitchen floor. Per usual, Chuck looked guilty as hell while Penny spun in circles, hoping to charm her way out of trouble.

"Yup. Full moon drama. Guys, I am taking up Shane's suggestion of obedience classes at Watchdog for the two of you."

On top of the day he'd just had, Elias should've been pissed. But the thought of what might be in the envelope cured him of that. He quickly cleaned up the mess, declining 'help' from Chuck, then read the note:

Dear Hostage Negotiator,

You drive a hard bargain, so I'm forced to send you a second hostage. This time, I'm including proof that said hostage does truly belong to me. Since you'll probably refuse to wear this hostage as well, I guess I'll just have to wear them both—if I get them back. How's that for incentive?

See you at the hostage swap tomorrow. Say 10:00?

Your Shameless Clothesnapper,
Wren

ONLY ONE PHOTO THIS TIME, but it was a doozy. Wren from the waist up, lying back against a pile of pillows, lazy smile on her face, eyes at half-mast. She wore a gauzy top that plainly showed a lacy bra underneath, the same emerald color as the panties.

And again, at the bottom of the envelope he found a tissue paper-wrapped bundle. Elias admired the bra before placing it on his dresser beside the pair of panties.

Then he got to work on a reply.

Dear Clothesnapper,

I have received the second hostage and taken it into custody. They are resting comfortably in an undisclosed location until

"Until I can get you back into them," he said out loud.

an agreement is met tomorrow. Unless you're busy stealing someone else's clothing (and I hope you aren't) feel free to come earlier than 10:00. Breakfast is at 8:00, just saying.

Yours. Just yours,
Elias

FIFTEEN

Wren bounced on the balls of her feet with anticipation as she read Elias' email on her phone for the hundredth time.

Yours. Just yours.

Every time she thought the words, her heart thumped extra hard and her tummy grew warm. Over the past few days she'd had so much fun setting up and photographing his clothes—and even more fun photographing herself. Each time she stood in her makeshift darkroom—the spare bedroom in the townhome she was renting—developing the photos, she imagined the look on his face when he pulled them out of the envelopes.

I'm head over heels. Not even two weeks, and I'm absolutely smitten.

I love him.

Wren bit her lower lip, fighting back the anxiety that shouted it was too soon for love, that she was heading for one more heartbreak, one more good thing that wouldn't last.

She glanced at the time on her phone. 7:40 AM, time to go if she wanted to get to Elias' for breakfast. She took a deep breath.

"All right, you mean little voice. I don't care if it's been eleven days, or eleven months, or eleven years—I do love him. I don't know if he loves me back, but it doesn't matter. I'm taking the chance." She wrapped her arms around her torso. "He's worth it. He's worth the broken heart if I lose him, as long as I can have just a little more time with him."

Her phone buzzed with an incoming text, making her jump.

She looked at the screen.

> You at the Lion's Lair yet?

Wren grinned at Barbie's message. Last night, she'd filled her bestie in on everything that had happened since the last time they talked. She hit Barbie's contact button.

"I'm on my way out the door," she said as soon as Barbie picked up. She grabbed her tote and dug out her key ring.

"Truth, or are you just saying that?"

"Truth." She held up her phone with one hand and jangled her keys with the other. "Hear that? That's my car keys." She tucked her phone in the crook of her neck.

"I was afraid you were going to play it like you always do and back off."

"Not this time." Wren opened the door from her kitchen to her garage.

"Good! I'm proud of you, Wrenbird."

Wren got into her car. "I'm proud of me, too." She hit the garage door button to open it, started her car, and backed out.

"So when can I come visit you? I have some time off before Greta wants me on set."

"Anytime. You know that."

"Um, so how did the shoot go?"

"Already talked about that last night." Wren smirked. "Are you just trying to come up with things to talk about to distract me so that I don't chicken out and go back home?"

"Maybe? I mean, you can't blame me. You skipped out early the last time."

"I'm not going to this time." She turned west onto the road that would lead her straight to Elias' door. *Or rather, the Lion's Lair. Cute. I'll have to tell him that one.*

"You know what? I can hear in your voice that you aren't. Go get 'em, Wrenbird."

"Thanks, Barbie Doll. I'll let you know how it goes."

"I'm happy for you. And I can't wait to meet him."

"He's got a lot of hot friends, just saying."

Barbie laughed. "That's just *your* way of getting me to visit sooner."

"Maybe."

"I'd rather live vicariously through you for the moment. I'm too busy for a beau."

"Suit yourself. Byyyee!"

"Mwah. Byyeee!"

⸻

WREN'S HEART did that fluttery thing as soon as Elias' house came into view. The one that was always accompanied by what felt like a tiny sun warming her chest every time she thought of him. She pulled up in front and parked, then grabbed her tote and barely kept herself from sprinting to his front door. When she got to his porch, she could hear the clicking of Chuck and Penny's toenails on the hardwood floor, followed by Elias' footsteps growing closer. The sun in her chest grew warmer.

I feel like a teenager about to meet her favorite rockstar.

Then the locks clicked as he unlocked the door and turned the knob. The door opened, and there stood her Lion looking at her with those intense lagoon-blue eyes, so gorgeous she couldn't move. His white tee stretched across his chest, and he wore a pair of jeans identical to the ones in her tote. He was barefoot, and even his toes were sexy.

Okay, when did I develop a foot fetish? She giggled nervously.

Elias gave her a slow, lazy grin. "First laugh point of the day goes to me and I don't even know what I did, except answer the door. Is there something on my face? Or maybe my feet? You were staring at them."

"They're good feet." *Great. I'm the queen of lame comebacks again.*

He looked down as he lifted one and then the other. "Had them all my life." He pinned her with his gaze again, his eyes sparkling. "You're not planning on stealing them, are you?"

"Oh, I'd never. I keep my thefts strictly to clothing. Specifically, yours."

Penny chose that moment to squeeze past Elias and put her front paws on Wren's knee as she looked up at her, tail going a thousand miles a minute. Chuck whined behind Elias.

"All right, you two, enough upstaging me," Elias said. "Come on in, babe," he told Wren. He quickly swiped Penny and tucked her under his arm. Wren watched Chuck follow obediently behind Elias to their room. She laughed quietly at the trio as her heart swelled.

He'll make an outstanding father.

The sudden thought shocked her. And then, something even more shocking—she settled into the idea.

He wasn't mad at the dogs for getting in the way twice now. He hasn't raised his voice once with me. Even through this misunderstanding, he's been funny and sweet. I can see myself making a family with him.

She'd never been close with a man like Elias before. The few relationships she'd braved always in ended with yelling, assuring that she'd never look back—and never get close to another man.

"All right," Elias said as he came back down the hallway, big smile on his broad, lion's face. "Come here." He opened his arms wide as he crossed the room.

I love him. I never want to lose him.

Wren dropped her tote and closed the distance. She felt a magnet-like pull in her belly until she was safe in Elias' arms. Wren buried her face in the crook of his neck and breathed in his good smell. Sandalwood with just a touch of bright, clean citrus. Warm and comforting. A rumble in his chest like a great cat's purr told her he was happy holding her.

He feels like home. I'm home.

Elias shifted his head to nuzzle in her hair. "I'm so sorry I gave you a reason to think you somehow didn't measure up. I never want you to feel like you're anything less than amazing. If I ever do something that makes you doubt that, I want you to tell me and I'll stop whatever it is. Then I'll do everything to remind you how much you mean to me. If we just keep talking to each other, this won't happen again."

Elias shifted and tilted her chin up with his finger until she was looking into his eyes. "Is all forgiven, baby, or do you need me to do something else?"

Can this be real? Elias never yelled, never got defensive, never blamed her. Sudden tears sprang to her eyes.

Don't let him see you cry. What a turn-off.

Wren desperately wanted him to laugh.

"Some clothesnapper I am." She laughed quietly. "We haven't even gotten to the negotiations and you already have me in tears."

Elias didn't laugh. If anything, he looked even more serious as he gazed into her eyes.

"Sorry. I'm a mess," she went on. "Didn't mean to spoil the mood."

"You aren't spoiling a thing, baby." He gently brushed away the first tear that fell.

"It's stupid." Wren wiped her eyes. "I just don't like arguments. I'm usually okay, but sometimes it sets me off, like now."

"Hey, no need to explain." Elias stroked Wren's hair. His fingers felt so good running through the strands. When he got to the ends, he rubbed them between his fingers, sending tingles back up to her scalp. She snuggled in closer to his body, laying her head on his shoulder, loving the warmth from his strong arms encircling her. He held her until her heartbeat steadied.

Now maybe he'll laugh. Say something funny.

"When I was a kid, my parents yelled a lot right before they split up," she heard herself say instead. She never told anyone, especially a man she was involved with, about her family. But the words flowed.

"It was when the economy went to hell and tech companies were laying people off right and left in Seattle. Both my parents worked in tech and my dad got laid off first, and my mom lost her job six months later in the next wave of downsizing. Neither one of them could find work, and they didn't have much in the way of savings so they started skipping mortgage payments. Of course I didn't know what was going on, I just knew that all of a sudden, my parents seemed to hate each other. They'd go silent for days, then out of nowhere, one or the other would burst out screaming and yelling about whatever. So I'd go running to my room and put a pillow over my head."

Elias stroked Wren's hair. Amazing how much it calmed her— that simple touch that he did without even thinking. She lifted her head so she could read his eyes.

"I didn't get what they meant when I'd eavesdrop and overhear them talking about losing the house. How can you lose a house? Was the earth going to open up and swallow it? Was it going to slide down the hill and into Puget Sound? I decided that was it, that was why they were yelling. They were afraid the house was going to slide down the hill."

Elias gave her a warm grin. "Little kid logic."

"Right?" She chuckled. "So, using my little kid logic, I went into the side yard, the one on the opposite side from the Sound, and took some clothesline and tied one end around the faucet sticking out of the wall. Then I looped the other around one of the pickets in the fence. I pulled the rope as tightly as I could, then tied the other end to the faucet. I ran in and made my parents come out to see my brilliant solution. I told them that we didn't have to worry about the house sliding down the hill anymore."

Wren grinned as Elias chuckled. "Cute."

"They both laughed, too," she said.

Elias' smile changed from amused to considering. "I bet you kept making them laugh after that."

Wren's eyes widened and her heart bumped at his observation. "You know what? I did exactly that." She thought for a moment. "Yeah. From that point on, I did everything I could to keep their laughter going. Silly, stupid kid stuff. I borrowed every joke book I could find from the library and memorized them. I got really good at predicting when the next outburst was going to happen, so I'd try and distract them by telling a joke, or just acting goofy. Anything to get them to laugh."

"Did it work?"

"Kinda, yeah. It did." Wren nodded. "Not every time, but enough that it became my default way of communicating. I got to a point where everything that came out of my mouth was meant to make someone laugh. It got me peace and quiet at home, and earned me friends at school." Wren grinned. "The teachers didn't always appreciate my commentary but some did. Some would crack up right along with the rest of the class."

"Wren Stapleton, class clown."

"Guilty as charged." She took a deep breath and let it out in a long sigh. "Eventually, though, nothing made my parents laugh. We were probably three or four months behind on the mortgage. That's when they split up and put the house on the market. I stayed with my mom as we went from one motel room to the next. One week, we were short on money, so we lived in the car."

Elias' looked heartbroken. "That must have been scary."

"It was." She took in a deep breath that was half sob. "Mom didn't get along with her parents and I'd never met them. But she was desperate so she called them. We moved in with them until the house sold and we had some money again. My grandparents were yellers, too."

"I'm sorry. I'm sorry you had to go through that." He kissed her forehead.

Wren shook her head. "Actually, it wasn't bad. They didn't yell at me. They doted on me. Thought I was the funniest thing going. I loved them, I really did. They were just loud, you know? Arguing was a way of life, a way to get your point across. I didn't understand that there wasn't malice behind it. They never said things like my parents did, they never said 'I hate you' or 'It's all your fault.' But by then, any yelling made me anxious. But loud laughter didn't. So I kept them in stitches."

She laid her head against Elias' chest, suddenly exhausted. And yet, she also felt like a burden had lifted from her shoulders. Elias didn't push her away. He just kept stroking her hair.

"Baby, I don't ever want you to laugh when you really want to cry. When you laugh, I want to know it's real, that it's because something has tickled you. Because I've done something goofy that's made you happy."

Wren nodded against his chest. "You do make me laugh for real, I promise. Just please don't question me or yourself every time I do laugh. That'll take the fun out of everything."

"I promise, so long as you promise to always tell me when you aren't comfortable." He tilted her chin up again. "I know how your parents messed you up with their fighting. That doesn't need to be us. I don't like yelling at the people I care about, either. Maybe if we keep on treating each other like friends, with respect, then it won't ever come down to fighting like that."

Wren grinned at him. "Friends with benefits I hope."

"Friends with many, many benefits," he told her. Then he moved in for a kiss.

SIXTEEN

Oh, this woman.

So much heartache hidden under layers of laughter. And yet, she revealed herself to him. Stripped herself of her defenses. Trusted Elias not to hurt her when she was most vulnerable.

So brave.

Elias gave Wren his sexiest smile as he dipped his head and brushed his lips across hers. "Mmm." He brushed her lips again. On the third brush, he licked her bottom lip and she made the sexiest sound as Elias felt his heart speed up. She wrapped her arms around his neck and found his nape. Wren parted her lips against his, letting him enter her mouth and explore. He groaned and pulled her closer, then broke off their kiss, savoring her sounds of protest.

"Right now, I'm going to show you just how many benefits you have."

And with that, he slid his hands down her body and lifted her. She wrapped her legs around his torso and giggled all the way down the hall as he carried her to his bedroom.

"Hey! It's your hostages," she joked when she saw her panties and bra on his dresser. Now that he understood her, Elias didn't have to question if she was joking because she was anxious. When she got anxious, she sucked her cheeks in. Right now, her other tell was right there—that gorgeous sparkle in her eyes whenever something made her happy.

"We'll discuss the hostages later. Right now, I need you too much to stop and let you put those on." Elias laid her down on his bed then covered her with his body. He leaned down and growled, "I'd only rip them right back off of you."

Wren moaned and arched up, pressing her body against his erection. He straddled her and pulled his shirt off over his head and tossed it into the corner as she watched. God, he loved being watched by her. Loved seeing the raw, naked desire in her hazel eyes. Her salty-peach scent rose up, tantalizing him.

Her hands went to his waist and she began undoing his pants. Her fingers brushed him—sheer torture as his cock strained against his boxer briefs. He moved off the bed then pulled off his jeans and boxer briefs, revealing his weeping cock. Wren sat up and pulled off her V-neck tee, revealing a pink silk bra with dark gray lace and trim. Elias could see her dark nipples—hard little pebbles under the thin fabric.

"Take your jeans off for me right now," he growled. "Make it fast."

Wren got to her knees and undid her jeans. But instead of pulling them off, she ran her hand down her belly until her fingers disappeared into her jeans. Elias groaned as he watched her hand move, imagining her fingers gliding over the silk barely covering her sweet pussy. Her eyes twinkled, full of equal parts of joy, mischief, and lust as she teased him.

"Do you trust me to make you feel good?" he asked.

"Always," she answered in a throaty voice.

"Then stop. That's mine to play with right now. Jeans off."

Her half-masted eyes widened as she licked her lips. "The panties too?"

"Not yet."

She kicked off her heels and peeled off her jeans and Elias got to see exactly what he'd hoped for. She'd soaked her panties for him.

"Oh, yeah, baby. That's what I wanted."

When he reached toward his nightstand to get a condom, Wren grabbed his wrist.

"No. I want you inside me without one."

Elias froze. "I've never done that."

"Never?"

"No. Not with anyone."

Her entire chest blushed red as she let go of his wrist. "Then we don't hav—"

"Not until now."

"Oh," she breathed.

"I never trusted anyone enough."

"I'm on birth control, and I'm clean."

Elias gave her a rueful smile. "Not that kind of trust. I never trusted a woman not to break my heart."

She blinked rapidly. "I won't break your heart."

"I know." He pulled his hand away from the nightstand. Then he covered her body with his. "I trust you completely." He dipped down and kissed her—another soft brush of his lips against hers. "My heart is completely at your mercy."

"I won't," she repeated.

He nodded. Then he kissed and nuzzled her neck and throat.

"God, I missed you," she whispered.

"Missed me?" he breathed into her ear, and felt her shiver.

"Yes. Not just the past few days but all my life. I didn't know you, but I missed you. Does that sound crazy?"

"Not at all. I'm here now, Wren. And I'm not going anywhere."

She gripped him as if a giant eagle was about to swoop down and carry him off.

"It's over now, baby. All that waiting for something good."

"Nothing good ever lasts for me." The sadness in her voice

cracked his heart open. Elias lifted his head and looked deeply into her eyes.

"That changes right now. Wren, I don't care that we just met. Like you said, I've been waiting for you, too, I just didn't know it. I love you."

He watched her lips part in shock.

I shouldn't have told her that. I messed up. I—

"I love you too, Elias." She gave him the sweetest smile.

He shook his head in disbelief. "It's a morning for firsts. That's the first time I've ever told a woman I love you, and the first time I've heard it said to me."

Her sweet smile turned sexy as hell. "Then let's get to that other first. Now you're the one who needs to hurry up."

Elias threw his head back and laughed. Her body felt good as she laughed under him.

"All right. But you can't stop me from doing one thing first."

"Yeah? What's that?"

He moved down the length of her body, then gazed down at her panties. He wasn't sure how it was possible, but they looked even wetter now. He bent his head and licked at the wet silk. He pressed his mouth against her, feeling her tight little clit under his lips, and growled. Wren moaned and gripped his hair, holding him in place.

"Let me up, baby," he breathed against her, and she let go. Elias wrapped his arm under her sweet, tight ass and lifted her pelvis. He pulled her panties off with his other hand and let her back down gently. Then he lowered his head down between her legs, breathed in the essence of her, and ate. He licked, and sucked, and held her down as she writhed under him. He reached up to her bra and played with her nipple, squeezing it just as he felt her body tighten under him. She cried out his name—the sweetest sound he'd ever heard.

Elias didn't hesitate. He covered her again until the head of his cock was aligned with her hot, soaking pussy. He thrust deep into her before her orgasm subsided. Nothing had ever felt this good as she pulsed and squeezed around his cock. He gritted his teeth against coming too soon and held still.

When she finished, he gave her long, gentle strokes at first, making sure to rub her clit with every thrust. Then as his pleasure built, he increased his speed until he was groaning, peaking, and she was right there with him, coming for him again.

Elias wrapped his arms around her and rolled until Wren lay on top of him.

"Was that good?" he asked.

"So good. The best."

He kissed the top of her head as she relaxed into his body.

"I promise, it's going to last."

"SO, tell me how you ended up in Colorado." They were sitting across from each other at the breakfast table, eating pancakes Elias had warmed back up in the oven. Wren wore yet another shirt she'd swiped out of his closet—a dress shirt with the top buttons undone so that he had a lovely view of her cleavage.

Wren licked syrup off her finger. "Well, you know I grew up in Seattle. I went off to school in Los Angeles to get out of the rain."

"Relatable."

Wren grinned and cut another bite of pancake. "I didn't know what I wanted to do, I just knew I wanted to see the world. Then I went to a lecture on travel photography and I was hooked. I declared my major and threw myself into learning everything I could about photography. My professor said I had a knack for photographing people and introduced me to a fashion designer who gave me a chance."

She shrugged and popped the bite of pancake into her mouth. "I started working shows, then magazines. I ended up flying back and forth between LA and New York all the time, so there was my travel."

She rolled her eyes. "Then I got tired of living half my life in airports, and decided to come to Colorado."

"Splitting the difference between the coasts." Elias took a sip of coffee.

"Never thought of it that way. But, I liked Colorado. I'd done a few shoots here in Vail and Aspen. I couldn't afford either place and realized it was the mountains and not the towns themselves that I loved, so I found Lyons. And apparently, a Lion as well," she joked.

Elias cracked a grin. "And I'm glad you did." He grabbed her hand and kissed it. "So tell me more. What was this project that you and Sandra worked on? She said it was a heartbreaker." He laced his fingers with hers.

Wren nodded and lifted her mug for another drink before she spoke. "It was." She sighed. "And I think it's part of the reason why I've been so moody."

Elias stroked his thumb over hers. "Babe, if you're referring to this morning, that wasn't moody. That was sharing a hard part of your life with me." He brought her hand to his lips again, brushing them across her fingers and loving the way she reacted—goose bumps rose on her arms. "I love that you did."

She ducked her head, smiling.

"So let me guess. It has something to do with losing a home."

"It does. I'm working with a reporter from *Mile High Marker*. Kit Larson. She's doing an exposé on people who have lost their homes due to medical debt. Not the same story as mine growing up, but close enough that I've let it bring up all my old insecurities."

Elias nodded. "How are you doing now?" He watched for her to suck in her cheeks, telling him she was uncomfortable, even if she joked.

"I'm much better. Talking about it helped." She gave him a wicked grin. "So did everything after."

She's not lying. My baby's feeling good for real.

"Then I guess we'll have to do a lot of that. I want you feeling good." He nodded at her shoulder. "I noticed your shoulder's not bothering you as much."

She unlaced her hand from his and rubbed it. "It is better. I sneaked in a yoga class with Stephanie this week and she helped me with my posture. Plus, I laughed so hard, I think I loosened the rock." Her expression turned soft. "And maybe talking got rid of most of it this morning."

Warmth spread through Elias' chest—a mix of tenderness and desire.

"I love you, babe."

"I love you, too, Lion." She grinned at his nickname. Then she blew out a breath. "Now, I do need to get some work done today. That's the joy of owning your own business—it owns you."

Elias grinned. "No worries, so long as I get to spend the whole day with you." He stretched his arms over his head, loving the way Wren's gaze went straight for his abs. "What kind of work?"

"I have to touch up some of the photos. I want to push the shadows a little more."

"What do you mean?"

"Oh, here, I'll show you. Where did I leave my tote?" She looked around and spotted it by the door where she'd dropped it when Elias took her into his arms. "Oh yeah, there it is. No idea how I could have lost track of it." She giggled as she winked at him, and he loved the blush that crept into her cheeks. She got up and brought her tote back to the table. Elias cleared the plates in the meantime.

"I can do the dishes first if you want," Wren said.

"Nope, they can wait." Elias stacked their plates in the sink. "I have to unload the dishwasher first anyway."

"I'm telling you, you're making me feel guilty for not washing them. Whoever doesn't cook, washes the dishes." She took her laptop out of her tote and set it on the table.

"So you have said." Elias grabbed his chair and came around the table with it. He kissed her temple, then they sat down in front of the laptop.

"Well, it's the new rule here." She stopped and covered her mouth.

Elias chuckled as he felt his heart swell.

"I mean, if you want. It's your house."

Elias draped his arm around her. Wren leaned into him and he kissed her temple again. "I'm glad you're comfortable enough here to make rules. Only," he nodded toward Penny in her doggie bed, "she has the final say around here."

"Oh, of course." Wren looked at Penny. "She says it's fine so long as she gets to lick the plates first."

"Ugh!" Elias grimaced and Wren burst out laughing. "I'm never eating off those plates again if that's the case."

"No problem. She'll take the new plate budget out of your minion pay."

"Great. How generous."

Wren giggled as she clicked on an icon and opened a photo, but grew serious once it loaded. "This is Matthew and his son, Arthur."

"Cute kid." Elias studied the contrast between laughing son and somber father. "What's their story?"

"Matthew lost his wife, Lena to a stroke. He was on top of the medical bills, then he wasn't. It sounded hinky. The hospital where she passed away is called Milestone." She made a disgusted sound. "The next guy I photographed was a sweetheart. He was a patient at Milestone, too. Same deal with the medical bills. He calls it Millstone."

"As in a millstone tied around his neck."

"Exactly."

Wren closed the photo of Matthew and Arthur. She clicked on another file.

When it opened, Elias felt adrenaline hit his system the way it did every time he was part of a search. He was looking at a familiar face.

"Wait a minute. What's his name?"

Wren looked at Elias. "Evan. Why?"

"Holy shit. Hang on." Elias got up and found the paper Gabe had given him. He came back and smoothed it out on the table. "This is him, isn't it? Evan Roy."

Wren compared the photos. "Yes." She looked at Elias in confusion, then tapped on the paper. "What is this? Why do you have a picture of Evan?" Her brow furrowed. "Wait, is that Stephanie with him?"

Elias beamed as he kissed Wren full on the lips. "This is the reason why we had that meeting at the rec center. Evan is friends with Stephanie and when he stopped showing up there, she asked us to find him."

"Why all of you? Why not the authorities?"

"She tried going that route and got nowhere." He paused. Wren had shared her secret with him. She was already friends with Ellie, April, Stephanie, Rochelle, and Sandra.

I'm safe telling her.

"Steph asked us because we...help people out. People who can't get justice any other way."

"People who can't get justice?"

He nodded. "We just helped out a little girl who had to testify against her abuser. We came to the courtroom, told her to look at us, not at him. Then his family wouldn't leave her alone and the police couldn't keep up. So we helped with that, too."

"People who fall through the cracks. Who can't defend themselves."

"Yeah. Sometimes, restraining orders don't mean anything to a predator. We make sure they stop, by any means necessary." He searched her eyes, trying to gauge her reaction, his pulse quickening. "Do you know what I'm saying?"

She nodded slowly.

"Are you good with that?"

Wren took his hand in both of hers. "No."

This is it. I've lost her. The fleeting thought whipped through his heart, leaving scars in its wake.

"Nope. I'm *great* with that, Elias."

He closed his eyes in relief. He felt Wren scootch forward, then her lips met his. A soft promise that said she accepted who he was and what he needed to do.

Elias opened his eyes and laid his hand against her cheek. Her soft skin grounded him.

She covered his hand with hers. "But you'd better promise me you'll always be careful."

He gave her a soft smile. "I can't promise you that, baby. But I will promise I won't hide what I'm doing from you. And I'll always come home to you."

"If you can't promise you'll be careful, then how can you promise me that?"

"Because my brothers always have my back."

He watched her consider that, his heart beating just a little faster as he waited for her response.

"Ellie and Rochelle know, too?"

"Of course. T-Wolf and Bear would never keep what they do a secret from them."

"Then, the next time you...do what you do, I'll have them over to my home. We can support each other, you know?"

"That sounds great, baby."

And if I have my way, your home will be here, with me.

Elias tapped her screen. "Do you or Kit know how to get a hold of him?"

"Yeah. He's got a room at the Y in Denver, where I took the photos."

Elias stood up. "I gotta call Gabe. Let everyone know he's been located." He planted a kiss on the top of her head. "Steph's gonna be so relieved." Elias started for the kitchen where he'd left his phone.

"Elias, wait. He doesn't want to be found."

Elias stopped and turned. "He doesn't?"

"No." She ran a hand through her long, chestnut hair. "He feels ashamed." She chewed on her lower lip. "He doesn't want to face the nurses who saved his life. He wishes they hadn't."

Elias clenched his jaw and looked away. He didn't want Wren to see the rage in his eyes, or hear his voice raised in fury. With a few deep breaths, he got himself under control. Centered, he said, "No one should *ever* be made to feel that way. And for such a stupid reason." He pulled at the hair on top of his head in frustration. "I was one of the EMTs who was there that day. Waylon, too. We didn't think he'd make it. We were so relieved when we got the news that he lived." He took another deep breath. "You can't take your patients home with you up here." He tapped his temple. "But some you never forget."

"Maybe I can talk to him," Wren said quietly. "Please. Otherwise, I feel like I've betrayed his confidence."

"It's not your fault. You had no way of knowing."

"No," she said half to herself as she looked at Evan's face on the screen, then back down at the photo on the table. "He looks so happy there. Must have been before the bills." She clenched her fist. "It's not right. He shouldn't be going through this alone."

She looked back up at Elias, fierce determination in her eyes. "Yeah. Let me talk to him. Maybe I can convince him to let his friends back into his life. Go ahead and let everyone know he's found and he's in a safe place. But maybe you could also explain the situation? Tell them to give me a chance to warm him up to the idea?"

"Of course, baby." He paused. "What do you think he'll say?"

"Well, he is going public in the article. So, I think there's a part of him who wants to be found, whether he admits it or not. I'll approach him that way. Speak to that part of him."

Up until that moment, Elias didn't think he could love or have more admiration for Wren. But seeing her look so determined made his heart overflow. He was only beginning to know her, and everything he learned made him love her more. His woman was strong, with a big heart.

If anyone can reach Evan, it's her.

"You'll convince him," Elias told Wren.

She stood and crossed the room until she was standing right in front of him.

"You believe in me."

He took her hands. "I do. Always."

SEVENTEEN

An hour later, Wren and Elias stood outside the Y.

"I'll wait for you down here," Elias told her as he leaned against the concrete planter. He'd insisted on coming with her and he'd put off calling Gabe until she'd had a chance to talk to Evan.

Wren rolled her neck, trying to loosen up the tense muscles in her back. "Wish me luck."

"You don't need luck. You've got this." He kissed her and opened the door for her.

Wren approached the front desk, relieved that the same receptionist from the other day was on.

"Hi, Carrie," she said smiling, which got the woman's attention. "Do you remember me from the other day? I'm the photographer. Wren Stapleton."

"Of course," Carrie said, brightening. "How can I help you? Did you leave something here?"

"No, but I'd like to talk to Evan if he's in? Just a follow-up to the story."

"He is. He came down for his mail about an hour ago and went back upstairs. Let me call up to his room." She picked up a phone receiver, dialed his number, then covered the mouthpiece and whispered, "He's such a sweetie."

Wren beamed. "He really is."

Carrie uncovered the mouthpiece. "Hello, Evan? It's Carrie downstairs. You have a visitor, Wren Stapleton the photographer." She paused. "She's here for," Carried looked at Wren, "a follow-up to the story."

Wren nodded, still smiling, while her nerves turned her stomach into a bowling ball, hoping that Evan would invite her up to talk.

"Shall I send her up to your room?" Another pause.

He's telling her no.

"All right, I'll let her know." Carrie hung up the phone.

Maybe I can wait for him in the parking lot. Like a stakeout. I bet Elias knows how to do those, but of course I've seen enough TV shows that—

Carrie held out a lanyard with a card on it. "He's in number twelve, third floor. It'll be on the left toward the end of the hall. You'll need this for the elevator, and I need to sign you in."

Wren blinked. "You mean I can go up?"

"Yes, he said he'd love to talk. Between you and me, he needs visitors."

Wren hung the lanyard around her neck. "I agree. And who knows? Maybe I'll be the first of many." She held up the card that identified her as a visitor. "Thanks."

Wren went over what she planned to say on the ride up. She walked down the hall to number twelve. The door was open a crack but she knocked anyway.

"Evan? It's Wren."

"Yes, yes." She heard him shuffling to the door. He opened it with a smile. "Come in, come in. I was just making tea. Would you like a cup?"

"That sounds good, thank you." She stepped into the little room. His only furnishings were a bed, a desk, a chest of drawers, a mini fridge, and two chairs. A small sink took up one corner. A beautiful quilt covered the bed. Two large cardboard boxes sat stacked on top of the chest of drawers and another acted as a makeshift nightstand, holding several medicine bottles, a glass half full of water, and a book. A hotpot sat on the desk beside a china teapot and two matching cups and saucers. The room was neat as a pin.

"Come sit." Evan pulled one of the chairs out for her beside the desk, then went to the fridge and opened it. She noticed his insulin bottles beside a carton of milk, which he took out and set on the desk.

At least he can afford his meds. Unless he's rationing them. Damn those bastards at 'Millstone.'

Evan sat in the chair opposite hers. "Do you take milk and sugar? I have my sweetener but I also have a wee bit of sugar left from making the fudge."

"Yes, both, please. And thanks again for the fudge."

Evan fixed them two cups of tea. It was strong, hot, and good.

"So," he started. "You wanted a follow-up? Another photograph?"

"No. I left my camera at home today." Wren set her cup down. "The follow-up isn't so much for the story, but for you. For your life."

Evan frowned, puzzled. "I don't understand."

Wren gave him a gentle smile. "I live in Lyons. I've been to the rec center, and I've met Stephanie West."

Evan looked away. "I see."

Wren softened her voice. "Evan. She has people looking for you. I just happened to find you first."

He looked back at her. "Have you told Stephanie?"

Wren grinned and leaned forward. "Do you *really* think she'd let me come here without her if she knew?"

Evan chuckled. "I suppose not."

Good. I've got him laughing.

"I wanted to talk to you before they find you, because they will. I've met the men she's asked to find you and they are very capable and determined. I know you don't want Sue and Fran to blame themselves for what happened after they saved your life. I don't think they will. But Evan, they *will* be hurt if they find out you didn't want their help."

He shook his head as his gaze settled on the cup of tea on the desk in front of him. "I'm just so embarrassed."

"I get it. I lost everything once, just like you did. My home. My happy childhood. I felt shame, too, for things that were out of my control. I spent years not telling anyone what happened because I was carrying the fear that they would leave me. I was afraid of losing everything all over again so I kept all the people in my life at arm's length. And I've missed out all this time. *Please*. Let me tell them where you are. Stephanie cares about you. The nurses too, and they'll all want to help you get back on your feet. It's okay to let them."

Evan nodded as he looked into the middle distance.

Finally, he met her gaze again and said, "Don't tell her."

THE REC CENTER was unusually quiet—the gorgeous Colorado weather keeping everyone outside—when Wren pushed the door open. Stephanie looked up from her book and watched her come in, Elias right behind her.

Helping Evan keep steady as he walked.

Stephanie's mouth opened as she stood up. "Evan? *Evan!*" She dropped her book and practically sprinted to them. "Where have you been? Are you alright? Sue and Fran thought you'd moved without telling us, which was weird."

Wren's instinct was to shield Evan from Stephanie's onslaught of questions. But he surprised her when he smiled at Stephanie.

"I moved, yes, but not because I wanted to. It's a long story, and you'll be reading about it soon enough in the *Mile High Marker*. I heard you were looking for me, so I decided to come find you instead."

"You bet I was, Evan." She pointed at Elias. "So was he, and I guess he found you."

"No, it was all Wren," Elias said. "A stroke of luck."

Evan laid his hand on Wren's arm. "I'm here now, thanks to this kind lady who talked a bit of sense into me. She was going to tell you I was coming in, but I wanted to surprise you myself."

Stephane beamed as she looked back and forth between Wren and Evan. "Let's head into the conference room where we can sit. I'm calling Sue and Fran and telling them to get their buns over here, ASAP. Oh, and *Gabe!*" She shouted Gabe's name down the hall. "Come here, right now! I've got a surprise for you."

"Oh dear," Evan said. "I didn't think to make a batch of fudge."

Stephanie laughed and pulled him into a hug. "I don't think they'll mind just this once."

WREN SPENT the rest of the weekend with Elias. She only stopped by the townhouse Saturday night to check on it and pack a weekend bag. She couldn't keep stealing Elias' clothing indefinitely. What would he wear?

Not that she would mind watching him walking around naked all day.

She considered *not* packing a weekend bag.

They spent their days talking, with Elias pelting her with questions about herself. What was her favorite color? Red. What was her favorite food? Taco Tuesday, duh. When would she like to move in with him?

She surprised both of them with her answer. "As soon as my lease is up."

It felt right. Like finally finding her forever home.

Tuesday, Elias went to work. Wren got up early when he did and insisted on frying up some eggs and making toast before he left, since he'd cooked every meal up until then. Wren had always heard that firefighters were good cooks, but Elias had them beat. He'd told her during their first dinner together Saturday night that he'd learned how to cook at the fire station where his ambo was based.

"Well, the student has surpassed his masters," Wren had said as she patted her tummy. "Good thing I belong to the rec center."

Now this morning, she set plates of eggs and toast on the table, both dogs at her feet. Elias was getting dressed in his bedroom.

Make that our *bedroom soon. Wow.* Her tummy warmed inside.

"Listen, guys. I'm moving in," she told Penny and Chuck. "I hope that meets with your approval."

Chuck sat down and thumped his tail against the floor. Penny stood on her hind legs and twirled in a circle.

"You're just doing that because you're hoping I'll give you that extra plate of scrambled eggs I happened to make, aren't you?"

Penny yipped. Chuck thumped his tail faster.

"I thought so."

"Are you kidding? Penny understood every word," Elias said as he came into the room. "She's as thrilled as I am and so is the Chuckster." He took Wren into his arms and kissed her. Like every other kiss, it lit up all the cells in her body at once. Her cootchie tingled, even though it was pleasantly sore. Elias had pelted her with questions by day, but he'd pelted her with multiple orgasms by night.

"Is this *my* scrubs top?" She plucked at the back of his collar.

"Hell no. That one smells like you and I want to keep it that way. Same with the tee." His smile turned devilish. "And the jeans, little Miss Goin' Commando."

Wren laughed and kissed him again. "So naughty."

"Yes, you are." Elias winked as he let her go and they sat down to breakfast. "What are your plans for the day?"

"Well, I've got another real estate shoot with Chase over in Boulder, then I'm calling Kit to tell her the good news about Evan. I think it will lend the article a bit of hope, and God knows we all need that."

Evan was going to be alright. Sue took the guest cottage—a converted carriage house behind hers—off the B&B site she used to rent it to tourists and insisted Evan move in immediately. He put up a token protest, but in the end, Elias and Gabe helped him pack up the rest of his things, loaded them into Elias' other, modern truck, and moved him in by the end of the day.

"I wish we could do more for Matthew and Arthur, too." Wren sighed.

"Just wait," Elias said. "If Kit's article doesn't change things, Gina and Lach will."

While the guys were busy moving Evan's belongings, Wren was meeting more of Elias' friends—specifically Gina Smith, Lachlan Campbell, and the man who ran a local security company called Watchdog, Kyle McGuire. Wren was familiar with the Watchdog Security branch in Los Angeles. Many of the celebrities she photographed used them, including Barbie and Bette Collins, the number one star in Hollywood. Gina, Lachlan, and Kyle had worked together at the LA location before Kyle set up his branch in Colorado.

But that was about all she knew about Gina and Lach—besides the fact they and Kyle were all big-time dog people. Each brought along their own dog. Lachlan's dog was an older boy named Sam who nevertheless looked healthy and easily kept pace with the others. Kyle had a black-and-yellow Lab named Camo who could probably give Penny a run for her money in the brains department. Same with Gina's dog, Fleur. If ever a dog and her owner resembled each other, it was those two. Both had the most amazing golden-amber eyes, bright with intelligence.

"They were quite interested in Evan's situation, but I'm not sure how they can help. For some reason, Lachlan kept reminding Gina they were retired. He was insistent about it."

Elias almost spit his coffee out. "Yeah, I bet he was."

Wren narrowed her eyes. "What?"

Elias shook his head and zipped his finger and thumb across his mouth.

"You can't tell me."

"Nope. Not beyond their jobs in *security.*"

"Ah, okay, gotcha."

Damn. Now I'm really intrigued, she thought. *Government maybe, or wait—black-ops. No—assassins! Oh, who am I kidding, this isn't a Kris Michaels novel.*

"You're overthinking it, babe." Elias stood and picked up their empty plates.

"Stop reading my mind. And give me those. You need to get to work." She made a grab for the plates but he lifted them up out of reach.

"Nope. You cooked, I wash." He smirked. "Your rules."

"Stupid rules." She pouted at him, then went to divide the scrambled eggs between Penny and Chuck's food bowls. "I'll just ask them straight-up what they did for a living when I call to see if they liked the house. Chase showed them the one near Bear and Ellie's yesterday."

"Good luck with that." Elias put the second plate in the dishwasher and dried his hands on a kitchen towel. "Hope they liked the house though, for their sake. Ellie's dying for them to move close, and Bear makes sure that what Ellie wants, Ellie gets."

"Aw, poor maligned Bear. He's really a big marshmallow."

Elias only smiled. "Not always."

***

BACK AT HER TOWNHOUSE, Wren had just finished packing up essential bathroom items—all the things Elias referred to as chick stuff—when her doorbell rang.

Probably another package. At least it arrived while I'm here.

Wren went to the door and looked out the keyhole.

Kit Larson stood on her porch.

"Kit," Wren said when she opened the door. "Come on in. I was just about to call you."

"Hey, Wren." The best way Wren could describe Kit's voice was

unenthused. Actually, that was being generous. Kit looked like she'd
lost her puppy.

This'll cheer her up.

"Hey, if you haven't finished the story, I have a new, incredibly
happy ending concerning Evan Roy." She closed the door behind Kit,
who sat down on the couch.

"I don't need it." Now her voice sounded flat with a heaping side
of angry that made Wren's stomach clench.

"What's wrong?" She sat beside Kit. "Don't tell me you want to
end on a sad note, for sympathy?"

"No. There will be no ending, sad or otherwise. Or a middle. Or
a beginning for that matter."

"I don't understand."

Kit played with the strap of her purse. "My boss, the features editor,
asked to see an early draft, which I thought was kind of odd. He knows I
still want to conduct a couple more interviews and he's always been good
about waiting until I'm done. So, I sent him what I had so far. Then, he
wanted to see all my research. I gave it to him, thinking I was in trouble
with one of the fact checkers. But no. They did a catch and kill on me."

"A catch and kill?" Now dread filled Wren's belly.

"Yeah. He told me to drop the story, said we won't be publishing
it. He wouldn't go into why, just said it didn't fit the *Marker* anymore,
which is bullshit." She twisted the purse strap around her hand.

"I have a feeling that editorial decision comes from higher up,
maybe even the publisher himself. I can't sell the story to another
paper without losing my job. Though, after this, it's tempting just to
quit." She laughed bitterly. "Can't afford to lose my medical insurance though."

Wren scoffed. "Can you say ironic?"

"Right?" Kit sighed.

Wren seethed. "This isn't fair. You're right—this is total bullshit.
People need to know about this...this *predatory* hospital. Who do you
think told the publisher to kill it?"

Kit blew out a hard breath and stared at Wren's coffee table, looking like she was debating with herself. Then she nodded slightly and looked at Wren.

"My boss was excited when I first pitched the story and whenever I gave him an update on my progress. But when I let him know at our last meeting that I wanted to interview Milestone's CEO, that's when he got back to me saying he wanted to read my current draft. Next thing I knew, the story was dead."

They were silent for a moment, both staring off into the distance, sharing their anger.

"Dead for you, maybe," Wren said quietly.

Kit curled her lips in and huffed through her nose. "So, are you saying that if you were walking somewhere, eyes on the ground, and you happened to see a thumb drive just lying there, you'd get curious, pick it up, and see what's on it?"

"I would."

"And, let's say it was full of research on a story you'd just photographed."

"Well. I think I might take up writing or find someone who knows how to write up a feature already."

"Interesting." Kit stood up. "Well, it's been great catching up with you but I've got to run. I'll see myself out."

As she walked toward the front door, she reached into the front pocket of her purse, then stretched her arm straight out to the side and opened her hand. A thumb drive bounced on the carpet.

"Oops," Kit said without slowing her stride. "Clumsy."

Wren didn't waste time picking up the drive, or her breath telling Kit she'd dropped it. She stood in her doorway watching Kit walk away.

"Thanks for stopping by," Wren said. "It's been educational."

Kit turned and waved. "Can't wait to see your next project."

EIGHTEEN

Wren stood in the middle of her living room and studied the thumb drive lying on her palm.

Two hours later, back at Elias' house, she finished looking at Kit's research, which came to the same conclusion she'd reached. She stared at the name on the screen as if it were at the end of a tunnel. Don Weisser. CEO of Milestone Hospital.

And a right bastard.

Then there was the second name, one she hadn't thought of. But it all made sense.

Her head throbbed. Wren was beyond mad. Beyond furious.

She needed to talk to someone. To do something. Elias was busy with his shift and she didn't want to bother him.

I'll talk to him tonight. Maybe he and his friends can help. She grinned. *They kinda owe me one.*

She got up from the kitchen table and went to the couch. Chuck and Penny followed her. Chuck sat on the floor within ear-scratching range and Penny jumped up beside her.

"We need a plan, Penny."

The terrier yipped in agreement.

"God, I wish you spoke English. Or that I spoke Dog. I bet you could think of something."

Penny sneezed.

"Okay, I get it, you've already got it all figured out. But until I can speak Dog, I need to think of one myself."

So she set her mind to planning.

When she came up with an inkling of a plan, she called Barbie and told her everything.

"I'm just so fucking frustrated that Weisser intimidated the publisher so badly that they killed the story."

"Bribed is more like it, hun," Barbie said, the voice of experience. "Or, maybe both."

Wren paced back and forth, from the kitchen at one end of the house to the bedroom on the other, Penny clipping along at her heels while Chuck watched from the couch. "I can't give up on this story. It's way too important. I've looked into the eyes of these people who have been hurt by this man, people who were already at their weakest. And he took advantage of them. I can't let it stand."

"So you need to get in to talk to him. Is that what I'm hearing?" Barbie asked.

"That's exactly what I'm saying. And I have no idea how to do it, not without tipping my hand."

Barbie paused and Wren could practically hear the gears shifting in her head.

"I think I have an idea. Let me get my people to set something up."

Wren stopped pacing.

I should have known.

"Barbie, I didn't call you to get you *involved* in this. I just called, I don't know, to bitch."

"Wrenbird, don't worry about me. No, I think I know how to handle this guy, and I have the time to do it."

"No. Way. No. Huh-uh. Penny, tell her she can't jeopardize her career, or her *safety*."

"Wait, Penny?" Barbie asked. "You're at Elias' house?"

"Yeah. That's the other thing I need to catch you up on, after you tell me you're not getting involved with my insanity."

"Fine, I'll set things up, then I'll let you do the dirty work. But I'll worry about you the entire time and that'll give me gray hair and I don't have time for gray hair. So you better not screw up, hear me?"

"Promise."

Barbie outlined her part of the plan. Halfway through, Wren's head stopped throbbing. Her heart started pounding instead. When they were through, Wren looked up Milestone's main phone number, took a deep breath, and called.

Once she got to an actual human, she said, "Yes, could you please put me through to Mr. Weisser?" Then she waited.

I can do this. I have to do this.

"NO WAY AM I letting you do this." Elias grabbed his hair and pulled it into an even crazier mess than it already was when he got home. They were still sitting at the table right after dinner—a massive bone-in ribeye that cost a fortune and that Wren hoped would soften him up when she told him what she was up to.

No such luck.

"How 'bout we try that again?" she said calmly. "How about, no way am I letting you do this *alone*."

"Well, that's a given. You are not going up against the CEO of a massive hospital *or* his backer. Jesus, Wren. You have no experience. You have no guns—"

"How do you know that? For all you know, I have a stack of rifles and I qualified for the Olympic biathlon."

"Did you?"

"Well, no." She folded her arms. "But that's not the point. The point is, I can do this part of the plan."

"No. Let someone else do it who is qualified."

"I can't. I already talked to him. He knows my voice. He'd be suspicious if he was suddenly dealing with someone else. But... I'd like you and your friends' help with the rest."

She mumbled her next words as she shifted her gaze away from his.

"What was that again?"

"I said, and Gina's help."

Elias blinked rapidly as he stared at her.

"Probably. If she can be helpful in that way. Which, from what you pointedly have *not* said about her former career, I think she can."

He covered his face with both hands and blew out a breath between his palms.

"Furthermore, I think she'd want to, if she knew the full extent of how badly Evan and Matthew got screwed over. And it's about to get a lot worse for many more people, according to Kit's research. You want to read it yourself?"

"I don't have to read it myself." Elias dropped his hands. "You know your stuff and so does Kit." He shook his head "I can't stop you. That's not a question, that's a statement."

"Right-o."

"And Barbie's sure she can make it happen?"

"Yup."

Elias studied her, his expression unreadable. Wren stood her ground.

Finally he said, "Okay. I'll talk to my brothers. *And* Gina. We can both talk to her if you want. Pretty sure she likes you."

Then he smirked. "You can go ahead and breathe again."

Wren let out her breath. "So that's why my lungs were burning. I had no idea."

He snorted.

"One point for me. That was a laugh, mister."

He grinned. "Fair."

She gave him a small smile. "Thank you."

His grin turned into a full-fledged smile. "No need to thank me, baby. I'd move heaven and earth to protect you."

"I know. That's not why I'm saying thank you."

His smile turned to a perplexed frown. "Then why?"

"Because we just had a big argument and you didn't raise your voice at me once. Not. Once. Not even close."

He shrugged. "I told you. I don't hurt the people I love if I can help it. So I'll never raise my voice in anger with you, because it would hurt you."

"I love you."

"Enough to marry me?"

Wren froze. She stared into his lagoon-blue eyes. He was serious.

"Enough to marry you."

She was serious, too.

"MS. GREENE? Mr. Weisser will see you now." Don Weisser's personal secretary glanced up from her desk and smiled at Wren.

"Thank you, Cherise. And please, call me Brooke."

Wren smiled back as she set aside the demitasse cup and saucer Cherise offered her when she walked into the suite on the top floor of Milestone, ten stories up. The espresso sat sour in her stomach as she followed the secretary down a short hallway. Her brown-colored contacts darkened the hallway a little, like sunglasses. She adjusted her wig quickly before Cherise could see. The borrowed black Louboutins with their five-inch stiletto heels pinched her toes but at least she didn't wobble. She'd practiced walking in them the entire week before the meeting. They changed her gait—which Gina told her was the point.

Gina had also coached her for ten days, then declared her a natural.

Wren had a better idea now what Gina used to do for a living.

Cherise opened a door at the end of the hallway and smiled at a man sitting behind a large desk. The surface was bare except for a blotter, a laptop, and a pen set—Mont Blanc if Wren wasn't mistaken. Don Weisser's silhouette was dark against the brutal, late-afternoon Colorado sun shining in behind him, making Wren thankful for the contacts. His window-lined office offered three panoramic views. To his left off in the distance rose Denver's skyscrapers. Directly behind him, planes took off and landed at a regional airport while the distant mountains looked cut from blue-grey construction paper in the summer haze. To the south stretched the high plains dotted with strip malls and subdivisions.

Cherise closed the door behind her, sealing Wren in the office with Weisser, who smiled but didn't bother to stand.

"Impressive view," Wren said as she took a seat.

Weisser nodded as his eyes briefly flicked to her cleavage, enhanced by a padded bra that added two cup sizes. "Ms. Greene." He folded his hands on his desk. "I understand you represent Barbie Gillis. I'm disappointed that she couldn't come herself."

I'm sure you are, she thought as she studied the man. Mid-fifties, neatly-trimmed salt-and-pepper hair, manicured nails, obviously worked out regularly. A little soft around the face with the beginnings of jowls on either side of his mouth. She was surprised he hadn't done something about that yet.

"She's disappointed not to be here too, trust me. Making this donation is a dream come true for her. If you know anything about Barbie, she came from a hard place. Not a lot of money growing up. She nearly died from a congenital heart defect as a baby and is grateful to the hospital that saved her life, thanks to its generous charitable funds." Wren adopted a convincingly sad smile. "Unfortunately, that hospital no longer exists."

"Probably wiped out because of those funds they gave out." He chuckled. "Cardiac surgery has never been cheap."

Wren took on an equally convincing, indulgent smile that said she understood perfectly where he was coming from. "Exactly. With the sale of her cosmetics company combined with the revenue from her latest Netflix series, she's now in a position to offer a high eight-figure donation to be made into a trust fund that would help subsidize cardiac patient bills."

Weisser's smile brightened. "And of course we specialize in cardiac care, so it's a match made in heaven."

Wren held up her hand in a not-so-fast gesture. "So, to ensure that Coloradans in need can afford quality healthcare, Ms. Gillis is sending me around to interview hospital CEOs to help her make a final decision where to donate her money."

His sudden frown was a beautiful thing to behold. "*Other* hospitals? I was not aware that Ms. Gillis was considering other places for her donation."

Wren pursed her lips. "Oh yes. She wants to make sure the right hospital is receiving her considerable contribution." She leaned forward and lowered her voice as if Barbie were standing close by and Wren didn't want her to overhear. "I have to tell you, right now she's leaning toward splitting the money between the children's hospital and CU's medical program, to pay off student loans."

Weisser unfolded his hands and grabbed the Mont Blanc pen out of its old-fashioned holder. He held it in his fist with his thumb clicking the end over and over like he was pressing the button on a remote desperately trying to change the channel.

"I see. You're here to see what Ms. Gillis gets for her money."

"Gets for her money?" Wren played dumb.

"We're expanding the hospital as well as adding clinics and ERs around the city. Would she like one named after her? Maybe one that specializes in pediatric services? That would be good publicity for her. Or, if she'd like, we could name the new wing after her." He set the pen down and opened his desk drawer. "I have some architectural renderings in here I was planning on framing, but if she'd like to look them over and choose—"

"I don't think that's necessary. Barbie isn't looking to put her name on anything."

He closed the desk drawer as he looked up, confused. He picked up the pen. "I don't understand. This is an anonymous donation?"

Wren's lips curled into a devious smile. "Barbie Gillis didn't get to where she is now by giving away things for free, Mr. Weisser. She made deals, both personal and for her business. She doesn't lift a finger for someone else unless she can get a substantial return on her investment." The lies about her sweet bestie tasted bitter in Wren's mouth.

Weisser took the bait. "Kudos to her PR team then. She comes across as an angel."

Wren looked offended. "Thank you, but she *is* a very good person. She knows that this will benefit patients who have no recourse otherwise."

"Of course."

"But you can't expect her not to want something in return. Her empire didn't build itself on charity."

"Despite what the media says? You're giving me a different picture of Ms. Gillis. I was under the impression that she donates the majority of her income to good causes."

Wren tsked. "And yet she still has more to give. No one ever does the math. They just see her carefully crafted persona and think she's a selfless sweetheart with a money tree hidden away somewhere." Wren narrowed her eyes. "She makes deals, Mr. Weisser. And I broker those deals. I have a tremendous amount of influence over her."

Understanding dawned on his face. "Ah, I see. You broker your own deals alongside hers, don't you."

Got him! Now to reel him in carefully.

Wren crossed one leg over the other and sat back in her chair. She looked past Weisser to watch a plane coming in for a landing against the blue-gray mountains beyond. "I never take more than what I'm owed from her donations, for doing good business. Call it a finder's fee." She looked back at him, capturing his gaze. "I'm discreet. I have to be, or I'm out of business as well. But, I look for opportunities where I can make a little more on top of that."

He blinked slowly, considering. "What is it you want to see that would convince you—I mean, Ms. Gillis—to bestow her donation on us?"

"Numbers."

"You want a shareholder's report for our parent company? I can get you that," he scoffed like she was wasting his time.

Wren smirked as if she were talking to a very dense person. "Let me tell you a story, Mr. Weisser. My uncle ran a dealership in Washington state," she lied. "He sold cars, both new and used. His salespeople used to practically break down in tears in front of customers during negotiations because my uncle worked on such a thin profit margin that he was practically giving cars away at cost. To get that amazing deal, all a customer had to do was take out their loan through his dealership. Sign on the dotted line and drive off the lot with a car they practically stole."

Weisser's growing smirk told her she was speaking his language.

"My uncle wasn't really selling cars, Mr. Weisser. He was selling high-interest loans. But his customers were so bedazzled by the low prices and the salespeople's theatrics—sellers who, by the way, did quite well on the back end—that they didn't stop to check the math or read the fine print."

The pen clicking sped up, like maybe it was now the button that detonated a nuke and he couldn't wait for doomsday. "What does this have to do with me, Ms. Greene?"

She swept her arm through the air. "You have a fine hospital here. The personnel, the doctors, the nurses, they're doing an amazing job saving lives, and from what I hear, they have a good bedside manner to boot. They're using cutting-edge technology in the cardiac unit. Everything is top-notch. I'd send my parents here. Heck, I'd seek treatment here if I needed it." She lowered her chin and looked him straight in the eye. "But I'd let myself die before signing a loan with the sharks the hospital's website sends patients to."

Wren watched him squeeze the pen and was surprised he didn't dent the metal. Before he could kick her out of his office—or maybe throw her through one of the windows and watch her plummet to her death—she gave him another devious smile.

"I would, however, love a little piece of *that* pie. I'd even be willing to buy in with my cut from the donation."

"How much is that?"

"Above board, three percent. Below...another two percent. Which I'd happily turn over, in cash, as a buy-in."

She watched him do the math. Then she watched him bluff.

"One-point-five million is a substantial amount of money, but it's short-term. What you'd get in return is long-term, and frankly, a much larger sum. I'm not sure that's going to work for me."

Wren nodded as if she fell for the bluff. She ignored the bile in the back of her throat for what she was about to say.

"Barbie would love to come and visit the hospital and hold a press conference. It's great publicity. She'd get her fans to match contributions. They love that sort of thing. Before you know it, that donation grows all by itself."

She reached across the desk, wrapped her hand around his, and the clicking pen stopped. "And all it would take is letting me in."

Weisser's face went blank as he studied her. "How well do you know Barbie Gillis? How close are the two of you?"

Wren tried not to crumble under his gaze. Was he seeing through her lies and trying to call *her* bluff?

"She trusts me implicitly. She doesn't make a business move without talking to me first. If I don't like it, she doesn't do it, period."

"Hmm." Weisser pulled his hand back and dropped the pen into its holder. "Then I want a meeting with her in person. Before any press conference gets announced."

"Of course."

"Alone."

Wren couldn't stop her eyebrows from shooting up, but she quickly got her face back under control. "Define alone, Mr. Weisser."

He gave her a lascivious smile. She could practically see the drool just waiting to spill down his chin. "I want proof that you are who you say you are to Barbie Gillis. I want you to call her up right now and tell her where you are. And I want you to set up an in-person meeting."

Wren sniffed. "Barbie can choose to donate her money anywhere. I'm not a madame, Mr. Weisser."

"Sure you are. Or if you aren't, you will be, if you want a piece of pie." He folded his arms and leaned back. "I want my pie, too."

Ugh! So gross.

He massaged his chin. "And you just told me you hold sway over Barbie, that she won't make a move without your approval. Do you want a deal for yourself or not?"

Wren sighed and frowned. "Fine. But we'll talk numbers first. Five percent of every loan for five years. We'll renegotiate after that."

Weisser laughed. "You think you run the hospital? That's what I get."

Ha! Thanks for telling me that, idiot.

Wren laughed to cover her glee. "You can't blame a girl for high-balling. How about two percent?"

"How about half a percent, the one-point five mil, and a meeting with Barbie?"

"How about the money plus that meeting *alone* with Barbie, for one percent?"

He pulled the Mont Blanc back out of its holder and squeezed it. "Call her. Right now. I want proof this can be done."

Without breaking eye contact with Weisser, Wren reached into the Birkin bag tucked at her side and pulled out her phone. She tapped in her code to unlock it. She hit one button and put the call on speaker. Three rings echoed in the office before Barbie picked up.

"Brooke? Have you got good news for me, sweetie?"

Wren smiled triumphantly. "I do. Mind if I put you on screen? I'm in Don Weisser's office. Milestone Hospital."

"Right. Yeah, absolutely."

Wren hit another button and Barbie's face filled her phone's screen. She turned it around to show Weisser, who was turning bright red and trying to smooth his hair back.

"Mr. Weisser?" Barbie purred as she looked him up and down. "So lovely to actually *see* you."

"Don, call me Don."

"Of course. So, has my incredible Brookie talked you into taking my money?" Barbie laughed.

Weisser chuckled. "I think we're closing in on a deal, yes. But, I'd love to do this in person. It feels so cold making this deal without you here. I'm a caring person, that's why I got into healthcare."

Wren tried not to gag.

"Oh, me too!" Barbie said. "Sure. When would you like me at your office? I'm tied up today and tomorrow, but I can get Brooke to set up a date."

"Well," Weisser drawled. "I was thinking it would be more comfortable to have you at my house. I can cook. I'm an excellent cook."

Gag gag gag!

"Oh!" Barbie trilled. "I love a man who can cook. Brooke? Can I see you for a sec, hun?"

Wren turned the phone to face her. "Yeah, hun?"

"Are you good with him?" Barbie let a little insecurity into her voice.

"Absolutely. We've been discussing how the money will one-hundred percent be used for the patients, minus my fee, of course."

"Okay, good. Not like that last offer you told me about."

"Nope, that was a bad one. I feel good about this one. About Don." She looked up and gave him a playful wink.

"Okay then. Set it up and tell me when and where to sign."

"Perfect. Love you, sweetie."

"Love you more! Gotta go. Mwah!" Barbie disconnected.

Wren's smile turned smug as she quietly placed the phone back in the Birkin. "There, see?"

"And you say you aren't a madame."

"I'm not. Barbie's a big girl and she's coming off a nasty break-up. She just said she likes a man who can cook."

"Did I look all right?" He frowned. "I wish you'd given me a warning."

"You look very distinguished. She likes that in a man, too."

She also likes men who aren't narcissistic monsters, so good luck with that, chump.

Wren folded her hands on Weisser's desk as if it were hers now. "Let's talk about my one percent. I also want assurance that the loans will go up over time."

Weisser was still high from talking to Barbie, judging by the color in his cheeks. "Between you and me, those loans are about to skyrocket."

"With the new hospital wing?"

He looked at her like she was a naïve child. By now, she felt blanketed by his constant condensation. "Oh no, Brooke. Like you, I have my own well-placed friend. And he's working on doing me a favor that will benefit us."

NINETEEN

"And that's when he filled me in on his good buddy, Senator Lorne Robbins," Wren said.

Elias sat on her right hand side at a table in Watchdog's main conference room as she recounted her meeting with Weisser earlier that day. Kyle sat to her left, at the head of the table. Across from her sat Lachlan next to Gabe, who looked like he was reading Wren's lips as she spoke. Gabe had offered his chair to Gina before the meeting started, but she shook her head and leaned against the wall instead.

"Old habits die hard," she'd told him with a grin.

"Her knees don't bend during meetings unless she's pacing," Lachlan clarified. "Isn't that right, Sunshine?" He winked at Gina, who rolled her golden eyes with a laugh.

Waylon sat by Gabe, then Ben next to Waylon. Bear sat at the other end of the table, taking up all of it. Shane sat on Elias' right side with another Watchdog bodyguard who Kyle introduced to Wren as Charlene King, better known as Charlie. Elias had met her before—she had served with their friend Badger as a SWCC in the Navy. Charlie was a stunning woman, tall and all lean muscle. Elias caught Ben eyeing her more than once.

Elias squeezed Wren's hand under the table. He was so damn proud of his woman because holy shit was Wren smart and brave. She handled that son of a bitch Weisser like a pro, got him slobbering all over himself to spill everything, and all because he wanted to get his dick wet with a celebrity—which of course would never happen. Wren told them Barbie had laughed about the phone call when Wren called her from a rental car on the way to Denver International Airport, where Gina somehow sneaked her back out after Wren had gone through security.

Bet the only thing that man can cook is books Barbie had told Wren.

But along with Elias' pride in her came alarm. "Are you sure your disguise worked, babe?"

She touched the black-haired wig still on her head. "Did you or did you not walk right past me at Riversong yesterday?"

Elias jerked back. "Wait. You were at Riversong?"

"I rest my case." She gave him a smug grin. "Gina taught me well."

"Like I told you, you're a natural, Wren," Gina said.

"In addition to the disguise," Kyle said, "You'll both be guests of Watchdog's finest safehouse until this blows over."

"Appreciated," Elias said, dipping his chin.

"So, we have confirmation of the link between Weisser and the senator that Kit suspected," Gina said.

"Yup," Wren confirmed. "And now we know the deal. Senator Robbins is getting a percentage from the loans too, through a shell company. And he's about to make sure those loans get worse. We're talking nightmare-level worse."

"How so?" Lach asked.

"He's pushing for two pieces of legislation in Colorado. The first supposedly protects patients' HIPAA rights but actually makes it harder to reveal these predatory loans. The second is where the real nightmare comes in."

"What nightmare?" Kyle asked.

Wren cleared her throat and took a big drink of water with lemon slices from a glass tumbler. She'd been talking for nearly an hour and her voice was showing it.

"Okay, imagine this. You've been diagnosed with cancer. You go to Milestone, which has just opened a shiny new oncology wing."

"Named after Barbie Gillis?" Waylon joked.

Wren snickered. "Yeah, right. In Weisser's wet dreams." She crinkled her nose in disgust and squeezed Elias' hand tighter.

I'm going to give her an extra-long massage tonight followed by a string of orgasms until that foul image is obliterated from her head.

Wren continued. "No surprise, your insurance won't cover everything. You don't want to die, but you also don't have ten thousand dollars in spare change lost somewhere in your sofa. So you take out a loan from the hospital to cover the difference. The hospital loan is zero-percent interest and you have a long time to pay it back. Sounds great, right?"

Gina started pacing. "Too great. What's the catch?"

"The catch is when Milestone gives your account to LastSave Lenders. You keep paying on time but then months later, you begin receiving late notices, even though you're making payments. Turns out your payments are only being applied to your surgery, not your medical appointments, or maybe your hospital stay. It doesn't matter —you're past-due.

"And that zero-interest offer goes away," Gina said.

"Yup, that zero-interest offer goes away," Wren confirmed. "And they don't tell you right away. They let those bills pile up for a few months without sending a notice. Then, you get hit with late penalties and an interest rate that is just under the legal maximum limit."

Gina looked sick. Her expression matched the feeling in Elias' stomach. "They purposefully neglect bundling everything and they don't tell you, or give you any warning."

Wren nodded. "Exactly. And the patient is also getting bills from the oncologist, *and* the anesthesiologist, *and* the PT person, *and* probably the dog next door. They do any number of things to make the payments more confusing. And if *that* doesn't work, they've already gotten you to sign a 'Surprise Billing Protection Form'—which is anything but—at the beginning of your treatment. It allows them to get around the No Surprises Act."

"So, Robbins is working on legislation that will make all this a reality?"

Wren shook her head sadly. "Oh, no, Gina. This is *already* reality. And Robbins is about to make it so much worse. Colorado passed legislation that says a hospital can't put a lien on your house. However, LastSave Lenders can and does. Robbins wants a bill that streamlines the process. LastSave Lenders forgives the sad little ten grand you owe them, but they have your home. Robbins calls it The Secure Healthcare Lending Initiative."

Gina looked horrified. "Let me guess. Alongside the HIPAA legislation he's pushing, it will be impossible to get the evidence to prove that the lending company is targeting patients who own their homes, or show that they are engaging in predatory lending practices. The legislation will prevent patients from entering the evidence with the excuse that they are 'protecting their privacy' for their own good."

Wren tapped the tip of her nose. "You got it."

Gina grimaced and closed her eyes. "Disgusting."

"Utterly. But." Wren's expression changed from disgust to triumph. She bent down to pick up one of the Louboutins she'd kicked off the minute she'd sat down. "Thanks to you, I've got it all recorded here." She tapped the side of the shoe. "Thanks for letting me borrow these, but my God, I'm never walking in them again."

Gina laughed. "It's been a while since I've had to wear them, and I have not missed the pinched toes."

Lachlan scoffed. "I didn't even know you still had those."

"Oh, I kept quite a few toys from my previous life."

"Can I see?" Elias asked. Wren handed him the shoe. He turned the wicked-looking thing in his hands. *How does any woman wear these?* "I don't see anything out of the ordinary."

Gina came around the table and took the shoe from Elias. "It's under the leather bow on the back." She fiddled with the bow until it lifted, revealing a tiny port for a cable. "The recorder is at the top of the heel at its widest. The mic is located at the toe, here." She ran her finger down the side of the shoe to the pointy toe.

"I crossed my leg to lift the shoe and pointed the toe at Weisser the Weasel as soon as we started talking," Wren said. "I hope it worked."

"Oh, it did, trust me," Gina said. "The mic's good, probably even picked up all the noise from the airport."

She set the shoe on the table. "Now for the next step. *Mile High Marker* killed the story and I have a feeling that other publications in Colorado would, too. Maybe even further afield. Milestone is part of a network of hospitals spreading across the country and they all use the same loan company."

"So how do we get the word out there?" Wren asked. The frustration in her voice made Elias stroke his thumb across the back of her hand.

Gina's eyes shone as she looked at Lachlan, who nodded. "We have a friend. She's a journalist with her own platform who specializes in stories like these. Kyla Lewis Dean."

Wren's eyes and smile both got a whole lot bigger. "She's a legend. Wait, she hired Watchdog, didn't she? When everything went down with her a year or two ago?"

Humor danced in Gina's eyes. "Yes. But first, *I* was investigating *her.*"

Wren covered her mouth. "Was that before Kyla went..." she trailed off.

Gina nodded.

"Can someone clue me in?" Elias asked.

Wren tilted her head. "You don't listen to podcasts, do you?"

"What's a podcast?"

She rolled her eyes. "Smartass. Kyla used to be a reporter in Los Angeles. Now she has a huge following on her podcast, *Up She Rises.* She exposes all sorts of corruption."

"If she can help us, that's great. I might even listen to her podcast."

Gina patted his shoulder. "If you start with episode eight, *Rumors*, you'll know her story. Well, at least the parts she can tell without endangering or incriminating anyone. Including me."

She tapped the shoe. "Let me listen to this first, then I'll contact Kyla. She'll want in on the story for sure." Gina looked at Lachlan again. "Lach insists I'm retired now—"

"Because you are, lass."

"—but that doesn't mean I can't pass a little info about the loan sharks along to the Los Angeles Watchdog office. We have quite the hacker there. Once she looks into LastSave Lenders and gathers proof —and rest assured, she will—she'll have no problem redistributing funds much quicker than the law will, if they do so at all."

"You mean give the money back to Matthew and Arthur," Elias said.

Gina nodded. "And Evan, and anyone else they've robbed. The money will also be untraceable, if needed." She gave the room a wicked smile, her gaze dancing from Gabe on down to Bear. "You gentlemen are not the only ones who know how to help people who've fallen through the cracks."

AFTER THEY FINISHED DISCUSSING the third part of the plan—which truly made Elias feel uneasy—the meeting adjourned.

Kyle led Elias and Wren—happily out of her disguise and back in her favorite cowgirl boots—on a picturesque walk through Watchdog's property, an entire forest-covered stray foothill east of Lyons. The sun had set but the path through the trees was lined with lampposts.

"Here we are," Kyle said when they reached a clearing that turned out to be a backyard. "Watchdog Protection's finest safehouse. I took you the back way because it's shorter than using the road."

"It's cute," Wren told Kyle.

"You sound surprised."

"I guess I was picturing some sort of bunker situation."

Kyle chuckled. "Negative. Watchdog bought the few houses scattered on the foothill, including my wife's small ranch further up the road. Arden will be down in the morning to meet you, Wren, and make sure you're comfortable. She loves visitors."

"Oh, good! Ellie was telling me about her."

"They're good friends." His grin lit up his ice-blue eyes. "I think you're gonna fit right in."

"Bear actually fixed this place up," Elias said. "And it's where he—"

"Met Ellie," she finished. "She told me all about it."

"I'll leave you two to get settled in," Kyle said. "You've got the key, brother?"

"Right here." Elias took the house key out of his shirt pocket. He'd been by the house earlier, bringing Penny and Chuck and a couple suitcases. His truck was parked out front.

"Thanks, Kyle." Wren hugged the tall man, catching him by surprise, Elias thought, judging by the look in his eye.

"Good night." Kyle gave them a chin lift and headed for the front yard and the road up to his home and Arden.

Elias turned and pulled Wren into his arms.

"I've wanted to do this all day, baby." He swayed her gently while the crickets sang around them and the first stars glittered in the darkening blue sky above. He nuzzled in her hair as she lay her cheek against his shoulder, right where it fit perfectly.

"I know you're worried about the next part." Her breath was soft and warm against his neck. "But I'll be all right. Today was way more risky, honestly."

Elias disagreed. Strongly.

But that was not tonight's problem. Tonight was all about pleasuring his woman.

Right after something even more important.

Wren lifted her head. "Your heart suddenly sped up. Please don't be worried and give yourself a heart attack."

"Well, if I did, I know what hospital I *wouldn't* go to."

Wren barked out a laugh and immediately covered her mouth. "Oh God. I'm slap-happy enough to laugh at that. So inappropriate."

"It's just gallows humor. You'd be shocked and appalled by what we say back at the station after a rough shift. But it eases the tension."

Wren dropped her hand and frowned up at him. "I'm sorry you're so tense about what's going on."

He shook his head. "It's about not that, baby."

"Then what?"

"It's about this."

Elias dropped to one knee.

Wren's hands flew back up to cover her mouth. "I thought you already did this like ten days ago after that amazing "marry me" ribeye I cooked for you."

He pulled her hands down away from her face and held them. "Baby, that was not the proposal you deserved. I'm not sure this one is, either. You deserve to be proposed to on a tropical beach, or some-place fancy and romantic like Paris. And by someone way better than me, because you are, in all ways, far above my paygrade."

"I don't want someone way better than you. I don't like guys who are way better than you. Because they actually *aren't* way better than you." She closed her eyes and threw her head back. "I'm spoiling this with my babbling, aren't I?"

Elias successfully fought back a laugh.

"Open your eyes and look at me, Wren Stapleton."

Using her full name got her attention. She looked back down at him.

"I realize we've only known each other for a month. But I knew from the moment you made me laugh that you were the one. And if you do me the great honor of marrying me, I swear that I will always break your rules by cooking you dinner *and* doing the dishes."

She giggled.

"And I will fill my closet with clothes for you to steal."

She snickered.

"And I will make sure your life is full of laughter. Because I really want all those laugh points."

She bent in half with laughter. And when she finally looked up, her eyes were full of happy tears.

"I love you so much, Wren, for so many reasons. So please." Elias reached into his shirt pocket, pulled out the ring he asked Ben to design and create, and held it up. "Please say you'll marry me."

Wren wiped her eyes. "I knew you were the one the minute you made me forget that I'd just escaped from a burning building. The entire world disappeared except for you. So, my answer's the same, my Lion. Yes, I will happily marry you."

He slipped the ring onto her finger. A perfect fit.

Wren wiped away another tear. "But right now, I have to tell *you* something very important."

Elias' heart hitched. "What is it, baby?"

"We're..." She sniffled. "We're...tied on the laugh points right now because I lost track, and I am not giving up that rule."

Elias laughed as he swept her up off her feet. He laughed as he spun around with her. And he laughed all the way across the yard as he carried Wren to the safehouse.

TWENTY

"My God. I can't tell the difference between the two of you." Wren looked back and forth between Barbie and Gina.

"So long as I'm wearing colored contacts and these tinted glasses," Gina said. "The eyes are always the hardest thing to fake, so we do our best to camouflage them as much as possible."

Barbie had come to Denver from Aspen three days before. She came quietly and incognito after posting on her social media that she was going to make a big announcement in a few days, but that for now, she was kicking back in her California home.

Gina had contacted someone she called 'one of my friends from my old life' and asked her to come to Watchdog. Gina had referred to her old friend as a makeup artist. But looking between the two of them now, Wren realized Nettie was so much more.

The first thing Nettie had done was make a couple slip casts of Barbie's face, which she used to create latex prosthetics. Then she applied them to Gina's face. Besides the eyes, the biggest difference between Barbie and Gina was the heavy makeup Nettie applied to help further hide the prosthetics. The real Barbie kept her face makeup-free when she wasn't in public, like now. The only time she went without makeup in public was if she wanted to run out and grab a meal with a friend without getting recognized and mobbed.

While Nettie made the prosthetics, Gina practiced moving and walking like Barbie. Barbie was a smidge taller than Gina, but she fixed that by concealing lifts in her shoes. She even borrowed one of Barbie's outfits that she'd worn on her social media a couple weeks previously.

Now with the shoes, the clothes, the glasses, and the prosthetics in place, Gina stood beside Barbie in the safehouse's living room and Wren was amazed. So were Elias, Shane, and Charlie as they looked back and forth between the two women.

"You did an incredible job," Elias told Nettie as she fiddled just a little more with Gina's wig.

"She always does," Gina added.

"Thank you. I do love my job. There." Satisfied, she stepped back and looked them over. "I think we've got it."

"Perfect." Gina picked up Barbie's trademark Birkin bag off the couch and slung it over her shoulder.

"Okay, I'm off to the airport. I'll take some selfies and post them on your social, Barbie. Weisser's subscribed to all your sites. What he'll see is a woman he thinks is you coming into Denver to make her big announcement about the hospital donation. I'll have the glasses on, and the photos will be from just enough of a distance that we can obscure my eyes a bit. Seeing photos of me in your most recent posts will help sell the deception once he sees me up close. Celebrities always look a little different in person, and he's never met you before, so he doesn't have a comparison."

"Can't you just stay here and drop in a fake background?" Barbie asked. "What if someone stops you thinking it's me and asks for an autograph?"

Gina grinned, which looked so weird to Wren. She'd even learned to smile like Barbie.

"That's actually what I'm hoping for. If there are videos of 'you' walking through the airport on other people's pages, it lends that much more credibility. And, if I pass as you up close," she patted her fake cheekbones, "it'll confirm that this face works."

"What if you don't pass?"

"Don't worry. I have a long track record of passing for other people." Gina looked at Charlie who stood beside the front door, looking every inch like a total badass. "And that's where Charlie comes in as my bodyguard. She'll make sure nobody lingers too long and that we move through the airport at a good clip straight to the waiting SUV."

"Driven by me," Shane said, grinning. "Your courteous and professional local Watchdog bodyguard."

Charlie cleared her throat as her eyebrows rose. "Ah-*hem*."

"Sorry. I meant your *other* courteous and professional local Watchdog bodyguard."

Charlie smiled. "That's better."

Gina crouched down to take Fleur's face in her hands. She looked tenderly into the dog's eyes.

"I have to go to work without you, sweet girl. You be good and behave yourself here while I'm gone."

"Penny and Chuck are more likely to misbehave, but we'll make sure they don't get Fleur into too much trouble," Elias said.

Penny, who was lying beside her new doggie bestie and intellectual match, looked appalled. Chuck snored in his doggie bed, completely oblivious.

"Telling you, brother," Shane said. "Take advantage while you're here and bring your pups up to the kennels. Alex will have them trained in no time."

Gina gave Shane a smile that wasn't hers but Barbie's.

"That is *so* uncanny," Wren said. She turned to Barbie. "How do *you* feel? You must be more weirded out than I am."

She nodded. "I've had body doubles before, but not like this."

"All right," Gina said. "This is the fun part." She looked almost giddy.

Charlie put on her sunglasses and opened the front door for Gina, Winnie, and Shane.

"I'll give you a lift over to Kyle and Arden's, Winnie," Shane said.

"Thanks."

Through the front window, Wren watched Gina and Charlie get into a nondescript car while Shane and Winnie took one of Watchdog's SUVs.

Barbie laid her hand on Wren's shoulder. "Are you ready for tomorrow, Wrenbird?"

"I am." *As long as I ignore the fluttering in my gut*, she thought.

Elias crossed the room. "I'm ready for it to be over." He put his arm around Wren's shoulder and she leaned into him, loving how warm and solid he felt.

Barbie smiled at them. "You guys are too adorable." She stretched. "If you need me, I'll be in the shower, then my bedroom." She turned and walked toward the hall. "But I don't think you'll need me."

Wren didn't want to go over every last detail of tomorrow's plan for the thousandth time with Elias so she cut him off before he could even start.

"Barbie approves of you."

"I'm glad, or this house would feel really small right now. Well, small-*er*." He pulled her in close, smiled and nodded when the sound of water came from the bathroom, then slid his hand up her side until his fingers found her nipple, which hardened immediately under his touch.

And that's not all that's hard. It took no imagination whatsoever to figure out what the waist-level bulge suddenly pressing against her could be.

"*Finally* alone," Elias murmured.

Wren laughed. "Do you know how many men would kill fluffy baby ducks to be in your position right now?"

"I'd have to kill *them*," he growled. "You're mine. That, and baby ducks are cute. Those sick assholes."

Wren laughed again. "I'm not talking about *me*, you goof. They'd kill to be sharing a house with Barbie Gillis."

"Well, not me." Elias tipped her chin up and kissed her until she melted. "You are the only woman who exists in my world, Wren."

"I know." She tried to sound flippant.

"No, baby, I'm being serious now. I mean it. There will never be another woman, Wren. Never. I met you and you took my walls down."

"No." She shook her head. "I didn't take them down, because I never even saw them after that first day. And the walls were there only because you were trying to be a professional while I was playing for laughs. I wanted to see you smile, see those gorgeous blues of yours light up. Because of me."

She watched his blue eyes flash, then fill with desire.

"Tell me again why Barbie is staying here?" he growled.

"Because someone else is hiding out in the other safehouse, and the third house is undergoing renovations. And, Barbie doesn't want to be a bother so she's not staying with Kyle and Arden like Winnie is."

"I thought you were going to say she's staying with us because she wants to keep an eye on *you*."

"Right, that's what I just said." She let a slow smile spread across her face. "Don't worry, you'll learn to speak the BFF language."

Elias looked toward the direction of the bathroom. "Does she take long showers or short ones?"

"It depends on the situation." Wren ran her hand over his jeans and felt his cock jump. "She's my bestie and she approves of you. So today? Pretty sure she'll take a long one and then go for a long walk."

Elias wasted no time in carrying Wren to the bedroom.

SHANE DROVE the SUV slowly through the expensive neighborhood past fake Italian villas and houses that could have doubled for a huge ski lodges. Somewhere behind him drove an unmarked car that would be joined by several marked SUVs after Gina and Wren were in place. In addition to sending Kyla all the evidence, Gina had contacted the police and filled them in. What Wren was learning about her new friend was that Gina knew all the right people to get shit done fast. At the precinct with the lead detective, Wren signed about eight thousand consent forms and then learned more than she ever thought she'd know about sting operations.

Charlie rode shotgun. Wren and Gina sat behind them, with Elias and Lachlan in the back, behind tinted windows. Wren was dressed in business casual. Gina had borrowed one of Barbie's more provocative dresses. She hoped it would provide enough distraction to keep Weisser's attention on her body rather than on her face.

Wren didn't think that would be much of a problem.

"Almost there," Shane said from the driver's seat. "Are you two ready?"

"Ready as I'll ever be," Wren said as she adjusted her dark wig then wiped her damp palms on her black linen skirt. She patted her satchel. In a follow-up phone call, Weisser told her to deliver one-point-five million dollars in bearer bonds—untraceable and way more portable than stacks of hundreds. After that, she was to come up with an excuse to leave "Barbie" alone with him for the rest of the night.

Of course that's not what's going to happen.

"I'm sorry you have to wear those shoes again." Gina nodded her chin at the toe-murdering stilettos.

"I'm the one who has to record him taking the bribe." Wren shrugged, trying to make the gesture look nonchalant, as if she dressed up and played super spy once a day and twice on Sundays. "You're not supposed to know I'm cheating you out of millions, Barbie."

"I'll try and give you the opportunity to be alone with him as quickly as I can without looking suspicious." She tapped her ear, where a tiny comm hid. Wren wore one as well, as did the rest of the team tonight. "I'll be able to hear every word. If there is the smallest hint that things are about to go sideways, I'll be right there, even ahead of the police."

Elias growled from behind her, then laid his hand on Wren's shoulder. She tried to entwine her fingers with his, but he covered her hand with his instead and squeezed. He ran his finger over the band of her engagement ring. She still couldn't get over the craftsmanship. Her ring was similar to Ellie's and Rochelle's rings—Ben had made theirs as well as Gabe and Bear's wedding bands. Only instead of mountains like Rochelle's or stars like Ellie's, Ben had covered her ring with flames, symbolizing the fire that had brought Elias into her life.

And one carefully carved scrubs top.

"I'll be all right," she told him.

"Any sign that you're in trouble, I don't care. I'm charging in."

"Elias," Wren warned. "You can't do that ahead of the police. It breaks every protocol and this will be for nothing." She looked at Gina for support but it was Lachlan who spoke instead.

"Can't tell you how many times I've been in this position, hoping Gina comes back to me unharmed. This sting is nothing compared to what she and I have faced before. Does that make it easier to watch her walk up Weisser's driveway and into a situation that I can't control? Of course not. But every mission I've seen her on was one meant to save lives. Tonight is no different. I have to stand ready to protect her, but also stand back and let her work for the greater good. She's had to do the same with me."

"It's not the same," Elias argued. "We're military and Gina is also a professional. Wren is not."

"But I'm surrounded by amazing people, Elias. I trust Gina. I trust Shane and Lachlan and Charlie. And I trust you the most. I'll be safe. I've got this, baby. *We've* got this. I can't live with myself if someone loses their home because I sat on the sidelines. You know that."

He took a deep breath and blew it out, hard. "I know." He squeezed her hand again. "Just come back to me safe."

"We're here." Shane turned up a long driveway and parked in front of a particularly ostentatious house. Charlie got out first to open "Barbie's" door.

"Ready?" Gina asked Wren. She had already shifted into the voice she'd use for the night. Not only did she look like Barbie, but she sounded like her right after a bad coughing fit, or recovering from a cold. The rasp was meant to work just like the lightly tinted glasses and obscure what little bit Gina couldn't mimic perfectly.

"I'm ready," Wren answered. "Let's go nail the bastard's balls to the wall."

"Proud of you, baby. Love you," Elias said as he gave her hand one last squeeze before letting go.

"Love you." Then she was out of the car and meeting Gina around the front. Charlie escorted them up the driveway toward the huge wooden double-doors under a portico.

"Scrubs, Soup. Acknowledge, over," she heard Lachlan "Soup" Campbell call her by her brand new nickname over the comm.

"Scrubs, Roger, Soup," she breathed, knowing she'd botched the prowords. *Fuck it.* "I hear you loud and clear, over."

"Acknowledged, over."

She listened to everyone else verifying that their comms worked as she walked beside Gina and Charlie up to the front doors.

Before Wren could ring the bell, one of the doors opened and Weisser popped out like a demented Jack-in-the-box. One doused in heavy cologne.

This is it. Either he'll fall for Gina's disguise or we're DOA.

Wren held her breath as Weisser's gaze skipped over her like a rock skipping over a pond and landed squarely on Gina. He gave her body the same quick appraisal he'd given Wren when she'd first walked into his office.

Come on. It's Barbie, it's Barbie, it's Barbie, you gullible ass.

Then he smiled so broadly every single one of his teeth went on display as he laughed through them. His lips, his mouth, didn't move, and his laughter was a staccato series of *ha-ha-ha-ha-ha's.*

Asshole's got a laugh like the world's creepiest uncle.

"Ladies! Lovely, lovely. Welcome. Come inside. The bottle of Cristal champagne is at the perfect temperature."

Wow. Feels like he hired us for the night. Oh, wait, he did hire Barbie for the night.

Weisser frowned at Charlie, then looked past her at the SUV still sitting in his driveway. He shot Wren a murderous look and she could practically read his thoughts—*I said, bring Barbie Gillis alone.*

Gina touched his arm, immediately reclaiming his full attention. "Oh, don't worry about them, Don," she said in her raspy-Barbie voice. "Charlie, I told you, in *this* neighborhood, we'll be fine. Honestly. Just go wait in the car with the driver, please."

Charlie nodded. "Yes, ma'am." She turned without another word and walked back to the SUV.

Gina smirked. "There. They know I might bring them a doggie bag if they behave."

"Ha-ha-ha-ha-ha-ha-ha!"

Gah! Abort mission! His laugh is killing me!

Unless his cologne gets me first. Gag. Just under the cologne, she could smell the bourbon on Weisser's breath. She hoped he'd had two big belts of it right before they showed up. That would help.

Wren stepped inside first, followed by Gina, Weisser's hand gripping her upper arm.

"What's wrong with your voice?" he asked, stopping Wren's heart in the process.

Gina cleared her throat but continued the rasp. "Oh, you know. I pick up some sort of airport crud every time I travel. I'm *fine* though, Donny! Can I call you Donny? I can't wait for that champagne."

"I know just what you mean." Weisser closed the door, cutting Wren and Gina off from the rest of the team. Wren's heartbeat, already clipping along at a fast pace, decided it was competing in a sprint.

"Follow me, ladies. It's a beautiful night, so I thought we'd sit out on the back patio."

Weisser looked to be a trophy hunter, judging by the inordinate number of antlered elks, bucks, and big game heads mounted on the great room's walls and the—*yikes!*—lion-skin rug in front of the fireplace. Wren recalled her comment to Elias the day before.

I wonder where he's hiding all the dead baby ducks he killed to spend the evening with Barbie.

The aroma of meat cooking on a grill wafted in through the open doors leading out to the backyard.

Oh, maybe that's what's for dinner.

"What a beautiful home!" Gina gushed. "Who is your decorator?"

"Just me, ha-ha-ha-ha-ha!"

Seriously. It's like being strafed every time he laughs.

The intimidating man sitting in his high tower lording over his hospital had been reduced to an awkward teenaged boy in front of his crush.

We've got this Wren told herself. *So you can quit with the sprints anytime now, heart.*

They stepped out onto a wide patio overlooking a yard manicured to within an inch of its life. His patio furniture looked like it belonged inside. And Wren was mistaken—it wasn't a backyard grill she smelled but a full-on outdoor kitchen.

"Here we are. Make yourself comfortable. Barbie, why don't you sit on the loveseat?" Weisser made a beeline for a bucket full of ice holding the bottle of Cristal upside-down, like it was mooning everyone.

Gina shot Wren a look that said *Are you all right?*

She gave her a quick thumbs up right before Weisser turned back around, the bottle in his left hand.

In his right, he held a saber.

Oh, Mother of Mercy, you're kidding me.

"Stand back," he said, despite the fact that Gina was sitting on the loveseat as requested and Wren was in an armchair.

"Oooo!" Gina clapped her hands and bounced—something that the real Barbie would never actually do if faced with this spectacle—but it kept old Donny fired up and distracted.

Which was a good thing because Lachlan's voice came over the comm just then.

"Soup, Spooky, over."

Weisser was looking straight at Gina.

She hunched her shoulders, tucked her chin, put her palms together like she was praying and lifted them until they blocked most of her wide, excited smile.

"Go ahead, over." Wren heard Gina's voice whisper over the comm. The visible corners of her lips never wavered from that smile.

"Police are in place on standby, over."

"Acknowledged, over."

Okay. I've got to get him alone, ASAP.

Weisser brandished his saber and readied the champagne bottle for its dramatic uncorking.

Here we go. Champagne and broken glass everywhere, in—

"Three, two, one!" Weisser shouted, then swept the blade down the bottle and *Pop!*

Wow. He actually did it.

Weisser set the saber aside, thank God, and quickly poured the foaming champagne into two flute glasses waiting beside the bucket. He picked the flutes up and carried them over to Gina. Weisser handed her one, then sat down next to her and clinked his glass against hers and drank.

"I guess none for me."

"Oh." Weisser acknowledged Wren for the first time since the front door.

"It's all right, I'm doing a dry summer anyway." Wren patted the satchel full of fake bearer bonds. "Actually, if I could use your restroom?" She grimaced. "I'm not feeling well all of a sudden."

"Oh dear," Gina said. "I hope you haven't caught my cold."

"Maybe that's it." She patted the satchel again, hoping Weisser would catch her drift.

"I'll show you to the restroom, otherwise you might get lost." Weisser set his champagne aside. He grabbed Gina's hand and kissed the back of it. "Be right back, my dear. Drink up, drink up! We're celebrating here."

"Oh, I will." She lifted her untouched champagne glass and took a big sip. "Mmm," she said through a closed-lip smile.

Satisfied, Weisser stood up, as did Wren, clutching the satchel's handle.

"After you," she said. As she followed Weisser inside, she glanced back and saw Gina spitting the champagne back into her glass as she stood up, preparing to follow them in at a discreet distance.

Then she listened as Gina told the team to prepare because Scrubs was about to deliver the goods.

Weisser didn't lead Wren to the bathroom but to his office instead. He closed the door and Wren's heart beat triple-time as claustrophobia kicked in. One more barrier between her and help. Then there was Weisser standing between her and the door. His face was bright red with fury.

She heard Gina update the team, telling them which room Weisser had taken her to.

They have a set of this godawful house's blueprints and know right where I am. To calm herself further, Wren pictured Gina silently hurrying down the hall and stationing herself right outside the door. Wren walked backward until her butt hit his desk.

Weisser lunged forward, grabbed two handfuls of her silk blouse, and pulled it up. His eyes roamed her body. Thank God she and Gina had rehearsed this possibility.

"What are you doing?" she shrieked as she whacked his side with the satchel. She listened to Lachlan alert the team over her comm. The police were surrounding the house, getting ready.

He let go of the blouse and shushed her. "Looking for a wire."

"Yeah, right. I'm recording us right now just so you know, because I really want to go to jail. Asshole." Her voice dripped with sarcasm as she mentally did a victory dance.

Now it's on the record that I told him he's being recorded.

Weisser just glared. "I thought I told you to bring her *alone*, Brooke."

"Without her security team? Oh, yeah, right. That wouldn't look suspicious at all. She always keeps them outside anyway."

"Fine. But here's how it's going to go. You're going to tell Barbie you aren't feeling well and need to leave and then you're going outside and getting rid of her security team. I don't care how you do it, just get them out of here." He looked at her satchel. "The money's in your bag, correct?"

"Yes."

He grabbed it and dumped the bound stacks of fake bearer bonds onto the desk. "This doesn't look like all of it."

"It's not. It's only a down payment." Wren moved until Weisser was no longer between her and the door as she listened to the team coordinate with the police. Then she tuned it out to focus on her job.

"That wasn't the agreement," he snarled.

"Neither was feeling me up for a wire. You think I'm going to give you everything you want without a guarantee that you're going to let me in on the deal you made with the lenders?" She folded her arms. "Actually, I want more. I want six percent of every loan."

He gawked at her. "Are you fucking crazy? That's a percentage point over what they're giving me."

"You're getting five percent from every single loan you direct to them when all you did was put a link to their company on Milestone's website." Then she went straight for his oversized ego. "An untrained monkey could have done that."

His eyes grew big as saucers as his face turned white, mottled with red blotches.

"Bitch, you think that's all I did? I did way more than *put up a link on the website*," he said, mocking her voice. "This was my brainchild." He ticked off on his fingers. "I gave them the idea. I structured the payment plan to make sure patients would miss payments and accrue interest." His chest puffed up. "I helped a goddamned *senator* draft those bills. I set the whole thing up. Now get me the rest of my money or..."

"Or what?"

He gave her a feral smile. "Or I tell Barbie what you're doing."

Oh my God, this guy's insane.

"Tell Barbie what exactly?"

"That you're taking money out of her donation to bribe me."

"She won't believe you."

Weisser gestured at the stacks of bearer bonds. "She will when I show her the goddamned bribe sitting right here on my desk."

This is it. Please.

"A bribe that you don't seem to want to take. I want six percent," Wren said coolly, despite the fear sweat dripping down her back.

Weisser snorted. He picked up one of the stacks and brandished it at her. "Oh, I will take *this* money, and then I will take the rest of it from you, and you will get nothing."

"Soup, now, over." she said calmly. Then she stepped out of the stilettos.

"What's now over?" Weisser asked. "Besides you?"

"Scrubs, Lion, hit the floor and roll to the wall, over!"

Wren dropped like a stone and rolled.

Weisser's look of triumph turned to confusion.

"What are you—"

The door burst open. Uniformed officers flooded the room, guns drawn.

"Police! Step away from her! Hands where I can see them!"

Wren watched as Weisser froze. The stack of worthless paper slipped from his fingers as his face drained of color. An officer grabbed him and turned him around to handcuff him.

Then Elias was there, sweeping her up and carrying her out the office and into the hall where she caught a glimpse of Gina standing right outside the door, where she'd had Wren's back the whole time. Elias sprinted as he carried her down the hall, through the great room, and back out into fresh air as the police took over. He didn't set her back on her feet until they were at the Watchdog SUV, now parked down the street and out of the way.

Elias cupped her face in his hands, his eyes searching for any injuries.

"I'm fine, Lion. I'm not hurt. I'm okay. You kept me safe."

He shook his head, dismissing his part. "My God, baby. That was fucking brilliant in there."

"Told you she was a natural." Gina, looking like Gina now that she'd removed the prosthetics, seemed to appear out of nowhere.

Must be why they call her Spooky.

"And great teamwork, Lion. Pleasure working with you." She looked around until she spotted Lachlan, then left them to themselves.

Elias didn't hesitate to take advantage of the situation. He cupped her face again, and proceeded to kiss her down to her soul.

TWENTY-ONE

Two months later

ELIAS WATCHED as April's son, Kevin dashed around like a mini-tornado, weaving through a sea of adults gathered at Gina and Lachlan's housewarming party. Poor April was run ragged chasing after him, tossing out apology after apology as guests lifted their drinks and dodged out of the way. No one was upset about it—Kevin was a cute kid, just rambunctious—but that didn't seem to matter to April, judging by the mortified expression on her face.

"Kevin, stop running!" she pleaded.

"I'm looking for Shane so we can play with the dogs!" he yelled back as he whizzed past Gina.

"Hold this for me, please." Wren handed him her virgin Bloody Mary. She was working with Chase later so she wasn't drinking. Another house through the trees a few acres away was about to go on the market and Chase was the sellers' agent. He'd become the neighborhood's unofficial Realtor after Gina and Lach paid cash for the house near Bear and Ellie's place.

Wren cupped her hands around her mouth. "Hey, Kevin!" she shouted. "Come here, I want to show you something."

Kevin barely acknowledged her.

"I guess you don't want to see my drone."

He skidded to a stop and whipped around, then charged straight at her.

"Incoming." Elias quickly set the drinks aside and caught Kevin right before he barreled into Wren, sweeping him up in an arc over his head while making airplane sounds. Kevin stuck his arms out to the side, laughing as he 'flew' through the air.

I want a son. Or a daughter. I want kids. The thought had been popping up so often lately that it didn't freak him out anymore. Now he just needed to bring it up with Wren and see where she was at.

Elias set Kevin down, but before letting go of him, he said, "Okay, if you want to see the drone, you have to sit crisscross applesauce on the grass."

"As soon as you're sitting I'll run to my car and get the drone," Wren added. "But you have to still be sitting when I get back. Think you can do that?"

Kevin nodded like a bobblehead.

"Okay, start counting and see how fast I can go." Wren crouched like she was on the starting line. "And...go!" She took off sprinting and Kevin started counting. In the meantime, April jogged over.

"You and Wren don't have to watch my kid," she told Elias.

"No, it's no problem. Go grab a drink or a burger. We've got him."

Wren came running back, carrying the drone case.

"Are you really going to show him that?" April asked her.

"Yup, I said I would."

April dropped down beside Kevin. "I'll just—"

"No." Wren waved April off. "Go take a break. Enjoy some adult time. We've got him."

April looked close to panicking. "All right, Kevin, you listen to every word Wren says. Do *not* touch the drone. Do *not* touch the landing pad. Don't touch anything. As a matter of fact, sit on your hands."

"April, it's okay, I promise," Wren said gently as she set the case on the ground and sat cross-legged. "He won't break anything, and my drone's insured anyway. Besides, it's really pretty tough."

"Mom," Kevin said. "I won't break it. Promise."

"See? You have his word. He won't break it." Wren pointed toward a table across the yard where a bunch of their friends were talking and drinking wine. "Now, take a break and go have some fun for once."

"Okay, fine." April stood up. "But your next five lattes are on me."

"Just vamoose." Smiling, she waved April off.

"Vamoose, Mom!" Kevin laughed and threw his head back like a howling wolf. "Vamooooose!"

April put her hands on top of her head, fingers spread across her scalp as she walked away. "You've been warned."

"All right, Kev." Wren opened the drone case. She took out a controller and popped her phone into it. "This is how we control the drone. We can see what the drone sees with this app right here on my phone, see?"

Wren took the launch pad out and spread it on the ground. Then she picked up the drone and unfolded it. She pointed out all the parts one by one and what they did.

Elias watched her sitting cross-legged on the grass, talking to Kevin like he was a little adult. The boy hung every word.

She's so good with kids. He smiled and took another sip.

Doesn't automatically mean she wants them though. He frowned.

Over the past two months as he'd gotten to know her better, the more he learned, the harder he fell in love. But the one thing they hadn't discussed was starting a family. It never seemed to come up in conversation.

"And this is my favorite part on the whole entire drone," Wren said. "The camera."

Kevin had sat spellbound and silent the entire time she spoke. A miracle.

"What makes the drone go?" he asked.

"It's got a battery. See, here's an extra one." She took a battery out of the case and handed it to him. He turned it carefully in his hands and Wren grinned.

"What happens if the battery dies when it's way up in the air? Does it crash?"

"Nope. But that's a great question." She picked up her controller and tapped her phone screen. "See these numbers here? These are called coordinates. That tells the drone where it is and where it needs to go. Every little spot on earth has coordinates. Let's see where we are right now." She did something with her controller. "There. Those are our coordinates." She pointed at the screen.

"So to answer your question, I can program in emergency coordinates, and if for some reason the drone loses touch with the controller and the battery is close to dying, the drone knows to stop what it's doing and fly right to this spot where it can make a safe landing, and I know right where it is so I don't lose it. Here, I'll show you."

Kevin's eyes lit up. He squirmed, but he stayed sitting, as promised.

Instead of standing, Wren kept sitting next to him as she readied the drone. She set it on the launch pad, worked the controller, and it lifted thirty feet straight up, catching everyone's attention. Wren circled it around the house.

"Now, pretend the battery's about to die," she told Kevin. "It would do this, but without me doing anything." She tapped the screen, then set her phone aside. The drone stopped circling and started beeping as it changed direction and headed straight for the landing pad.

Wren held up her hands. "Look, no hands." Kevin laughed.

The drone made a perfect landing and everyone clapped, Kevin loudest of all. Wren stood and took a bow.

"Kevin," April called. "Tell Wren thank you and come get a burger."

"Thank you!" He jumped up and *zoom*. Off he went like a hummingbird.

"Thank you," April shouted to Wren. She looked much more relaxed.

Wren picked her controller up and looked at her phone.

"Whoops. I lost track of time. I've got to hurry if I don't want to be late for the shoot. At least it's close by." She stooped and picked up her drone, then packed everything up.

"Let me carry the case for you, Scrubs," Elias said. She gave him a big smile every time he used her new nickname, so he used it often.

"I will let you do that, Lion, over. Did I do it right this time?"

"Close enough for guv'ment work," he joked as he picked up her case.

They headed for her car. They'd driven up separately so that she could go to work, then come back to the party when she was done.

"Chase will probably stop by too when we're done. At least I'm going to try and talk him into it," Wren said. "Oh, and I have his wedding invitation on the dash since I knew I'd see him anyway." She looked back over her shoulder at the party. "Don't know why I bothered buying and sending wedding invitations when pretty much everyone we invited is here. I could have just stood on a chair and made a general announcement."

She pretended to yell, "Hey, everybody, wedding in two weeks. Ellie and Bear's place because they insisted it's *the* wedding spot. Be there or be square." She shook her head. "We could have saved a bundle if I'd only sent them out to my old colleagues, a couple college friends, all the parents and step-parents. Barbie already knows because duh, she's my maid of honor. And, let's see." She pursed her lips and looked up at the sky, thinking. "Yup, that's everybody."

"Oh, don't give me that," Elias teased. "You loved hand-addressing every single envelope." They reached her car. "Besides," he set the case down and took her in his arms, "you only get to do it once."

She gave him her warmest smile. "Very true. By the way, do you know what today is?"

"Well, let's see." He pretended to think about it. "I believe that on this day three months ago, I was... What was I doing?"

"Keep thinking. It'll come to you."

"Oh, right. I was de-quilling a porcupine."

"Yeah, something like that."

"A mostly naked porcupine, if I recall."

She rolled her eyes. "You're still a pervert."

"Happy anniversary." Elias tangled his hands in her hair and kissed her lips. He kissed the sensitive spot on her neck below her ear.

Sweet peaches and salt.

He pressed his forehead against hers. "Hurry back, Scrubs."

"Why? So we can leave early and celebrate our anniversary alone?"

"You read my mind."

"I love the way you think."

"I love *you.*"

She kissed him one more time and got in the car while he stowed her drone in the trunk. He closed the trunk, banged on the top twice, and waved as she drove away.

———

"YOU LOOK GOOD, BROTHER," Waylon told Elias back at the party.

"I feel good, brother." They clinked beer bottles and drank. "You buy that tux yet? Wedding's only two weeks away."

"Still hoping Scrubs is gonna steal one for me."

Elias smirked. "She's out of that game, so I guess my best man's gonna show up in his underwear."

"Naw, you're in luck. I'm renting the same damn tux I wore to the last wedding."

"Telling you. If you buy it, you'll save money." Elias nodded at the scene across the lawn. A pack of dogs made up of pets—including a very happy Chuck and Penny—and working dogs from Watchdog, were taking turns doing tricks for Shane while guests clapped and cheered then returned to their conversations.

No surprise, the most enthusiastic audience member was Kevin.

Shane gestured to the kid, who came tearing up to him. Shane crouched down, told Kevin something while he pointed at the dogs, then handed him a dog treat.

Kevin shouted, "Peetie," and Shane's working dog broke from the pack and trotted up to Kevin. The boy told him to sit, then he balanced the treat on Pete's nose. He shouted another command, and Pete flipped the treat high into the air and caught it in his mouth.

Kevin lost it. He clapped and shouted and jumped up and down while Shane practically glowed with pride, watching the boy. Then he turned in time to see April walking up to him.

"See?" Elias said. "There's your next wedding."

Watching April, Shane glowed brighter.

Until April walked right past him to Kevin.

"We need to go now," she said flatly.

"Mom, no! I was just getting started."

"*Now*, Kevin."

He stamped his foot. "No!" Tears ran down his cheeks.

Guests murmured then pretended nothing was happening.

"Kevin, listen to your mom, buddy," Shane said, dropping down to the boy's level. "I can teach you more tricks at the wedding reception, but not unless you do what she says, and do it with respect. Not because I'm trying to punish you. But because good dog trainers know how to control themselves first, or no dog will ever listen to them."

Kevin wiped his arm across his face and sniffled. He looked from Shane to April as he gave Pete a scratch behind the ears.

"Okay," he said. He turned and gave Pete a kiss on the head. "Ready."

"Then go to the car, please," April said calmly.

Kevin ran toward the line of cars parked along the quiet road. It looked to Elias like their ride was parked damn near halfway to the house where Wren was.

Shane straightened. "April," he began.

"*Goodbye*, Shane." She stormed off after her son, leaving Shane to watch her retreating figure.

Waylon looked at Elias. "You were saying something about buying a tux?"

Elias shook his head. "Okay, maybe not the *next* wedding. Give it time, that's all I'm sayin'."

They sipped their beers.

"I listened to Kyla Lewis Dean interview Wren about medical bills and bankruptcy on that *Up She Rises* podcast," Waylon said. "Saw her photo essay that went along with the story, too. Man, she's got talent. Those photos." Waylon shook his head. "Heartbreaking."

"The good part though, is that the lenders are now under investigation, too. Those people are gonna get their money back, one way or another."

"Are Gina's friends one of those ways?" Waylon asked.

Elias nodded. "Sure are."

Waylon paused, then said, "Wren looked happy today."

"Yup."

"She doing all right?"

"Yeah. She's distracting herself from the trial with the wedding plans."

"Think she's gonna have to testify against Weisser in person next week?"

Elias shook his head. "They're still saying she doesn't, that her written statement's good enough. They aren't even releasing her real name. And she recorded the whole confession anyway."

Waylon raised his eyebrows. "It's admissible?"

Elias chuckled. "The one in his home office for sure. She told Weisser he was being recorded and he didn't get it. We'll see about the first meeting they had at Milestone. Plenty of evidence to convict him though, just from that second meeting. She left the recordings at the crime scene for the police to pick up, so the chain of custody's preserved."

Plus, she never did like those damn shoes.

"They're trying to get him for attempted rape, too. Gina saw him slip something into her glass as he was pouring the champagne. It tested positive for one of those fucking date rape drugs."

"Fucking hell. So maybe justice will be served, for once," Waylon said.

Elias didn't say anything, just took another swig of beer. It looked bad for Weisser, who was shouting from the rooftops about how he was framed. Nobody was buying that. He was looking at significant prison time.

Then again, Elias had seen bad men walk free too many times to have unshakable faith that Weisser would be convicted. The son of a bitch *might* see time, but then again, he had the money to hire an expensive lawyer who was doing everything imaginable to twist the law. The lawyer managed to convince the court that Weisser was not a flight risk or a danger to anyone, so he was under house arrest instead of rotting in a cell.

As for Senator Robbins, Gina's friends told her what was going down and she passed the news along to Elias and Wren.

Robbins got a better deal than Weisser—withdraw his support from the proposed bills and table them, pretending to be shocked and appalled at how they could be abused, or be exposed and face charges for accepting numerous bribes, among other things.

Guess who tabled the bills?

"Only one of the many reasons why I'm happy to be *mostly* retired," Gina had commented. "Too many politicians get off scot-free."

Kevin's shouts coming from the direction of the parked cars took

Elias out of his thoughts. They turned to see the boy running full tilt back toward the party, a huge smile on his face. His red-faced mother was trying to catch up to him.

"Oh Lord. Poor April," Waylon said.

"It's Wren's drone! I saw it! I saw it!"

Elias grinned as he shook his head. "Kid's as crazy about that thing as he is about dogs, man."

"It's coming this way!"

Elias frowned. "You mean it's circling, right?" He twirled his finger. "Overhead?"

"Nuh-uh!" Kevin skidded to a halt on the grass where Wren had demonstrated flying the drone less than an hour before. He bent over, hands braced just above his knees, trying to catch his breath. "It's going straight. It's gonna land here. I wanna see it."

This isn't right. He pulled out his phone to call Wren.

Waylon caught his brother's unease. "What's happening? Why'd she send it back here?"

Elias held up a finger as her phone rang.

"Hello!"

"Wren, what's—"

"Thanks for calling Wren Stapleton Photography. I'm busy on a shoot right now but if you'll leave your name and number I'll get right back to you. Have a picture-perfect day!"

It doesn't mean anything. She always sends calls straight to voice-mail when she's working.

His fingers flew as he texted her to call or text him back ASAP.

He heard the drone before he saw it. Elias scanned the sky in the direction of the other house and spotted a little black dot growing bigger.

"Elias, what is it?"

"Kevin's right. It's coming in for a landing here. Just like it's supposed to if the battery runs low and the pilot doesn't bring it in, which Wren would do. Or if it loses contact with the controller."

He looked at Waylon. "Code six, brother."

"Fuck. I'll get the others. Go! Go!" Waylon pulled out his phone as he started toward the back patio and the majority of the guests.

Elias ran toward his truck. He passed Kevin, then April as she caught up. He thought she called his name.

But all he could think was how as kids he and his brothers had come up with their own secret codes, ones that they still used to this day.

Code six. Eminent danger. Come at once.

TWENTY-TWO

Elias reached his truck. He nearly tore the door off its hinges, jumped in, shoved the key in the ignition, and flew down the tree-lined road.

"Fuck-fuck-fuck. Please, Wren. Please let this be a stupid misunderstanding. Please call me and say your stupid controller isn't working and did the drone land all right? Please, Wren, be there. Be okay."

Up ahead, he saw her car and Chase's parked along the road to his left, directly across from the house. He pulled off to the side of the road while still out of view of the house and killed the engine. He checked his phone. No call, no text.

There's a good explanation.

He checked the timestamp. Five minutes since he'd tried to call her.

You're going to embarrass her in front of Chase.

He put his phone on silent.

Look at my overprotective fiancé, she'll say.

Elias grabbed his gun and its shoulder holster from under the seat.

"She'll just have to deal with having an overprotective fiancé."

Elias put the shoulder holster on. He grabbed his flannel shirt off the seat beside him and put it on over his tee, concealing the gun. He slipped quietly out of the truck and dashed into the trees to the right. Under forest cover, he quickly and silently approached the house until it came into view. He stopped just inside the trees lining the manicured yard, about thirty feet from the end of the driveway. No movement, no voices, no obvious sign of a break-in. No drone case in the front yard, though she'd told him she usually flew them from the back.

Keeping just inside the protection of the trees, Elias ran around the near side of the house to the back yard where Wren would normally be—

Will be. She will be there. She is there.

—and stopped. A lush lawn stretched green and empty to the edges of the forest surrounding the house.

No Wren.

No Chase.

Seven minutes since he'd called.

The drone case lay at the edge of the lawn beside the round red launch pad, opposite Elias' position. He spotted something small resting on the grass about two feet away from the case.

The drone controller with Wren's phone still attached.

Fuck.

Nine minutes.

Who has her?

The possibilities flashed lightning-fast through his mind.

Weisser?

No. He was under house arrest with an ankle bracelet, so he wasn't going anywhere without the police tracing his ass and catching him real quick.

He could have hired someone.

No. How would he even know who Wren was? He only knew Brooke Greene, who worked for Barbie Gillis, had black hair, dark brown eyes, and stood three inches taller than his chestnut-haired, hazel-eyed Wren.

Senator Robbins?

No. This wasn't even a slap on the wrist, though he was losing plenty of money. And again, he didn't know Wren, had never even met her as Brooke.

Someone from the lenders?

No. They knew even less about Wren's involvement than Weisser. She had no other enemies.

Could it be...

Chase?

Did he secretly want her? Was he obsessed enough to kidnap her before she could marry another man?

Elias checked his texts and watched three dots bounce. A new group text from Ben appeared.

> At your truck. SITREP.

Elias responded:

> Backyard. Scrubs gone. Check roads.

He watched the three dots.

> T-Wolf and Bear checking roads.

A moment later, Elias watched Bear's truck drive past the house.

> Hold position. Coming in behind you.

It killed him to wait even a moment but Ben was right—he'd be stupid to go in alone, crossing the lawn, fully exposed. He wouldn't be a damn bit of good to Wren with a bullet in his head.

Elias tried to calculate how much time could have passed since Wren disappeared. She was in a hurry to return to the party, so she wouldn't dally, didn't even program in a new emergency flight path.

Thank God, or I'd still be at the party shooting the shit with Waylon while my woman—

Stop that thought right there.

He estimated that it took her fifteen minutes to arrive at the house, say hi to Chase, and set up the drone. Its fly time was thirty minutes max before the battery died and it dropped out of the sky like a brick. The drone had started its emergency flight path when it still had enough juice to get to its pre-set landing at Gina and Lach's place. Considering its speed, the drone had been aloft for twenty to twenty-five minutes total. Kevin spotted the drone—

He checked the time.

Ten minutes ago.

If someone grabbed her right after she launched the drone, she'd been gone roughly twenty-five minutes. If the drone was coming back in from its flight and running on fumes when she was taken, then that happened ten to twelve minutes ago.

She could be twenty-five minutes away by car. Or, she could be only ten minutes away. Roads were few and traffic non-existent up here in the sticks. God-willing, Bear or Gabe would find and follow any car they found on the road, and she'd be in it.

Elias had been within sight of the road the entire time Wren was gone. He didn't recall seeing a strange car pass Gina and Lach's place.

They could have driven the other direction, in which case he wished Bear godspeed. T-Wolf would have gone the opposite direction to search.

He typed quickly:

> T-wolf they didn't go your direction. Circle back. Bear look out.

The other possibilities? Wren was still in the house.

Contained. Good.

Or anywhere in the woods.

Not good.

Ben, Waylon, and Shane appeared like shadows at his side. A fourth, shorter shape accompanied them. A Malinois, one of Watchdog's retired military working dogs no doubt.

Twelve minutes since the phone call.

Ben used hand signals. *House first.* He pointed to himself, then Elias, then the back door. Shane signaled the dog to heel as he and Waylon followed the tree line toward the front of the house.

Weapons drawn, Ben and Elias started across the open space between the trees and the back patio, crouching as they moved. They were exposed, but at least they were in the shadow of the house.

So help me, if Chase has her inside, if he's hurting her—

The back door opened. Ben and Elias froze.

Chase stepped out and walked to the edge of the patio. Looking to the left toward the drone case, he stopped.

"Wren?" He lifted his hand to shade his eyes from the late-afternoon sun stretching across the lawn. "Where'd you go? I'm done inside," he called. "Did she go to her car?" he added as he scanned the yard. "Wren?"

Ben and Elias shared a look. By now, Shane and the dog would be at the front door, waiting for the message from Ben to breach the house. They holstered their guns and stood up straight. Ben took out his phone and texted Shane. They approached Chase.

When he looked in their direction and saw them he startled, then relaxed as he recognized Elias. Chase frowned.

"Whoa, not cool. You guys can't be here on the property like this. Wait, is Wren with you?"

"No," Elias said. "When did you last see her?"

"Why? What's going on?" His eyes darted from Elias to Ben. "Who are you?"

"Just answer the question."

"I don't know, maybe half an hour ago?"

"Half a fucking hour she's been gone maybe. And we're fucking around here." Elias could barely keep his anger in check, dealing with this fool.

"Elias, calm." Elias' shoulder nearly disappeared underneath Ben's huge hand.

"What's wrong? Is she all right? Guys, I'm sorry, I was inside for—"

Chase jumped when Waylon, Shane, and the Malinois stepped outside from the back door.

"Clear," Shane told Ben. "She's not in there. No one is." He looked at the dog. "Willow, alert."

"What are you doing?" Chase shouted "You can't just walk through someone's house like that. I'm responsible—"

"Wren's drone followed an emergency flight path to Gina and Lach's," Ben told him. "We came to investigate and she's gone."

"And we're wasting *time*." Elias reset his mental timer to Chase's last confirmed sighting. "You last saw her half an hour ago and she disappeared sometime after that, and we're surrounded by forest."

"Shit," Chase said. "What can I do to help?"

"Did you hear or see an unfamiliar car drive by or stop in the past half hour?" Ben asked.

Chase shook his head and spoke quickly. "No. I was in the garage with the door down but I still would have heard. The owners are in Virginia and they texted asking me to change the battery on the garage door sensor because it wasn't responding. I told Wren to come in when she was done with the drone shoot. Took me forever to find the extra batteries, then I was in the garage fixing the damn sensor. I didn't hear any cars go by while I was in the house or the garage."

"You positive?" Elias asked.

Chase looked at Elias. "Yeah, there's no traffic up here so I would have noticed."

Elias exchanged looks with Ben and Shane. "The forest."

"Is there a security system with cameras facing the back yard?" Ben asked Chase.

"Yeah, but that camera needs batteries, too."

Fuck.

There weren't any other houses close enough to capture anything on camera, either.

Except...

"Cover me." Elias didn't wait. He bolted across the lawn to the controller. He did a quick scan of the ground surrounding it. No trampled grass indicating a struggle, only two oblong-shaped spots next to the case and launch pad where the short, springy grass was still bent.

The size of Wren's feet. That's where she stood while she worked the drone. It looks like she was standing there a while.

Elias updated the timer in his head. Judging by the impressions in the grass, Wren wasn't taken near the beginning of the drone flight but toward the end. Maybe as little as fifteen minutes ago.

Nothing else caught his eye. No torn-up spots indicating a fight. No other impressions.

No lines from dragging her body.

Stop. You don't know what happened.

He picked up the controller and looked around. If anyone had a gun, he was fully exposed.

He turned to see his brothers with their weapons drawn, covering him. Ben looked particularly furious.

At me. He'd understand if he had a woman. The uncharitable thought rose unwelcome in his mind.

"Get back here before you get your ass shot," Ben shouted.

Yeah, by friendly fire.

Elias ran back to his brothers and one horrified-looking Realtor.

"What the fuck, Lion? You're not gonna be any good to Wren with a damn bullet in your head."

"Sixteen minutes she's been gone. Maybe a little more. She's near, but she's in the woods. Might as well be a needle in a haystack." He glanced at the dog. "She a tracker?"

"Damn straight, Willow's the best. Give her the controller to get Wren's scent."

"Hang on." Elias tapped the screen on Wren's phone. "We can give Willow—and us—a starting point if I can open her phone." He was shit out of luck if it was bio-locked and needed her fingerprint.

It was only password-protected.

Thank God. Wren had a chance if he could guess the numerical password.

"We don't have a camera on the house, but we might have something else," Elias told them.

"With any luck, the drone filmed the kidnapping."

Ben nodded, then turned to Chase.

"If your help's at an end, you might want to head on home right about now. Maybe even drop this listing."

Chase turned white as a sheet. He looked at Elias and his brothers. Their weapons. The determined looks on their faces.

"I never saw a thing." He turned to go into the house then stopped.

"She's a good person and that's rare anymore. When you find her, tell her I still have work for her."

He left without looking back or saying another word.

TWENTY-THREE

Wren had just sent her drone into the air when Chase's phone buzzed. He looked at the screen.

"Hey, that's the owner texting."

"Is there a problem?" She watched the live footage from her drone on her phone.

"Only a small one. One of their sensors in the garage is out." He finished texting a message back and looked up. "This might take some time. They don't remember where the spare batteries are."

"Oh, shoot."

"Tell you what. I know you want to get back to Gina and Lach's party and I don't want to keep you, so how about you keep going with the drone and I'll go battery hunting, and then if you get done before I do, come on in and you can get started on the interior shots."

Wren looked up from the screen. "Sounds good. Good luck finding the batteries."

"Thanks, I'll need it." Chase jogged across the lawn.

"And then we can both go to the party," Wren called after him.

"Yeah, yeah, I'll think about it."

"You need time off. A little fun."

"Selling houses is fun. Just ask my bank account." Chase reached the patio.

"You *are* coming to my wedding though."

"Of course. If I don't accidentally lose the invitation." He opened the back patio door and went inside.

"You'd better not!" Wren grinned and shook her head. She turned her attention back to the controller. She'd already gotten some nice footage of the house and front and back yards. The house's property extended far into the woods, all the way back to an old logging road, and she wanted to film the full extent of it, including the stream that ran through Ellie's property and beyond.

She checked the battery. She had about ten minutes before it reached eight percent, which was when she liked to start bringing the drone in for a landing. Ten minutes would be enough time to fly the drone around the woods to the road and back without risking it dying and falling into the trees, getting hopelessly lost or broken.

Wren sent the drone up high, stabilized it, and rotated it slowly for a panoramic view of the mountain peaks first. She snapped some stills, then shifted the camera lens down and tried not to get herself in the picture, though she could always delete the frames later.

On the screen, she thought she saw movement in the trees behind her. She resisted turning around to look and zoomed the camera in instead. She panned for a few seconds. Whatever it was, she couldn't find it now.

Probably deer. They're so hard to catch, they just blend right into the foliage.

She didn't have time to search if she wanted to get the drone to the logging road and back before the battery died. She sent the drone flying over the trees until the road came into view. Someone had parked their vehicle back there. Chase told her the owners said to watch for trespassers who sometimes sneaked onto their land to fish. Wren could attest that the brookies Bear caught out of their stretch of the creek were tasty. Still, trespassing to fish was technically stealing, so she zoomed in and got a nice, clear shot of the rear license plate just in case.

Her controller beeped a warning that the battery was nearing eight percent.

Time to bring her in.

Wren turned the drone and sent it higher to avoid a strong air current blowing just across the treetops in the opposite direction. The house and yard came into view and she watched them grow bigger. More beeps told her the battery was draining fast but it would be okay because the drone was close enough that she could see herself on the screen.

Someone broke cover from the trees behind her and was running straight at her.

Wren spun just in time to see her attacker's face.

You? How?

He knocked the controller out of her hand and pressed a cloth over her nose and mouth before she could scream. A horrible smell clogged her nose. The world tunneled in as she threw her head back to try and get away from it.

"Stupid bitch," he said as she struggled. "You and your precious photo essay."

The last thing Wren saw before the tunnel closed in was her drone hovering high above them.

WREN RODE in and out of consciousness—head pounding, stomach churning, wadded up cloth shoved into her mouth behind a gag, hands and feet bound, and slung across his shoulders like a deer carcass, as he moved with relative ease through the forest.

Right. He's a hunter.

Wonder if he's taking me to where he keeps all the dead baby ducks.

Dead duck. That's me.

She tried getting away but the black took her under again.

THE NEXT TIME she woke was when her arms and her back slammed against the hard ground, knocking the wind out of her. She couldn't breathe and at the same time, she had to fight from puking or else the gag in her mouth would cause her to choke on her own vomit. With her arms tied behind her back, she couldn't pull the gag down. She wheezed and gagged and tried to stay conscious. She tried not to panic, which would get her dead. The treetops above blurred from her tears.

His shadow fell across her.

Gone was the awkward buffoon fawning over a woman who would never have him. Gone was the cheat, the blackmailer. The coward.

Face painted, dressed in camo, this was the hunter.

Don Weisser.

He knelt at her side, leaned down until his mouth was beside her right ear.

"You're awake," he breathed. "If you want to live, you need to be silent."

She wheezed, trying desperately to draw in air.

"You're too loud. I need you *silent*."

Then you shouldn't have thrown me down like a burning sack of flour she wanted to scream at him. But that would probably make her head pound harder.

Worth it.

"Get yourself under control now." He shifted and she felt something cold and hard press against her jaw below her ear. "Or I shoot you in the head. Your choice."

She could argue the faulty logic that if he wanted silence, firing something literally nicknamed a boom stick to punish her for wheezing too loud kind of defeated his purpose. But she couldn't waste what little breath she had trying to cure his stupidity.

After what felt like ages, her chest loosened and she pulled a nice, long breath in through her nose. It cleared her head a little and helped with the nausea. Weisser pulled the gun away and straightened his spine. He still pointed the gun at her, even as he reconned the area.

Under the face paint, he looked worried.

He knows his way around the forest so he's not worried about that. He wants me completely silent. We've stopped moving and are hunkered down in the undergrowth beside a fallen log.

I'd say we're being followed.

A tiny spark of hope kindled in her heart.

Not followed. Tracked.

Hope roared to life, filling her heart.

By a Ranger. My Ranger.

Weisser had no chance.

"Not yet, not yet, not yet," Weisser chanted quietly. He wiped sweat from his brow.

She tried to figure out how much time had passed since he'd taken her. Wren knew light, knew how it looked at any given time of day in any season. The trees made judging the light difficult, but not impossible. The sun was still up and lighting the highest branches. She estimated twenty minutes, half an hour tops. Carrying her on his back through the forest, Weisser couldn't be covering too much ground too quickly, but she couldn't gauge how far they'd gone. It wasn't her specialty.

Elias, on the other hand, now he would know. He told me he was the best tracker growing up, that only Shane came close to his skill, and Elias only got better in Ranger school.

Despite the hope in her heart, she realized she was trying her best to find all the positives she could to fight off the panic that was telling her she was at the mercy of an unstable man. Who hated her guts. Who had at least one gun on him. Who had nothing to lose.

Panic would get her dead. Wren closed her eyes and concentrated on getting it under control.

Elias will bring his friends. Correction: our friends.

Elias with his tracking. Bear with his brawn. Gabe with his eagle eye. Ben with his tactics, Waylon with his daring. Shane with his—

Dog. Was that a dog? I think I just heard a dog.

She opened her eyes and braved a look at Weisser's face to see if he'd heard it, too. His eyes darted, his head swiveled, his breaths picked up the pace.

There's a dog loose in the woods. Bet I know where it came from.

Weisser turned his head in the direction of the sound, past the fallen log to Wren's left, and listened.

Weisser smiled. His white teeth glowed against the dark green face paint.

He looked down at her, an evil Cheshire Cat. He realized the gun barrel had drifted during his inattention so he pointed it back at her face.

"I knew they'd bring dogs. I'd be a fool not to know that. But the bait worked. It's drawing them off in the wrong direction. Away from us. If you make a sound, your blood will paint the trees. Doesn't matter if you're dead, you're still my hostage."

He looked up again toward the sound of the dog. Wren could make out a man's footsteps, too.

Shane? Shane, is that you?

Then other footsteps following the man and his dog, impossible to know how many.

Guys! Over here!

Wren fought the insane urge to shout, to stomp, to thrash her body, anything to get their attention as the sounds moved farther away.

Panic. Will. Get. You. Dead.

She and Weisser both strained to hear the men and the dog now. Weisser kept the gun pointed at her with one hand while he brought the other to his mouth. For one irrational moment, she thought he was going to whistle for the dog. Instead, he flattened his hand side-ways, shoved the side of his pointer finger into his mouth, and bit down. His body shook and Wren realized he was stifling a laugh.

Come on, you bastard. Laugh. Laugh hard. Think funny thoughts. I'm beaming them straight at your head.

Weisser was so focused on the dog, and Wren was so focused on Weisser that she almost missed the silent movement to her right, behind Weisser's back. She didn't dare turn her head or look side-ways, didn't dare break Weisser's concentration—his *distraction*, she realized—so she stayed still and watched the figure out of the corner of her eye.

Elias.

She watched him study them both. She watched him raise his gun.

She saw the bright muzzle flash. The sound was not as loud as she anticipated.

Weisser's head snapped forward. He crumpled.

Elias grabbed the back of his shirt, pulled his body off Wren, and shoved it aside. Waylon materialized out of the brush. "Clear!" he shouted.

Then Elias was beside her. He slid his arm under her head and lifted Wren. She realized her arms had gone numb from lying on them. As much as she'd wanted to thrash moments ago, now she could barely move.

Am I in shock?

Elias yanked the gag down and pulled the cloth out of her mouth. "Baby, are you hurt?"

She heard the others running toward them. Heard Shane shout, "Willow, heel."

"Talk to me, Wren." Elias was looking her over while he did something behind her back. When her shoulders shifted, she realized he'd cut her bonds. Waylon was at her feet, doing the same thing to the zip ties securing her ankles.

Their friends and Willow sounded closer.

"I can't feel my arms. Is that my voice? I'm a frog. Ribbit."

Elias' expression stayed serious as he pulled her shirt up and scanned her torso.

"Ribbit?"

All she wanted to do was make him laugh.

"No porcupine quills this time, but I did spot a deadly fire coming from a gun a minute ago," she said.

That did it. The hot medic smiled.

Because of me.

TWENTY-FOUR

People assumed Wren would want to postpone the wedding after her 'accident.'

They were wrong. If anything, she doubled her efforts to finish all the preparations in time.

Life was short. When good things came into your life you had to grab them and hang on tight. The wedding was the next good thing coming up and she wasn't about to let go of it. Because then she'd have to let go of the next good thing after that, which was a honeymoon to Hawaii. Besides, Barbie would be super-pissed that her wedding gift went to waste.

Even if she said she wouldn't be, under the circumstances.

"It's not a big deal, Wren. People return wedding gifts all the time," Barbie said. "Like when you get two of something."

"Believe it or not, I did not receive two honeymoons to Hawaii. And even if I did, you know I'd return the other one and keep yours, right?"

"You'd better keep mine instead or we aren't friends anymore," she answered as she poured aqua-blue M&Ms into another organza bag. Wren never understood why people did Jordan almonds at weddings. They didn't taste that great and they broke teeth. But chocolate M&Ms tasted better and didn't break teeth so she, Barbie, Ellie, and Rochelle were now sitting around Ellie's table filling little mesh bags for the reception tables.

Well, at least Wren and Barbie were filling them. Ellie and Rochelle kept stopping because they were laughing too hard every time Barbie or Wren opened their mouths. Now, however, Barbie was getting all serious, which annoyed Wren.

"I promise. I'm fine." She looked at Ellie and Rochelle. "Tell her for the hundredth time that I am fine, please?"

"She really is," Rochelle said as she reached for another bag. "Ellie and I have subjected her to non-stop cooked meals, flowers, and homemade talk-therapy and she survived it just fine."

"Yes. The talk-therapy," Wren said. "I'm being serious when I say it really did help, especially coming from you guys."

"Voices of experience," Ellie said. She set the big bag of M&Ms down as the color drained out of her face.

Wren reached across the table and grabbed Ellie's hand. "Oh, Ellie, I'm sorry, I didn't mean to bring up bad memories."

Ellie pulled her hand away quickly and stood up. "No, it's not that." Then she dashed down the back hall and they heard a door slam. The other three women looked at each other, confused.

"I upset her, I totally upset her."

Barbie shook her head. "She said it's not that, Wrenbird."

"No, it is. She's too sweet to admit it, that's all. I need to go apologize to her again."

Wren pushed her chair back and stood. She hoped Ellie wouldn't tell her to go away.

The door at the end of the hall opened and Ellie came back down the hall.

"Sorry," she said, still looking pale. "Almost didn't make it to the bathroom that time."

"Stomach bug?" Wren walked around the table to get to Ellie. "I can run get some ginger ale. We have it stockpiled for the wedding."

"There's already some in the fridge. Bear stockpiled it, too, because I'm gonna need it."

"Are you unwell? Oh no, not something serious, please."

Ellie gave her a sheepish smile. "Well, serious for nine months or so."

"Oh my God, I'm an idiot. You're pregnant!" Wren pulled her into a hug as Barbie and Rochelle clapped and cheered.

"We wanted to wait until after the wedding to say anything. Didn't want to steal the show."

Wren pulled back and looked into her friend's eyes. "It's not stealing the show, it's one more good thing adding to the joy."

WREN COULDN'T HELP but sing along with every song that came on the radio on the way home from Ellie's. Her friend absolutely glowed once she started talking about all the plans she and Bear were making. He was even building her a rocking chair and a cradle for the baby. Ellie had caught him quietly singing "Twinkle, Twinkle, Little Star" to himself in his woodworking shop.

Such a softie under all the grump.

Wren sighed. She'd had her own grump for most of the week. No, that wasn't fair, not at all. Elias hadn't acted grumpy, especially toward her. He let her win all the laugh points. She couldn't even finish a knock-knock joke without him already laughing and saying, 'Another point for you.'

Totally fake.

Because when he'd thought no one was watching, he didn't sing cute nursery rhymes. He brooded.

Of course it was related to what happened with Weisser. She knew the story, what he'd done to find and save her, because the police told her when she gave her statement. But it took three days before Wren could get Elias to tell her in his own words what happened.

They were lying in bed, after he'd given her a near-seizure-inducing orgasm. He thought she was asleep—those toe-curlers tended to knock her out—so he sighed and sat up at the edge of the bed, feet on the floor, head in hands.

"Are you upset because you killed someone?"

He lifted his head slowly. "Thought you were asleep, Scrubs."

She scooched over to his side, laid her head on his pillow, breathing in his good scent, and wrapped her arms around his waist. He dropped his hand into her hair and gently ran his fingers down the strands, bringing on the tingles.

"So, are you?"

"No, babe. I'm not. He was going to kill you. He knew he was going to prison and made a break for it. If he had just disappeared," Elias shrugged, "but he didn't. He took you as a hostage. He could have grabbed anyone, but he took you. Because he wanted to be free and he wanted you dead."

"You stopped him."

He turned his head and studied her face in the moonlight. "Are you sure you want to talk about this? You already know what happened."

"I want *you* to talk about it."

"I don't want to upset you."

"Babe, I'm good. I'm alive, I'm getting married in less than two weeks to an incredible man, then I'm going with him to Hawaii where I will chain-drink Mai Tais on the beach and stuff my face with mahi-mahi at every meal."

He grinned. "Even breakfast?"

"Yup. Mahi-mahi omelets. Mahi-mahi bacon. Mahi-mahi sausage."

"I don't think mahi-mahi bacon and sausage are a thing."

"Well if they are, I'm filling my breakfast plate." She shifted and sat up next to him. He wrapped his arm around her. "But first, I think you're hanging on to what happened, and we only have a two-suit-case limit, so we are not bringing along that baggage. Talk to me, Elias. Get it out."

He kissed her temple.

"We knew you had to be close by and that we had a better shot of finding you if the drone saw you. I just needed the numeric code to get into your phone. I know you're a romantic, so the first number I tried was the date of our wedding."

She smirked. "And it failed."

"Yup it failed, and my heart stopped dead. And then I tried a second number."

"The date we met."

Elias grinned. "Yeah. And I was in. From there it went quick. The last frame of the last video the drone recorded was still on the screen. I scrolled back until the drone was hovering over the yard. We watched him take you."

Elias paused, his jaw clenched, and Wren knew she'd done the right thing by making him talk it out or it would have festered.

"Bear called in to Ben right then. He knew about the logging road at the back edge of the property, so he and T-Wolf followed it on a hunch. They found an abandoned Beemer. Totally sketch. Not exactly something you go off-roading in." Elias' smile held no warmth at his joke.

"But thanks to the drone, we also saw where Weisser carried you into the woods—*away* from the car. If we hadn't seen that, we would have assumed he was hiding somewhere in between the house and the logging trail, trying to get back to it."

"Instead of the SUV he'd stolen and parked on a different logging road."

He nodded.

"We put Willow on to your scent with the launch pad, then I looked for where Weisser entered the forest. I found it and I tracked him. Then at one point, Willow decided she wanted to go in a different direction from where I was tracking Weisser. She was insistent."

"But you knew better." Wren brushed a stray lock of hair off his forehead.

"It was a gamble. I gambled with your life."

"No you didn't." She kissed his cheek. "You knew."

"Shane, Bear, and Gabe let Willow take the lead off the other direction. They made noise, just enough to let Weisser know he was safely hidden. Waylon and I kept following his trail. Until we found you." He grabbed his hair. "You were less than fifty feet from the SUV. He was so close to escaping with you."

"But you saved me, Elias."

He was quiet.

"Mission accomplished. So what are you carrying?"

"He never should have gotten near you."

"And somehow you're to blame?"

He nodded.

"Why?"

"He couldn't get to Barbie or Kyla. He knew Kit Larson had dropped the story so he wasn't interested in her. That left finding you. Well, finding Brooke Greene."

Wren covered her face. "And I was stupid enough to think I could publish the photo essay and let Kyla interview me. He recognized my voice." She shook her head. "I did the interview because I rationalized that he had ankle jewelry and was heading for prison. I didn't think he even had much in the way of internet access. Stupid."

Elias lowered her hand. "Not stupid, Wren. Weisser never should have been under house arrest. All it took was a two-dollar roll of tin foil to build a damn Faraday cage for the bracelet and block the real telecom signal. A spoofing service online pinged the police with fake messages telling them he was at home. The law failed you."

"Yes, it did. So, why are *you* carrying their failure?"

Elias tensed. "After his arrest, he became fixated on you, thought you'd been watching him for years, waiting to destroy him. It's all in his last journal."

She tsked. "Gotta love a narcissist."

"Wren." Elias shook his head. "I never should have let you put yourself into danger like that."

"Pfffth. You couldn't have stopped me."

"Wren—"

"No, Elias, listen. If you had told me I couldn't, I would have ignored you and done it anyway. Then, you would've been mad and we'd have broken up. But nothing would have changed with Weisser. Except for the ending. He would've still found me and kidnapped me. But I'd be dead now. Or worse, I'd be with him on the run."

She gently clasped his chin and turned his head so he was looking her in the eye. "But you respected my decision. You supported me. You *saved* me. And bonus, Weisser won't be stealing money from sick people anymore. Now it's Mai Tais and mahi-mahi time for me and you, baby." She smiled at him.

"One thing you got wrong though, Scrubs."

"What's that?"

"I never would have broken up with you. Never."

WREN PULLED up in front of her home. Chuck and Penny were looking out the window, tails wagging. She jogged to the door and let herself in. Elias was at the stove, and something smelled amazing.

"Guess what? Ellie and Bear are pregnant!" She did a little dance in place.

Elias smiled. "Little Bear cub."

"Little Bear *and Ellie* cub, mister. She's doing the heavy lifting." Wren crossed the kitchen and wrapped her arms around Elias from behind.

"Looks like you're excited about it, Scrubs."

"How could you tell? I'd better be the first person they call for babysitting. Of course, if they're smart, they won't because I'll spoil the little cubby rotten."

"You're good with kids," Elias said.

"Why, thank you."

"You like them."

"Uh, kinda goes along with being good with them."

"How about your own?" Elias said softly.

"My...own?"

"Well. Ours. But you'd be doing the heavy lifting."

Wren's heart lit up. "You saying you want kids? Little Lion cubs of our own?"

"Yeah. That's what I'm saying."

"I do, too."

After that, Elias stopped brooding completely.

"NO, YOU CAN'T MAKE ME."

"Wren, come on."

"I am *not* going in there. I value my life too much."

"Wren."

"Barbie."

Wren watched her bestie roll her eyes. So did the receptionist—sorry, the concierge—in the fancy new building. He hadn't taken his eyes off Barbie from the moment they walked through the door.

More like from the moment Barbie pushed Wren practically kicking and screaming through the door.

"I already spoke with him, Wren. He's going to apologize profusely, and then Serge will be giving you free acupuncture sessions for the rest of your life."

"The rest of my life? So I'll get half a session then."

"Stop it. We'll go together and he can work on both of us."

"Wow, I had no idea you were into murder-suicide."

"Nothing's going to happen. The fire was a freak accident in an old building." Barbie spread her arms and took in the three-story atrium, the huge windows, the ugly, expensive art on the walls. This place is so *nice*."

"Serge is ready for you now," the concierge said. "I'll take you to his studio."

"Thank you," Barbie told him, much to the man's pleasure.

They followed him down a hall filled with ambient light. The sound of windchimes and rain came from some unknown source.

"This looks like the tunnel to the afterlife."

Barbie ignored her.

"I smell smoke. Do you smell smoke?"

Barbie slapped her arm. "Stop it. Behave."

The concierge stopped at one of the closed doors, gave them a little bow, and returned to the lobby.

Barbie turned to Wren. "You're hilarious when you're anxious."

"I know. I swear, you put me in anxiety-inducing situations just to get new material."

"I won't deny that. After everything you've just been through, I can't believe *this* is freaking you out."

The door opened and a very repentant-looking Serge invited them in.

An hour later, Wren practically floated out into the hallway. Her body felt incredible.

"Did I not tell you?" Barbie said. "Little darts of love."

"You did."

"It was very sweet of you to invite him to the wedding tomorrow."

"Are you kidding? He's coming with us on the honeymoon."

THE NEXT MORNING, the morning of her wedding, Wren stood in Ellie's bedroom and listened to the murmur of people gathered outside while Ellie flitted around her, smoothing out her dress here and securing her updo with another bobby pin there.

"Beautiful," Ellie declared when she finally stepped back and looked her up and down. "Are you ready?"

Wren looked at herself in the full-length mirror. Yes, the dress was gorgeous, her hair looked great, makeup was perfect. But it was her eyes that drew her attention. They looked calm. Not the least bit anxious.

No joke.

She watched herself nod. "I'm ready." She turned and looked at Ellie, so pretty in her bridesmaid dress. "Let's go."

The other bridesmaids—Rochelle, April, Wren's college roommate Mary, and Barbie—were waiting in the front room with Wren's mom and stepmom, who both burst into happy tears the second they saw her.

Someone knocked on the door and Barbie opened it. Ben stepped inside.

"Excuse me. It's almost time. May I escort you to your seats?" he asked the moms, who were more than happy to each take one of his massive, muscular arms and let him lead them out the door.

Music drifted in through the window a few minutes later.

"That's *our* cue," Ellie said. "Everybody line up." Wren stepped back out of the way of her bridesmaids. Ellie opened the door, and one by one, they paired off with one of Elias' groomsmen waiting on the front porch, until Wren was left alone inside. The music changed to the Bridal March. Her dad and stepdad smiled at her, both ready to walk her down the aisle.

All the guests stood and turned to watch Wren. She only had eyes for one man standing up front, smiling at her and waiting patiently.

And that's when she knew.

This good thing was going to last a lifetime.

TWENTY-FIVE

Waylon "Ram" Ramsey

"WAYLON!" Stephanie waved him over to her desk the minute he stepped inside the rec center. Gabe stood beside the desk, giving Waylon a look that said *Good luck and beware, brother.*

Oh boy. With Stephanie, that look could mean anything.

"Yes, Steph?" Waylon asked when he got to the desk. "What can I do for you?"

"I've started a club," Stephanie told him, beaming.

"A club." Waylon looked at Gabe, hoping for some insight.

"An adventure buddies club! They meet every Saturday for the next six weeks. It's for members who maybe wanna go do activities and don't have a buddy to go along with them, thus the name." She pointed at Waylon. And *you're* signed up."

"Wait, what?" He looked at Gabe to see if this was some kind of joke, but going by his brother's confused expression, this was news to him. "I *have* friends. There's one of them now." He pointed at Gabe, who did him the courtesy of nodding. "If I wanted to go hiking and asked him, he'd come with me."

"That's true, I would," Gabe confirmed.

"So I don't need to be in a, what'd you call it? Activity Bros Club?"

"Adventure Buddies! Sheesh. I know you have friends, but it's this Saturday and I'm one person shy and I haven't had any takers. So, tag, you're it." Stephanie picked up a pen and wrote down Waylon's name. "I've got you paired up with Frank."

"Who's Frank?" Gabe asked.

"Frank hasn't been into the rec center since before you started here, Boss."

"Why do you need to pair people up for your club?" Waylon asked.

"The Adventure Buddies Club is done in pairs so that everyone has someone watching their back since some of the activities are gonna get rigorous. And since I'd hate to disappoint Frank after being gone so long, I've signed you up, Ram. Problem solved."

"Why me? Why do I have to do this?" Waylon asked.

"Because you don't want to let down an old lady, do you?" She stuck out her bottom lip into the biggest pout ever and fluttered her eyelids at him.

Waylon crossed his arms. "You have never once in your life thought of or called yourself an old lady, Stephanie."

"No, but I will do whatever it takes to get my way. Just ask Gabe."

"She's a monster."

"*Thank* you. You're my favorite boss again." Stephanie beamed at Gabe. "Now what do you say, Way?" She grinned at her own rhyme. "Are you on the bus, Gus? Is it a new plan, Stan?"

"*Stop.*" Waylon looked at the rec center ceiling then back at Stephanie.

She's going to be insufferable if I say no.

"Fine."

"Yes!" Stephanie fist-pumped the air.

"But only one time. This Saturday, and then that's it. I'm not doing this for six weeks."

She narrowed her eyes. "So then you're gonna leave Frank high and dry? Not cool. Actually, worse than not cool."

Dammit. He hated the way Stephanie was appraising him.

She's thinking of ways to make my life about as fun as jock itch if I don't agree to help.

"Fine. But, you have to promise me that you'll keep looking for a replacement, and the minute someone else signs up, I'm out, free and clear."

"Hmm." She continued to study him like he was a frog pinned to a board and she had a dissecting kit. Then she smiled. "Okay. Deal."

Waylon didn't trust that smile one bit. "You *have* to look for a replacement."

"Okay."

"*Actively* look. You can't hide the sign-up sheet."

"Fine."

"And you need to tell people you need one more person."

"Yup." Stephanie popped the P.

"And the second you find someone else, I'm out, no exceptions."

"Got it. No exceptions." She grinned in a way that murdered his trust.

"Do I have your word?"

"Sure do." Her grin got wider.

"Shake on it."

"Want me to spit in my hand first?"

Waylon flinched. "Please, no."

Stephanie stretched out her thankfully dry hand. "Deal."

Waylon shook her hand. "Deal."

AND NOW WAYLON was standing in the rec center at the beginning of his weekend when he should have been home nursing the hangover he'd worked hard to build the night before at Cocks and Strippers. At least he hadn't gone home with anyone, though he'd danced with not one but two gorgeous women and he wouldn't have minded sharing a bed with either of them.

"Adventure Buddies," he scoffed under his breath. "I don't need this."

But he kind of did now. Last night was proof. Bear and T-Wolf had long since stopped going to Cocks and Strippers unless their women came along, but that was okay, totally understandable. It was still great when it was just him and Elias looking to score, but that was the end of an era now that Elias and Wren were married. Shane was never part of the pickup scene, focusing on April ever since he got back to town. And Ben? Well, the meat market was never really Moose's scene, either. He tended to be the designated driver and the one who talked his brothers out of making bad choices a time or two. Waylon had been forced to talk himself out of last night's bad choices and where was the fun in that?

I wonder if this Frank guy is single. Yeah, probably, or he'd be out with his wife or girlfriend on a Saturday, right?

Maybe Stephanie knew his dating situation and that's why she'd signed him up. Frank might be in the same boat.

Sneaky woman! Maybe I'll find an adventure wingman while I'm here. Not bad.

And speak of the devil, there she was, popping out of a doorway and smiling like a kid with a new puppy.

"Come on back," Stephanie said as she cocked her arm and waved him down the hall. "We're all waiting for you, slowpoke. Frank's feeling like the odd man out."

Waylon reluctantly made his way down the hall. The room was full of people talking to each other in pairs.

Except for one person.

Whatever joke Stephanie was playing, Frank was a great, big nope.

Waylon definitely did not need a wing*woman.*

READ *about Waylon and Francesca in Blizzard on the Mountain*

GET A FREE SHORT STORY, *Tell It to the Bees – A Bear and Ellie Story*

AFTERWORD

Well, hello there! I always wonder who reads the afterward and acknowledgements, and why. I do for every book, because I love getting insights into what the heck was going through an author's mind while they were writing. It seems like we all have different methods to get to that world that only exists in our heads. And then carry that world back out with us in the form of words in order to share it.

It's a risky venture, at least for me, because sometimes trying to see where a story is going is like getting lost in a fog at midnight. Maybe I hear someone speaking, but I can only make out every third word, and I have no hope of figuring out who this person is. Sometimes, when I meet a character, they refuse to speak to me. They remain a stranger and it takes everything I've got to get them to open up.

Sometimes all the stars align. The road into my head is clear and bright. The characters I meet are real, and they say things that surprise me, delight me, scare me. They do things that I would have never thought of on my own. They are much cleverer than me. So all

I'm doing is chasing after them with my laptop, recording every word, every crazy situation they get themselves into and back out of.

Lion is one of those books.

The first chapter—Wren on the table getting stuck like a pincushion, came to me during my first acupuncture session, gosh, almost two years ago now. (I have to say right here that I was not left to die in a fire by my wonderful acupuncturist. She'd never dream of it. Her needles are truly little darts of love. Hi, Julie!)

I had no idea who Wren was. I didn't even have her name. But I watched her jump off the table in nothing but a sheet and dash out of the building only to meet the man of her dreams. I went home, sat down in front of my laptop, and that chapter just *flowed*.

This is the joy. This is the drug that hooks me. The flow that tells me that maybe—just maybe—I know what I'm doing. If only for one sentence, or one paragraph, or one chapter.

So, I reluctantly put that chapter away and went back to the book I was actually working on. I think it was *More Than Secrets*. Could have been Bear's book, which also wrote itself at the time. I say reluctantly because I was *in*—I had two characters, still nameless, who were eager to *live*, and that is not something I ever take for granted. Sometimes they get resentful that I abandoned them for another book (they can be possessive little suckers, let me tell you) and when you get back to them, they cross their arms, zip up their mouths, and pout. And then I have to woo them to get them to talk to me.

So when it came time to open that chapter back up, I did it with fingers crossed, knowing that there was a good chance Acupuncture Girl and Medic Dude did not want to be someone named Wren Stapleton or Elias "Lion" Hunt.

And what I found was that not only did they want to be those people—they already were. They'd gone ahead and gotten to know each other, and better yet, gotten to know themselves. And they were not resentful of me. They still wanted to *live*.

Wren especially. I can't tell you how many times she made me laugh. I could write her forever. She was so funny, so smart, and still so vulnerable. The more anxious she was, the funnier and cleverer she got, poor thing. I never wanted anything bad to happen to her.

But just like life, that's not how stories go, is it?

Luckily, she had a great bestie, and a whole squad of new friends to help her out. But first and foremost, she had Elias, who was so gentle, so open and supportive, who waited for her to get past the anxiety that warped her perceptions, that made her run from all the good things she wanted to keep in her life.

Dear reader, I did not want this book to end. I did not want to leave Wren, and Elias, and Barbie, and Stephanie, or any of them. I'm even a little teary now, and I have to tell myself I'll see them again in the next book. Just like Gina and Lach have been gracious enough to move into this series from the last one.

Writing takes a lot of faith, both in the story itself, and in my ability to string the right words together to tell it. And then, I have to have faith that you guys will see what I saw, hear what I heard, and most importantly, feel what I felt. And that you love it. I never want to waste your time. So, I hope, even more that I usually do, that Wren, Elias, Barbie, and all the rest delighted you. I hope you love them all as much as I do. We'll see them again soon.

It's time to start the next book. And I find that the stars are once again aligned. Waylon, who I got to know quite well in Lion, is eager to keep on going. And the woman who he meets has already told me so, so much about herself. She wants to live even more than Waylon does, as you'll see.

Until next time, Lovelies! xoxo Olivia

ACKNOWLEDGMENTS

This is not a solitary venture (thank goodness). No book ever is. These are only a few people who make sure I survive the journey.

Trinity Wilde, who is off having well-deserved fun. (So am I now!)

Amber Hamilton, who reminds me to do all the things that are not writing, if she's not already doing them for me.

Caitlyn O'Leary, who makes me laugh harder than Wren does.

Riley Edwards, who is the person I want at my side when it comes to investigating strange noises in hotels.

Bella Stone, may she win all the glitter wars!

Kris Michaels, for whom I will always run across very long rooms for hugs.

Susan Stoker, who, at this very moment, I'm on my way to visit (the aforementioned fun I'm having!)

Elle James, who is forever and always my dancing partner.

Syneca Featherstone, who makes all my books so pretty!

Owen, my own personal bookseller, who has taken all of this insanity in stride, and even takes on some of it now. Come meet him at a signing some time and let him sell you a book.

And most of all, thank you, Lovely, for reading my books. This is all for you.

FOLLOW OLIVIA

Follow me to catch my latest releases at:

Newsletter:
https://oliviamichaelsromance.com/

Amazon:
https://www.amazon.com/author/oliviamichaelsromance

BookBub:
https://www.bookbub.com/authors/olivia-michaels

Facebook:
https://www.facebook.com/oliviamichaelsauthor

Instagram:
https://www.instagram.com/oliviamichaelsromance/

Want more? Come be one of Olivia's Lovelies on Facebook. I can always use another ARC reader or two...

https://www.facebook.com/groups/639545290309740/

And for a FREE short story about Bear and Ellie, follow this link:
https://BookHip.com/KQSADJD

ALSO BY OLIVIA MICHAELS

Watchdog Security Series

More Than Love

More Than Family

More Than Puppy Love: A Christmas Novella

More Than Paradise

More Than Thrills

More Than Words Can Say

More Than Beauty

More Than Rumors

More Than Secrets

Watchdog Security Series Box Set, Books 1-3

Watchdog Security Series Box Set, Books 4-6

Watchdog Security Series Box Set, Books 7-9

Watchdog Protectors

In Susan Stoker's Special Forces Operation Alpha

Protecting Harper

Protecting Brianna

Protecting Sylvie

Watchdog Mountain Division

Bear On The Mountain

Timberwolf On The Mountain

Lion on the Mountain

Blizzard on the Mountain

Thunder on the Mountain

Avalanche on the Mountain

Free Mountain Division Short Story

Tell it to the Bees – A Bear and Ellie Short Story

ABOUT THE AUTHOR

Olivia Michaels is a life-long reader, dog-lover, gardener, and a certified beachaholic. When she's not throwing a Frisbee for her fur-baby, harvesting tomatoes, or writing, you can find her playing in the surf, kayaking, or kicking back on the sand and cracking open a romantic beach read.

www.ingramcontent.com/pod-product-compliance
Lightning Source LLC
Chambersburg PA
CBHW070636260626
47161CB00007B/2730